HOW *to* READ *the* AIR

ALSO BY DINAW MENGESTU

The Beautiful Things That Heaven Bears

HOW

to

READ

the

AIR

DINAW MENGESTU

RIVERHEAD BOOKS
a member of Penguin Group (USA) Inc.
New York
2010

RIVERHEAD BOOKS
Published by the Penguin Group
Penguin Group (USA) Inc., 375 Hudson Street, New York, New York 10014, USA * Penguin
Group (Canada), 90 Eglinton Avenue East, Suite 700, Toronto, Ontario M4P 2Y3, Canada
(a division of Pearson Penguin Canada Inc.) * Penguin Books Ltd, 80 Strand, London
WC2R 0RL, England * Penguin Ireland, 25 St Stephen's Green, Dublin 2, Ireland (a division of
Penguin Books Ltd) * Penguin Group (Australia), 250 Camberwell Road, Camberwell, Victoria
3124, Australia (a division of Pearson Australia Group Pty Ltd) * Penguin Books India Pvt Ltd,
11 Community Centre, Panchsheel Park, New Delhi–110 017, India * Penguin Group (NZ),
67 Apollo Drive, Rosedale, North Shore 0632, New Zealand (a division of Pearson
New Zealand Ltd) * Penguin Books (South Africa) (Pty) Ltd,
24 Sturdee Avenue, Rosebank, Johannesburg 2196, South Africa

Penguin Books Ltd, Registered Offices: 80 Strand, London WC2R 0RL, England

The author acknowledges permission to quote from:

Duino Elegies and The Sonnets to Orpheus by Rainer Maria Rilke,
translated by A. Poulin, Jr. Copyright © 1975, 1976, 1977 by A. Poulin, Jr. Reprinted by
permission of Houghton Mifflin Harcourt Publishing Company. All rights reserved.

"Pastoral" by William Carlos Williams, from *Collected Poems: Volume 1, 1909–1939*.
Copyright © 1938 by New Directions Publishing Corp. Reprinted by permission
of New Directions Publishing Corp.

Library of Congress Cataloging-in-Publication Data

Mengestu, Dinaw, date.
How to read the air / Dinaw Mengestu.
p.   cm.
ISBN 978-1-59448-770-5
1. Children of immigrants—Fiction.   2. Ethiopians—United States—Fiction.   I. Title.
PS3613.E487H69   2010   2010003045
813'.6—dc22

Printed in the United States of America
1   3   5   7   9   10   8   6   4   2

BOOK DESIGN BY AMANDA DEWEY

For Anne-Emmanuelle,

pour toutes les belles choses

You still *don't understand? Throw the emptiness in*
your arms out into that space we breathe; maybe birds
will feel the air thinning as they fly deeper into themselves.

RAINER MARIA RILKE, *Duino Elegies*

PART I

I

It was four hundred eighty-four miles from my parents' home in Peoria, Illinois, to Nashville, Tennessee, a distance that in a seven-year-old red Monte Carlo driving at roughly sixty miles an hour could be crossed in eight to twelve hours, depending on certain variables such as the number of road signs offering side excursions to historical landmarks, and how often my mother, Mariam, would have to go to the bathroom. They called the trip a vacation, but only because neither of them was comfortable with the word "honeymoon," which in its marrying of two completely separate words, each of which they understood on its own, seemed to imply when joined together a lavishness that neither was prepared to accept. They were not newlyweds, but their three years apart had made them strangers. They spoke to each other in whispers, half in Amharic, half in English, as if any one word uttered too loudly could reveal to both of them that, in fact, they had never understood each other; they had never really known who the other person was at all.

Learning a new language was, in the end, not so different from learning to fall in love with your husband again, Mariam thought. While standing in front of the bathroom mirror early in the morning, she often told herself, in what she thought of as nearly flawless diction, "Men can be strange. Wives are different." It was an expression she had heard from one of the women at the Baptist church that she and her husband had begun attending. A group of women were standing in the parking lot after the sermon was over, and one of them had turned to Mariam and said, "Men can be so strange. Wives are just different."

At the time she had simply repeated the words back, almost verbatim, "Yes. That is true. Men *can* be strange," because that was the only way that she could be certain that what she said was understood by everyone. What she would have liked to say was far more complicated and involved a list of sizable differences that by any other standards would have been considered irreconcilable. Regardless, since arriving in America six months earlier, she had pushed herself to learn new things about her husband, like why, for example, he spoke to himself when no one seemed to be looking, and why some days, after coming home from work, he would sit parked in the driveway for an extra ten or twenty minutes while she watched him from behind the living room curtains. On some nights he would wake up and leave the bedroom, careful not to rouse her but always failing because most nights Mariam hardly slept at all. He would lie down on the couch in the living room naked, and from the bedroom she would eventually hear him let out a small whimper followed by a grunt, and he would return to bed and sleep soundly until the morning. My mother learned these things and filed them into a corner of her brain that she thought of as being specifically reserved for facts about her husband. And in just the same way, she pushed herself to try new words and form new sentences in English, because just as there was a space reserved for her husband, there was another for English, and another one for foreign foods, and another for the names of streets near her house. She learned to say, "It was a pleasure to meet you." And she learned individual words, like "scattered" and "diligent" and "sarcastic." She learned the past tense. For example, I was tired yesterday, instead of: I am tired yesterday, or Yesterday tired I am. She learned that Russell Street led to Garfield Street, which would then take you to Main Street, which you could follow to I-74, which could take you east or west to anywhere you wanted to go. Eventually they would all make sense. Verbs would be placed in the right order, sarcasm would be funny, the town would be familiar: past, present, future, and husband, they could all be understood if given enough patience.

At this point in their marriage they had spent more time apart than together. She added up the days by rounding up some months, rounding down a few others. For every one day they had spent together, 3.18 had been spent apart. To her, this meant a debt had to be repaid, although who owed the other what remained unclear. Is it the one who gets left behind who suffers more, or is it the one who's sent out alone into the world to forage and create a new life? She had always hated numbers, but since most of the English she heard still escaped her, she now took comfort in them and searched for things to add. At the grocery store she calculated the cost of everything she brought to the register before she got there: a can of peas, seventy-eight cents; a package of salt, forty-nine cents; a bag of onions, forty cents. The smiling faces behind the register always offered a few words out loud before saying the total. All of them were lost on her, but what difference did it make if she didn't know how to take a compliment, banter, or understand what the phrase "two-for-one" meant. She knew the number at the end, and that number, because it didn't need translation, was power, and the fact that she knew it as she went up to the register filled her with a sense of accomplishment and pride unlike anything she had known since coming here. It made her feel, in its own quiet fleeting way, as if she were a woman to be reckoned with, a woman whom others would someday come to envy.

She never knew what her husband had gone through in the three years they had been apart, nor had she ever really tried to imagine. Say America enough times, try to picture it enough times, and you end up with a few skyscrapers stuck in the middle of a cornfield with thousands of cars driving around. The one picture she had received during those three years was of him sitting in the driver's seat of a large car, the door open, his body half in the car, half out. He kept one arm on the steering wheel, the other balanced on his leg. He looked handsome and dignified, his mustache neatly trimmed, his thick curly hair sculpted into a perfect ball that highlighted the almost uncanny resemblance his head had to the globe that her father kept perched on top of his chest of drawers.

When she first saw the picture she didn't believe the car was his. She thought he had found it parked on the side of the road and had seized the opportunity to show himself off, which was indeed almost exactly what he had done. Still, that didn't stop her from showing the picture to her mother, sisters, and girlfriends, or from writing on the back, in English: *Yosef Car*. She expected other pictures would eventually follow: pictures of him standing in front of a large house with a yard; pictures of him in a suit with a briefcase in hand; and then later, as the days, weeks, and months collided, and two years was quickly approaching three, she began to wait for pictures of him with his arm around another woman, with two young children at his side. She had secretly feared the latter would happen from the day he first left, because who had ever heard of a man waiting for his wife? The world didn't work that way. Men came into your life and stayed only as long as you could convince them to. She even named the children for him: the boy Adam and the girl Sarah, names that she would never have chosen for her own children because they were common and typical, and Mariam's children, when they came, were going to be extraordinary.

When no such pictures arrived, she wanted to write him and tell him to show her a picture of him in the middle of something, a square, a city park, a picture in which he played just one, minor role.

"Show me a picture of you doing something," she had wanted to write, but that wasn't it exactly. What she wanted was to see him somehow fully alive in a picture, breathing, walking, laughing, living his life without her.

On the morning they left for Nashville, my mother packed a small suitcase with two weeks' worth of underwear, three heavy wool sweaters she had bought at a garage sale for two dollars apiece, and pants and shirts suitable for summer, fall, and winter, even though it was the first week of September and so far the days had been nothing but mild, sunny, and occasionally even too warm for the thin cotton tank tops she had seen other women wearing as they walked casually through the aisles of the grocery store, through shopping malls, and down the deserted Main Street. Those women were neither slim nor graceful. They were plain, pale, and average, and to her eyes entirely indistinguishable one from another, which was precisely what she resented and envied the most. The trip was supposed to last from start to finish four nights and five days, but as she stuffed her suitcase to its limits, she decided it was best to always be prepared for the unexpected, for the broken-down car, for the potential wrong turn, for the long walk at night that for one reason or another never ended. She had packed up her entire life once before, and now six months later, if she had learned anything at all about herself, it was that she could do with far less. She could, if she wanted, get away with almost nothing.

Her husband, Yosef, was already waiting for her outside in the red Monte Carlo he had scraped and saved for more than a year to buy and now could hardly afford. It was not the same car as the one in the photo. She couldn't have said how or why, but it was less elegant, smaller perhaps, and even though the picture had been black and white, she thought of the Monte Carlo he was waiting in as being a shabbier shade of red than the one she imagined.

The car horn honked twice for her: two short high-pitched bleeps that could have gone unnoticed but did not because she half expected, half prayed for them. When they came she pictured a bird—a dove, or something dovelike—being set free, its rapidly fluttering wings disturbing the air. Had she known more words in English she would have said the sound of the horn pierced through the silence, *pierced* being the operative word here, with its suggestion that something violent had occurred.

If he honks one more time, my mother said to herself, I will refuse to go. It was a matter of principle and conviction, or at least something that so closely resembled the two that even if it was merely pride or rage in disguise, she was willing to fight and tear down the house to stand by it. She had, after all, waited for him for years—a virtual widow but without the corpse and sympathy. If she was owed anything now it was time. Time to pack her clothes, fix the straps of her dress, and take account of everything she might have missed and would perhaps potentially later need.

If he honks again, she told herself, I will unpack my suitcase, lock the bedroom door, and wait until he leaves without me.

This was the way most if not all of my parents' fights began. With a minor, almost invisible transgression that each seized upon, as if they were fighting not about being rushed or about too many lights having been left on, but for their very right to exist, to live and breathe God's clean air. As a child I learned quickly that a fight was never far off or long in the making, and imagined it sometimes as a real physical presence lurking in the shadows of whatever space my parents happened to occupy at that given moment—a grocery store, a car, a restaurant. I pictured the fight sitting down with us on the couch in front of the television, a solemn black figure in executioner's robes, a caricature of death and tragedy clearly stolen from books and movies but no less real as a result. Ghosts are common to the life of any child: mine just happened to come to dinner more often than most.

The last fight they had had before that morning left my mother with a deep black and purple bruise on her right arm, just below her shoulder. The bruise had a rotting plum color and that was how she thought of it, as a rotten plum, one pressed so fast and hard into her skin that it had broken through the surface and flattened itself out underneath. She found it almost beautiful. That the body could turn so many different shades amazed her, made her believe that there was more lurking under the surface of our skin than a mess of blood and tissue.

She waited with one hand on top of the suitcase for the car to honk again. She tried not to think it, but it came to her nonetheless, a selfish, almost impregnable desire to hear even the accidental bleating of a car horn crying out.

Just once more, she thought. Honk just once more.

She held her breath. She closed the lid of the suitcase in complete silence. With her hand pressing down on the top, she zipped it halfway shut. A tiny stitch of blue fabric from a pair of padded hospital socks picked up two weeks earlier peeked out over the edge. She pressed the sock back in with one finger, granted the zipper its closure, and with that, acknowledged that on this occasion her husband had won. He had held out long enough for her to complete the one minor task that stood between her and leaving, and despite her best efforts, that was how she saw it, as a victory won and a loss delivered. She was going. Even if he pressed on the horn now with all his might she would have to go, would have to walk down the stairs and apologize for having taken so long, because he had pressed her just far enough without going too far. Sometimes she suspected that he knew the invisible lines she was constantly drawing. There were dozens of such lines spread out all over their one-bedroom apartment like tripwire that, once crossed, signaled the start of yet another battle. There was the line around how many dishes could be left in the sink, another around shoes worn in the house, and others that had to do with looks and touches, with the way he entered a room, took off his clothes, or kissed her on the cheek. Once, after an especially rough night of sleep, she felt her husband's breath on the back of her neck. It was warm and came in the steady consistent bursts of a man soundly asleep. She didn't know which one she really hated—the breaths or the man breathing. In the end, she created a wall of pillows behind her, one she would deny having made the next morning.

The four large oak trees that lined the driveway were the last of their kind. The largest and oldest of the group stood just a few feet away from the two-story duplex that my mother and father shared with a frail, hunchbacked older woman with milky-blue eyes who hissed under her breath every time she passed my

mother on her way in or out of the house. The oak trees cooled
the living room in the summer, allowing the afternoon light to
filter through seemingly oversized leaves that Mariam thought of
as deliberately keeping the worst parts of the light out, leaving
only the softer, quieter shades. Now that it was September and
supposedly the harshest of the summer heat had passed, she noticed as she prepared to leave the apartment that the leaves nearest
the tops of the trees had begun to turn; a small pile of dead ones
had already grown around their bases. So this was *fall*. A woman
at the Baptist church had told her just a few weeks earlier, "Oh,
just wait until fall. You'll see. You'll love it." Her name was Agnes
and she wore a curly black wig to hide the bald patches in the
center of her head. A-G-N-E-S, Mariam wrote on the back of
a church pamphlet that went on in great detail about the agony of
Christ, which prompted her to write, after their first meeting,
A-G-O-N-Y, on the back of the pamphlet, and next to that, *Agnes
is in agony*, which was a simple sentence, with a subject and verb,
which formed a declarative statement that Mariam decided was
more likely than not absolutely true.

At the time my mother had thought to herself, I could never
love anything called "fall." There was fall and Fall. To fall was to
sink, to drop. When my mother was nine, her grandfather came
out of his bedroom at the back of the house wearing only a robe
with the strings untied. He was deaf and half blind and had been
for as long as Mariam could remember. He walked into the middle
of the living room, and having reached the center, where he was
surrounded on all sides by his family, fell, not to his knees, but
straight forward, like a tree that had been felled, the side of his
head splitting open on the edge of the fireplace mantel, spraying
the wall and couch with blood. That was one way to fall.

One could also fall down a flight of stairs, as in, your husband falls down the stairs while leaving for work one morning. She had this thought at least once, sometimes as many as three times a week. She pictured him tripping, stumbling, feet over head, just like the characters in the cartoons she had grown addicted to watching between the hours of one p.m. and four p.m. In those shows the characters all shook the fall off after a few seconds, bending an arm back into place here, twisting an ankle there. The cartoons made her laugh, and when she thought of her husband falling down the steps, his tall, narrow body perfectly suited to roll uninterrupted down the shag-carpeted stairwell, stopping perhaps briefly at the one minor bend that led to the final descent, it was only partly with those cartoon images in mind. When real bodies fell, as Mariam knew well enough, they did not get up. They did not bounce back or spring into shape. They crumpled and needed to be rescued.

Despite my mother's best efforts to resist fall, she found herself taken by the season more and more each day. The sun set earlier, and soon she learned, an entire hour would be shaved off the day, an act that she sometimes wished could be repeated over and over until the day was nothing more than a thumbnail sketch of its former self. The nights were growing marginally but noticeably cooler. Leaves were changing, and children who over the course of the summer had ruled the neighborhood like tyrants were once again neatly arranged in groups of twos and threes each morning, beaten (or so Mariam thought) into submission by the changing rules of the season. There was enough room in the shrinking day to believe that the world was somehow sensitive to grief and longing, and responded to it the same way she did when she felt convinced that time had been arranged incorrectly, making the loss of one extra minute nearly every day a welcome relief.

My mother could never have said she loved fall, but as she walked down the steps with her suitcase in hand toward the red Monte Carlo her husband had been waiting in for nearly an hour, she could have said that she respected its place as a mediator between two extremes. Fall came and went, while winter was endured and summer was revered. Fall was the repose that made both possible and bearable, and now here she was with her husband next to her, heading headlong into an early-fall afternoon with only the vaguest ideas of who they were becoming and what came next.

II

Six months before I left my wife, Angela, and began retracing my parents' route through the Midwest, my father passed away in the boardinghouse he had been living in for ten years. At the time I had effortlessly placed his death into the same private corner in which for many years I had buried anything I considered too troubling—a steadily growing category which by that point included even minor injuries such as casual insults and malicious stares from strangers. It had been three years since my father and I had spoken, and many more since we last saw each other regularly, a fact that I pointed out to Angela when she asked me, several days after news of his death arrived, why I was acting as if I wasn't even the least bit affected.

"You're doing it again, Jonas," she said. "You're going on as if nothing at all has happened. I can't stand it when you do that."

I remember we were sitting on the plush faded green couch in what doubled as our living room and dining room on a Saturday afternoon when we had that conversation. It was late July and I was beginning work on the syllabus for the freshman English literature class I once taught at a private high school on the Upper West Side of Manhattan. Angela was dressed in a light blue suit and had her hair, which she had recently braided into thick black locks, tied into a bun, giving her a grave, serious look that seemed unearned, as if she, with her oversized, almost fawnlike black eyes and slightly puffed, elevated cheeks, were merely playing the role of a busy lawyer who worked even on the weekends for a small-town production in which she was the star.

"We were never really close," I told her, "and besides, I'd been expecting this for a long time. What else do you want me to say?"

Many of the conversations that Angela and I had at that point fell along similar defensive lines. We had been married for three years, but we had spent much of the past six months hardly talking except to exchange pointed attacks at each other. It was common for Angela to accuse me of feeling nothing at all, just as it was common for her to spend long stretches of the day and night away from me and the small one-bedroom basement apartment that we shared. She was a lawyer at a midsized law firm in midtown Manhattan that dealt with second-rate corporate clients who didn't have the resources yet to hire one of the white-shoe law firms that occupied the top floors of the building she worked in. She hated what she did, and most of the people she worked with, but she took great pride in the job itself, having grown up poor and rootless in more than a dozen different towns scattered throughout the South and Midwest, from Tennessee and Missouri to the northern reaches of Ohio. She told me once that she could still remember how she felt the first time she looked in the mirror and told herself that she was a lawyer.

"It was strange," she said. "I had to say it three times before I really began to believe it."

It was Angela who found me my job teaching at the academy through one of the partners in her law firm. Before then I was working at a refugee resettlement center in Manhattan, which was where she and I met. The center was near the corner of Canal and Bowery and came with a fifth-floor view of the East River and the Manhattan and Brooklyn bridges. The center's clients often liked to stand in front of the double-paned windows for several minutes before seeing one of the lawyers, as if they knew already that given the laws and politics of the time, they might never have the chance to catch sight of such a view again. It was the sixth job I had had in two years, part of a string of constant upheavals that included new and progressively smaller apartments shared with strangers who remained throughout our time living together as thoroughly unknown to me as on the day we first met. I had held a couple of semipermanent jobs before then, but none that could be marked as a career, or even as preparation for one. After finishing college, I had thought vaguely of returning to school to get a Ph.D. in English literature, with a focus on modern American poetry, and had often said as much when asked by casual acquaintances or women I was trying to impress with what I did in New York, since often I did very little at all. A decade after graduating, however, I had yet to make any substantial effort to do so other than annually requesting a catalogue and application for the five or six universities that I said I dreamed of going to. I had been a waiter at two small but trendy coffee shops on handsome, tree-lined streets near the edge of the city's West Village, both of which prided themselves on their homemade jams, bread, and locally grown produce, and whose prices reflected the extent to which people were willing to pay for them. Our customers were often wealthy and on many occasions famous but were never gawked at. For promptly delivering coffee or toasted bagels with the requisite jam, I was paid twice what I earned per hour in tips and was twice offered unwanted and unnecessary investment advice, such was the slightly surreal air in which those places existed. Besides my multiple stints as a waiter, I had also held temporary jobs at middling midtown brokerage firms that occupied a quarter or less of a floor in a shabby, neglected building on an off-brand avenue. At least one was an elaborate tax evasion scheme for the city's very rich but nearly dead; the others were simply hustling start-up ventures, still too poor to hire more than a handful of people full-time, and which in their desperation for clients, or customers, often seemed to me to be little more than elaborate lemonade stands around which a dozen or so men and women sat waiting for their phones to ring. My sole tasks, regardless of what the companies did or how successful they were, were to speak little, eat quickly, and punch in several hundred numbers an hour, all of which I always did well, and for which in two instances I was, at least temporarily, said to be greatly valued.

Without ever thinking about it, I had become one of those men who increasingly spent more and more of their nights alone, neither distraught nor depressed, just simply estranged from the great social machinations with which others were occupied. After the forced intimacy of childhood was over, I found I had a hard time being close to others. The few friends I had made during college had all eventually moved on without me, not to different cities but to better lives within the same city where drinks and birthday presents, along with sex and intimacy, were casually exchanged.

Angela and I became close shortly after we began working at the immigration center together. She was one of the many volunteers, summer interns, and temporary employees who passed through the offices in any given year. Unlike all of the others who came and went without my ever knowing their last names, Angela and I had quickly found mutual points around which to bond. We were the only black people who worked at the center—anyone else of color in the office was most likely a former, present, or future client—a fact that Angela asked me about a few days after she began working there.

"Does that ever bother you? Especially since this is your full-time job."

"I almost never think about it," I told her. "And you?"

"No," she said. "It doesn't. But I wonder sometimes if it should."

From there we found that we had other cultural and racial obligations that we could be anxious about if we cared to.

"What about the Africans who come into the center?" she asked me a few days later. "Do you like them more or less than the others? Be honest."

"That depends," I said.

"On what?"

"Which part of Africa. If they're from the west coast, then to be honest it doesn't matter much to me. East coast, however, is a different story."

"We have a problem, then, here," she said. "Being of African-American descent and all . . ."

"I see what you're saying. Your loyalties—"

"West side all the way," she said.

We began to take lunch together in Chinatown almost every afternoon. It was Angela who suggested that we do so, even though she claimed she hated the sight of the ducks strung by their necks roasting in the restaurant windows.

"I'm part vegetarian," she said. "Which is sort of like saying I'm part white because my grandfather was Irish. It doesn't really count, and no one but me really believes it."

Over various bowls of shared noodles, we began to divide up our clients between the west side and east side. We split the

Africans first since they were the easiest. Benin, Togo, the whole western coast down to Namibia, and even large chunks of northern and central Africa went to Angela, from the Congo on west, which was fine, I said, because I had Somalia, "and no one wants to fuck with them." When we were finished we moved on to South Asia, which we cut in half evenly down the middle, which hardly mattered since all of our clients from that region were Pakistani to begin with. Central America was later carved up according to each state's proximity to the Gulf, and then there were the smaller pockets of the world that we settled on a case-by-case basis. A man from Fiji was given to Angela because she said he looked like an uncle of hers who lived in Boston; I took an entire family from Turkmenistan because their last name almost rhymed with mine. When we finished one week later, Angela had her imaginary west side crew, and I had mine to the east. If someone from my side was granted an asylum interview, it was a victory for everyone on my team. All I would have to say to Angela was "east side," and she would know what I meant. She could and often did the same, not just with me but also with the other lawyers and interns at the office, who stared at her puzzled when she smiled and said, "West side wins again." No one at the center besides us talked like that. When it came to conversations about our clients, the general mood was one of overwhelming sympathy buttressed by seemingly sincere, heartfelt statements such as "I can't believe they had to go through that." Angela could never talk like that, which was part of the reason why I admired her. Unlike almost everyone else who volunteered or worked at the center, she was happy with what she did there. "Refugees," she said. "How could you not love them? Who else do you know has it worse."

In the one year I had worked there before Angela arrived, more than a half-dozen volunteers and lawyers had come and gone, with nearly all departing for what would later be explained in group e-mails as personal reasons, or family reasons, when the truth, of course, was known to all who spent even the smallest portion of their lives there. We were losing all the time, on a weekly if not daily basis: clients abruptly disappeared, and many of those who did not were eventually scheduled to be deported; we were helpless in the face of both. One week a man from Honduras took flight; the next a family of four from Liberia whose asylum application was coming up for a review vanished into a corner of the Bronx. Like everyone else who came to us, they knew their chances, despite whatever reassurances they might have heard from the four full-time lawyers who worked there. Better than decent odds were never good enough—only full-on certainty could make those who had risked their lives or lost their fortunes getting here sit idle while someone else decided their fate.

Angela was the only other person besides Bill, the center's bald and rapidly aging veteran lawyer and director, who knew how to temper that loss with an appreciation for reality. Bill often joked that the real reason the center existed was to give people enough time to learn how the system worked before they vanished.

"And for that," he said, "the bastards don't even thank us."

Most of the victories that we could claim came easy; every month Bill chose a few cases whose outcomes could almost always be predicted in advance—the former doctor or lawyer from Cuba, the political dissident from China, or the recent victims of a particularly horrific African war that had briefly made its way into the headlines and had earned the attention of a senator or congressman. We knew that we could generally count on these to bolster our year-end report, in which we tallied up our wins and losses before doctoring the outcome in order to make sure we had come out ahead.

.   .   .

My job at the center was to read through the asylum statements as soon as they came in, although initially I was
hired only to answer the phone and deflect the frequent calls from
creditors who were demanding payment for whatever minor ser-
vices had been rendered to keep the office functioning. Money was
owed to multiple Xerox repairmen, along with several different
plumbers and one electrical technician who frequently threatened
to come down to our office. Undoubtedly it was my name more
than my English degree that had first gotten me the job and then
later the promotion that came with a change in responsibilities
and a monthly subway card. Jonas Woldemariam had a perfect
degree of foreignness to it for the center's needs, almost as deeply
vested in America from the sound of it as John or Jane, but with
something reassuringly "other" at the end. I could be Jonas, or
Jon, or J, and of course when Bill needed, Mr. Woldemariam, who
despite distance and birth, remained at heart an African. If many
of the clients, especially those who came from neighboring African nations, were disappointed at seeing me when they first walked
through the doors, they were undoubtedly relieved by the time
they met the white middle-aged lawyers who would perhaps someday stand next to them in court. It was one thing for our paths to
cross on the street or at a restaurant, behind the counter of a grocery store, and another thing entirely to stake our futures on one
another. I once heard Bill, who at fifty-three still hadn't learned
how to whisper when he meant to talk discreetly, tell someone over
the phone how lucky they were to find me.

"He's completely American," he said, "but you wouldn't nec-
essarily guess that from just looking at him. It's important for the
clients to see that."

When it came to the personal statements that each asylum applicant had to write, my job, at least at the beginning, was to assign them to one of two piles, which in my head I had listed as the persecuted and not so persecuted. The persecuted were the easiest to read through—the narratives almost always self-evident, and succinct—while the not so persecuted tended to ramble and digress and include statements such as "It's been a dream of mine" or "The opportunity to pursue . . ." There was never that sort of wishful thinking in the others—a cold, almost hard pragmatism was the rule of the day, with the governing philosophy simply stated as I have nowhere else to go or there is nothing for me to return to. Often there were such statements as: The village, city, town, country I came from, was born in, lived in for forty-five, sixty years was taken over, occupied, bombed, burned, destroyed, slaughtered, and I, my family, my sister, cousin, aunt, uncle, grandparents were arrested, shot, raped, detained, forced to say, tortured to say, threatened if we did not say that we would vote, not vote, believed in or did not believe, supported or denounced the government or movement or religion of X. In the end the consequences were always the same, and each ended with a similar emphatic note: We, I, can't, won't, will never be able to go back.

It was only Bill and the three other lawyers who dealt at any great length with the clients directly. I saw the clients mainly as they came and went through the dimly lit corridors of our offices, which were undoubtedly worn and in desperate need of new carpet. I often exchanged nothing more than a brief hello and goodbye with them. Had it not been New York, the range of faces that passed through our doors would have seemed extraordinary to me, but there was no chance of claiming that here. Any attempt to do so was thwarted by a greater chaos waiting outside. One of the volunteer lawyers who came down from the Upper East Side twice a month to work at the center once declared that our little office, with its vast range of clients, was the perfect microcosm of greater New York. After only a few months at the center, however, I was convinced that our office was not a microcosm of anything; it wasn't even a reflection of a larger whole, which in fact was a myth to begin with. Our African clients were all in the Bronx, the Chinese in a different section of Queens from the South Asians, while anyone from the Caribbean was in Brooklyn; all we had were thin, crooked, and fiercely territorial wedges stacked next to one another.

Those who came seeking help often did so with a faint trace of shame hovering over them—the sense that they were once again pleading to someone to grant them a right that everyone else they passed on the street, on the subway, and in traffic took for granted trailed them in almost all of their dealings and most likely made them more deferential than they had ever been. It was hard sometimes to look at them when they came in like that, and I would be lying if I didn't admit to averting my gaze, even though Bill had explicitly told me not to.

"How else will they be sure that you respect them, if you don't look at them honestly in the eyes?" he had said. The problem, however, was that I was never sure if I really did respect them— those that came in with those war-weary faces often seemed so desperate to please and to attach themselves to someone that all I could muster for them was pity.

On occasion I would try to match their faces to the statements I had read. Who among this haphazard and wandering tribe was Afghani or Pakistani, Sudanese or just pretending to be because they knew it made the process easier? If I didn't know for certain when they entered, I assigned them the narrative that I thought they deserved. A gray-haired and prematurely stooped man who tried to look his best in his donation suit was the Iranian professor whose statement I had read a few days earlier, even if there was no chance that could have been true. His real life had clearly been much harder. The difficult stories, the ones that came with death or prison and rape, I left alone. I never tried to imagine whom they belonged to. It made it that much easier to bring the clients coffee or tea or Coke before they had a chance to ask.

In time I was given the job of editing out the less credible or unnecessary parts of some of the narratives, while at the same time pointing out places where some stories could be expanded upon or magnified for greater narrative effect. I was seen as the literary type in the office, with my background in literature and my supposed desire to get my Ph.D. Angela, as one of the summer lawyers working at the center before her more profitable private-law career began, would pass stories to me that needed to be "touched" or "built upon." I took half-page statements of a coarse and often brutal nature and supplied them with the details that made them real for the immigration officer who would someday be reading them. I took "They came at night" and turned it into "We had all gone to sleep for the evening, my wife, mother, and two children. All the fires in the village had already been put out, but there was a bright moon, and it was possible to see even in the darkness the shapes of all the houses. That's why they attacked that night."

It was easy to find the necessary details; they resurfaced all over the world in various countries, for different reasons and at different times. I quickly discovered as well that what could not be researched could just as easily be invented based on common assumptions that most of us shared when it came to the poor in distant, foreign countries. Bill put it to me this way once: "When you think about it, it's all really the same story. All we're doing is just changing around the names of the countries. Sometimes the religion, but after that there's not much difference." It was his suggestion that I borrow from one story to feed another. "No one will ever know the difference," he said, and at least in that regard he was wrong.

After a few weeks of working together, Angela came over to my desk. She was holding one of my reports; it was the first time she had actually gone back and read what happened to one of them after they passed through my hands.

"What is this?" she asked. She handed me the report—the supposedly true-life account of a family driven from their home in Liberia. It had been one of my more dramatic and to my ears better efforts: the family, as I cast them, forced to take shelter for weeks in a church while outside a militia stood waiting for them.

"This isn't even close to what happened," she said. "They flew business class straight to Dubai. Who are these people?"

Angela wasn't angry so much as shocked at what I had done. One of the many things that we had easily assumed about each other was that when it came to the clients, we both saw them strictly for who they were, with no sentimentality attached to them or their plights. What I had done betrayed that belief.

"I didn't make them up," I said, which was true. Something similar had happened to someone else, although whether I had heard it in the office or read it in the newspaper I could no longer remember.

"This isn't what I wanted," she said. "Give me back the original."

I handed her back the one-page report that told the all-too-common story of a family forced to surrender its business and livelihood to another family that until then had neither. I tried to make the argument to her that it was only by a trick of the imagination that we saw this as special. We lose what we have and often try to take by force what we don't. When has this ever been news? When the report was passed up to the lawyer that would actually be representing the family, it was rejected immediately and passed back down to me with a note in Bill's handwriting stapled to the top that said "Do Something With This Jonas." Angela and I never spoke of it again, nor did we speak to each other for any great length of time for a couple of days. When I asked Angela if she wanted to join me for lunch, she simply said, "Sorry, Jonas. Not today," which was as close as she could come to saying that I had disappointed her, not because I had invented a new history for someone, but because I had seemingly no problem doing so. It was the ease with which I could lie that alarmed her. It wasn't until the end of that week, at a summer boat party the center had organized, that we began to find our way back to each other. All of the lawyers were there, along with a few of the volunteers and interns and the clients whose asylum applications had recently been approved. The mood on the boat was supposed to be festive—a sort of international goodwill tour of Manhattan, with food from all the troubled corners of the planet that we represented arranged on a buffet table with tiny tabletop flags from each nation.

Halfway into the cruise, Angela found me standing by myself on the starboard side of the boat staring out into what I guessed to be the very edge of the Atlantic.

"This is where you're hiding," she said.

"Can you blame me?"

"Not really. It's depressing in there. I think someone's getting ready to give a speech."

"Aren't you afraid you'll miss out?"

"I know what they're going to say already," she said. "'It's hard times. We've done the best we can. Our clients are an inspiration.'"

She slid her arm across the railing so that it was touching mine.

"Are you mad at me now, Jonas?"

"Not at all."

"Would you say so if you were?"

"Probably not."

"I didn't think so. That's not your style. You're a brooder. Bill told me that he's the one who told you to change the statements as they came in. He said you were very good at it."

"Lying comes naturally to me."

"Yesterday a woman tried to tell me that she had eight children, and that she needed to get visas for all of them. She said she was thirty-five."

"And how old was she really? Eighteen, nineteen?"

"Twenty, twenty-three tops. I tried to explain to her that it was impossible to use that story. No one, I told her, will believe you. But she kept shaking her head and insisting that everything she said was true. Eight children, she said. Over and over. She even brought along pictures. The oldest one was almost the same age as her. I wanted to tell her to go see you and then come back to me when she was done."

The boat approached the southern tip of Manhattan; as we neared the Brooklyn Bridge, more and more of the clients came out onto the deck. They had never seen the Twin Towers except in photographs and in highlight footage of the buildings as they were burning and preparing to fall. Most stood on the deck wondering just where exactly they would have been. A couple standing near us pointed to competing sites. One placed them just on the water's edge, the other closer to the very bottom where the ferries bound for Staten Island departed. Bill came over and corrected them both.

"They were right there," he said. "Just behind those buildings."
The couple focused their sights onto where he was pointing, and
I could see them trying to recreate from their television memories
an image of the towers, but the dense cluster of buildings that
were there kept getting in the way. A year or maybe two years earlier Bill would have stuck around longer and recounted to them
his own personal experience of that day. He would have said something like "I was on my way to work," or "I came to the office
early that morning." "I saw" or "I heard," something that placed
him squarely near the center of events, which was how he saw
himself—as a slightly heroic man standing on the front lines.
In this case, however, Bill wasn't alone. For a few years we had all
tried to stake our own personal claim on what happened that day.
That time had clearly passed, and the best he or any of us could
do was to try on occasion to set the record straight.

By the time the boat crossed under the Manhattan Bridge and
was firmly rooted on the other side of the city everyone had gone
back below deck except for Angela and me.

"What do you think is going on down there now?" I
asked her.

"Bill, Jack, and John are getting drunk at the bar and trying
to show off to one another by calling their clients over. The Paki-
stanis are sitting at a table by themselves barely talking to one
another because none of them really like each other. They just all
happen to speak the same language and don't trust the Liberians,
especially the boys, who have probably snuck a bottle of alcohol
out from behind the bar even though they're too young to drink."

"And if you were down there, where would you be?"

"With the Liberians, silly. They're practically family, you
should know that by now."

"And me?"

"That depends, if I wasn't there with you, you'd probably be sitting quietly in a corner by yourself."

"And if you were there?"

"Then I'd bring you with me to the west side, where you'd never have to sit around and sulk all by yourself again."

That was the first time Angela acknowledged my tendency to quietly slip away in the company of others; even if I was still in the same room, I often disappeared into a corner of my own making. The fact that Angela saw that as something she could address, perhaps even change, had only just begun to occur to us when she said as much that night. We had our first date two days later, although neither of us ever called it such. We were both leaving the office when Angela turned to me and said, "I don't want to go straight home yet."

"What do you want to do, then?"

"I want to have a drink after work. I've never done that before, but people do it all the time, don't they? I tried to do it once, but by the time I got to bar I didn't feel like it. I had a club soda and left without saying good-bye."

We settled on an Italian wine bar that had recently opened a few blocks away in what had been a Chinese fish market. They had kept both the wide bass-mouthed fish and the Mandarin script over the entrance.

"Clever," Angela said, and in case I missed out on the sarcasm, she added a deliberately over-the-top "Real clever," with a double wink behind it.

From the beginning I drank too quickly while Angela slowly sipped away at the same glass of wine for close to an hour. I wanted to impress her and to be taken seriously. When she asked me how long I planned on staying at the center, I had drunk enough to speak without any concern for the facts. I told her I was going to leave any day. I had bigger and more ambitious plans for my future.

"I'm finishing my applications for graduate school," I said. "I almost applied last year, but I wanted to have more real-life experience. It looks better on your application, especially for the best schools."

"And lying on asylum application forms counts as experience?"

"Of course it does," I said. "It's the best kind. It's fiction but real at the same time."

"Just like graduate school?"

"Exactly."

We ended up walking back to the apartment that she shared with two other women who attended the same law school.

"This is where it ends for now," she said. "I can't have my roommates thinking I'm easy."

From then on we met every night after work. Angela still had three more weeks before the summer was over, which meant that we spent the whole of our days and all but the last hours of our night in close proximity. At the office we found excuses to come in constant contact. Angela came to my front desk to search for pens, staplers, paper clips, erasers, and when she ran out of office supplies to request, she asked for the first thing she could think of.

"Do you have a map of Missouri, Jonas?" she asked me.

"No," I told her. "I forgot it at my apartment."

I found one at a used bookstore later that evening. Missouri was the place Angela most associated with home. "We lived in a lot of other places," she told me. "Most of which I'd like to forget. But Missouri was the first one I remember. I think we lived there the longest, but who knows. I was probably too busy sucking my

thumb to keep track of these things." I left the map wrapped on
her desk the next morning. She came by later to tell me that she
loved her gift, and this time there was no sarcasm or even attempt
at humor in her voice. She was genuinely moved, and it was important to her that I understood to what extent.

For the rest of the summer, when we left the office, we did so
ten minutes apart. We would meet outside the same wine bar we
had gone to on our first date, and from there we would wander
through the city for five or six hours since neither one of us had a
private place that we could retreat to. Walking out in the open for
so long only helped to draw us closer. There was too much space
on the avenues, and the side streets were often too crowded with
people and cabs hurrying to cut across town. To counter that we
held each other's hands and arms, ribs and waists.

Angela joked that we were like a pair of stray cats. "We used
to have them in the alleys when I was growing up," she said, "and
I always wondered what they did all night. Now I know."

Despite us both having lived in New York for years, neither of
us had formed any deep, lasting attachments to particular quarters of the city. There were no streets that we were especially fond
of, restaurants that we loved, or bars where we had once spent
many hours sitting alone. Angela had come in as a serious student
studying the law, while I had spent too much time wandering from
one neighborhood and borough to the next to claim my stake on
anything other than what was immediately before me. We deliberately set out to remedy that.

"I want us to have a café," Angela said. "Some place that I can
always go to and think of as being ours."

On our fifth night together we found a vaguely French-themed
café with marble tabletops and heart-shaped wooden chairs that
we settled on as belonging to us.

"Next we need a bench," Angela said. "You can't ever be an old couple unless you have a bench. It's one of the rules of life."

We dedicated several evenings to trying out benches across the city. It was as close as we would ever come to house hunting, although we didn't know that at the time. Instead we saw everything we did as a dress rehearsal for a future date in which we would join the ranks of young, happy couples who spent their days and nights searching for what they imagined to be the perfect home.

"I don't want a bench above Fourteenth Street," I said.

"And I don't want one near or on a busy street."

"It has to have armrests."

"And a nice view. There has to be some sort of grass or a tree nearby."

"What about amenities?" I asked.

"A restaurant with a bathroom not too far away would be nice."

"So would a bodega," I said. "I get thirsty if I have to sit still for a long time."

The benches in and around Union Square within walking distance of Angela's apartment were ruled out immediately—too loud and too crowded, and the crowds of war protesters who congregated there on the weekends made even Sundays a riot.

"No one ever seems to go home around here," Angela noted. "There's always people around. We need something quieter."

We walked farther east until we were at the bottom of the East Village. There, across the street from a housing project and a community garden filled with willow trees, we found a bench that seemed rarely occupied.

"This is perfect. This bench will definitely do."

"We can sign the lease tomorrow," I said.

. . .

When the summer was over, Angela began her real career at her midtown law firm. She took her first paycheck and moved into her own place—the one-bedroom basement apartment that we would come to share for the next four years. Angela had never been strong on boundaries, and on the day she moved into her apartment she had an extra set of keys made for me.

"You leave work before me," she said. "I don't want you wandering around like a cat anymore. I think we've done enough of that now. It's time we got a home."

I officially carried over the last of my personal belongings to her apartment two months later.

"We don't have to make a big fuss over it," she said, even as she handed me the new lease that she had drawn up herself to include space for both of our names. "People do this sort of thing all the time. Or that's what I've been told anyway. It makes sense. The only thing of yours that isn't here already are the rest of your clothes."

On the morning I moved into Angela's apartment we spent several hours deliberately mixing all of our belongings together.

"I don't want a yours and mine, a his and hers," she said. "I've never lived with anyone before, and if I'm going to do it now I want to do it properly. Here. Give me your suitcase."

I handed her the one black valise that contained all the clothes I owned. She opened it, tried to stifle a small laugh at how little was there, and then without any direction began laying all my clothes neatly in drawers next to hers.

"What if someone comes in and thinks that those are all my underwear?" I asked her.

"Then they'll know you spend too much on clothes. What else do you have?"

I pointed to the half-dozen boxes of books I had brought with me—the core of what had once been a sizable collection of paperback editions of poems and novels that had all but completely fallen apart.

Angela emptied her bookcase of the hardbound legal texts she had accumulated in law school and began to fill the shelves with my books, which stood in poor comparison to the formidable, well-bound texts that had once been there. When she was finished she shook her head and went back and cleared the ends of each shelf. She filled the empty space with thick, solid books on constitutional and tort law. It was an effort that we both admired.

"It's not too much, is it?" she asked. "I don't want it to seem too deliberate."

"It looks perfect," I told her. "And sums us both up just right."

For at least the first six months we lived together we remained fully committed to the principles established that morning. We were careful to talk always about the things *we* had, and that *we* owned, or that *we* needed.

"How much money do we have?" Angela would sometimes ask, not because she wanted an actual response but because she wanted to revel briefly in that plural possessive that she was free to employ whenever she pleased. Like a magic trick, we had doubled our meager belongings and our even more meager selves, and for a time there we both felt richer for it.

"I'm going to read everything you have," she said to me one afternoon. "Even the stupid books you don't want to tell me about."

"And I'm going to do the same," I said. I stood up and pulled from the shelf volume one of *U.S. Constitutional Law*. Angela, not to be outdone, went to the closet and pulled from the top shelf a thick hardbound copy of a thesaurus that had been a college graduation gift from my mother.

"I've heard it's really good," she said, "and by good I mean: exceptional, superb, outstanding, marvelous, wonderful, first-rate, first-class, sterling."

After that Angela carried copies of novels she had never heard of with her to work. She made a committed effort to read several of them on the subway, just as I also honestly tried to become a lay expert on the regulations governing international and human rights law, which she said were the only two things she could love about the law.

"The rest to me is bullshit," she said.

We continued on like that, albeit with diminishing degrees of conviction that everything we said was possible. Angela gave up on my books, and I did so on hers as well. We struggled sometimes to have dinner together more than twice a week, but then again, so did most busy young couples. It wasn't until I lost my job at the center nine months later that the first cracks in our relationship began to show. Bill called me into his office on a Tuesday morning and with a heavy, somber voice said there were some things we needed to talk about.

"You know we've been very happy having you here, Jonas," he began. He had always had a hard time standing still, even in the most mundane situations. He paced around the corridors of the office throughout the mornings and afternoons often muttering to himself. It was even worse now that we were in his cramped office, which came with a single window that looked directly onto a new apartment building that was going up. He didn't have enough space to diffuse his anxiety and found himself constantly hemmed in by the desk, the bookcases, the stacks of poorly arranged files that occupied the floor around him. He tripped over one and sent a stack of papers cascading onto the ground. When I bent over to pick them up, he told me not to.

"They're irrelevant," he said. "I should have thrown them away years ago. Like most of the files in here. Leave them where they are, otherwise I'll never touch them again."

He started talking then at great length about the challenges facing an office like ours. He repeatedly used the phrase "It's a whole new game out there."

"The laws. The immigration people. They're not like they used to be. It's a whole new game with them," he said.

"And as for funding, I can't even talk about how that's changed. It used to be that we could write a couple dozen grant proposals a year and we could almost be certain that at least half of them would come through. Now it's a whole new game. We write seven, maybe eight. And if one of them works we count ourselves lucky. Our private donors want to always know who exactly our clients are. They never say anything specific. That would be beneath them, but I know they're worried that we're trying to let the wrong people through. I tell them we have plenty of safeguards against that, but that's not what they're worried about. They're worried about being caught up in something that may someday look bad. They don't even know what that something may be or could look like, but they don't want to take their chances and so now they're dropping like flies, Jonas."

I let him talk like that without interruption for more than a half hour, during which he touched on everything from the Patriot Act to the FBI to how seriously fucked you have to be in your home country to get a visa in America. By the time he finally came to the reason why he had called me into his office I was hardly listening anymore. I knew the outcome long before then and had spared myself the misery of anticipation. I don't even remember him saying, "We're going to have to let you go immediately. There's simply not enough money left to keep paying you." By that time I had left the building and was picturing the walk I was going to take later that afternoon across the Brooklyn Bridge. It was a bright, almost spotless late October afternoon, brisk without being too cold, and I was certain there would be a good, strong wind blowing across the East River that would carry me across.

III

The trip to Nashville had been my father's idea, or not exactly his idea but his boss's, a slightly heavyset man with thick rolls of fat around the nape of his neck and a pale bald head that reminded Yosef of the moon before it had fully risen and hung low and dim, its stains visible to the naked eye. He knew my father had a fondness for country music and had told him multiple times that if he really wanted to hear and understand it, then he had to make his way to Nashville. My father's love of country music was one of the few things he had brought with him from Addis. Kenny Rogers had been the first American singer to break his heart, but there were others as well. As he was sitting in an outdoor café terrace along the city's main Bole Road in 1973, a song had snuck in from a parked car radio and through the idle chatter of the other men sitting next to him. He couldn't have repeated a single line, but that didn't matter, because he had understood the mood of the song, and he knew the spirit in which it had been written was the same as his. Decades later, when his English was fluent and he had learned all the standard clichés, he would tell me that the song "spoke to him." For now, though, there were better and more difficult ways of describing it, and he would have to say that the song reminded him of a certain type of sadness that came to him whenever he found himself alone. He had realized at a young age—eight, to be precise, in the weeks following his mother's death—that the world was a cruel and unfair place, and yet despite that, he hated watching it pass. He couldn't stand to see some days end, and that song said it all without having to say any of it.

My father had been dreaming of boxes since coming to America, and he hoped that this trip might end those dreams, which despite his best efforts had continued to haunt him. He saw the boxes folded and flat, stacked one on top of another in long, endless, elegant rows. He saw them made of cardboard and cement, paper, plastic, and wood. Boxes large enough to hold a man and small enough to fit under an arm, into the palm of a hand. His life had been made and unmade by boxes, and what he felt toward them could only be called a guilty obligation, one that hung hard and heavy around his neck like a debt that however much he tried could never be fully repaid. At night, in his dreams, he gave the boxes the consideration they deserved, granting them their full and proper place in his life. He spoke to them. He asked them questions and waited in vain for a response. He sized them up and determined what their contents could possibly bear: a hand-carved bed frame made in Dubai; a pair of woman's shoes, preferably Italian and a size 6 with adjustable leather straps for an ankle that may have grown an inch or two larger; two arms, half a torso, and one right leg of a thirty-five-year-old man who stood five-foot-ten and had been reduced to one hundred thirty-four pounds by a combination of hunger and illness.

He had learned by practice and observation how to measure the strength and interior scale of any one box simply by looking at it. Not all boxes were equal or could be trusted. Take two boxes of the same size and stare at them long enough and you learn to catch the stress fractures along one corner, the slight dent at the bottom that while suitable for short and light journeys—a trip, say, across the Gulf or up the Nile—could never handle long and difficult hauls. Styrofoam was better than cardboard, and cardboard was better than plastic. Metal was obviously the strongest, but there was little of that, and when it came, it did so with intense unwavering scrutiny by border guards and managers. Metal also trapped heat and, unless there were holes already drilled into the top, was impossible to breathe through.

The dreams began to come almost nightly shortly after my father arrived in Peoria. He had just begun work on a factory floor as the assistant to the deputy assistant manager of shipping and inventory, and there, for the second time in his life, he found himself circumscribed by boxes. When the dreams first came, he was driven from his bed into the arms of the worn green-and-brown-striped couch in the living room that had been given to him by someone at the Baptist church he now attended. (In Italy he had been a Catholic and in Sudan a third-generation Muslim, and now here in America he was a Protestant who kept his alcohol hidden under his bed.) The couch was too short to handle his outstretched body, which was fine because at that point in his life he no longer trusted the dimensions of any space. He was always crouching, curling, trying to reduce himself into a package smaller than the one he was made of. This was the problem with beds. They afforded too much space, granted the body too much permission. In a bed, even with a wife next to you, there was enough room to stretch out your arms and legs, to fold your hands behind the back of your head and stare mournfully at the ceiling. Some lessons in life deserved to be remembered, and if there was one rule that my father believed in, it was that space was not immutable. It could be stripped from you at any moment. For four months he had practiced contorting and conforming his body into the smallest state imaginable. At the port in Sudan he had practiced squeezing himself into empty oil barrels at the suggestion of a tall, nearly hairless dark-skinned man who told my father to call him Abrahim—"like the prophet," he liked to say. He had charged himself with getting my father out of Sudan, and was the one who had told him that with time and practice he would eventually learn that the body could endure and survive on much less than he had ever thought. And like a prophet, he predicted that before the year was over, my father would be ready to make the ten-day journey north, up the Red Sea buried in a box in the hull of a ship, to a new home in Europe.

Before the port in Sudan there had been a prison cell just outside of Addis, which was not acknowledged to exist or have been built, filled with dozens of men and boys, all of whom learned to sleep standing upright by finding a wall or trustworthy shoulder to press against. They sat in stages, squatting on the ground with their knees pulled all the way up to their chest, the oldest and youngest, of which he was neither, being granted the longest intervals. Eventually the floor was covered in shit and urine, but the men continued to sit anyway because despite how hard they may have tried, how much will they may have exerted, there was always a point at which the body had to relent. After he was abruptly released for reasons he never learned, there had been days spent crammed on the bed of a white pickup truck, hidden at times under a plastic blue tarp that if seen from above reminded you of a caricature of the sea, complete with ripples and waves, and so by the time he reached the port in Sudan two months later he was already well versed in the body's governing rules, nearly all of which he had already broken.

My father, Yosef Getachew Woldemariam, dreamed of boxes until the last days of his life. He dreamed of them in French, Spanish, Italian, Amharic, and English, of which only the last two he spoke fluently. His Italian had been reduced to *Ciao, bella*. His French to *Oui, ça va*. His Spanish to *Quiero tener*. At night, however, the missing words came back, and he continued to chatter away with the boxes in French, Spanish, Italian, and English— whatever they demanded—picking up the conversation that had begun thirty years earlier when he was a scrawny refugee working in a port in Sudan. He continued to ask the boxes where they were going, and how much they could carry, and most important, whether or not they had room enough for him, drawing on every language and country he had ever known, proving that language, like memory, suffered from the same need for context in order to survive.

During the last eighteen months of his life he granted the boxes permission to step out of his dreams into his day-to-day life, giving them the presence they had always deserved. It was a form of peace, long withheld and finally discovered in a one-room studio (itself a type of box) at a YMCA built close enough to the banks of the Illinois River to offer an occasional view of a passing cargo ship. Alone in that tiny room he drew pictures, some of which I still have, of three-dimensional boxes on the backs of take-out menus, on the rare envelope that found its way to his mailbox, on the backs of his social security checks, just under the space reserved for his signature. He collected discarded cardboard boxes from the trash and reassembled them in his room—an act that he thought of in near religious terms, with the same promises of rescue and salvation that a preacher brings to his flock. While the other widows and widowers who haunted the long fluorescent-lit hallways of the YMCA rescued cats, stray dogs, scraps of metal, aluminum cans, and empty bottles to be recycled, my father gathered the stained and worn boxes left outside restaurants and grocery stores. He brought them back to proper form, leaving them to dry in the sun, even taping up their battered edges when necessary so they could live again, this time without the burden of having to support any weight other than their own.

My father sat hunched over the wheel of his 1971 red Monte Carlo and watched as his wife of three years and one hundred twenty-three days walked down the steps of their two-story apartment building carrying far too many suitcases for such a short trip. She had retained her looks, and for that he had been grateful. After more than three years apart, without so much as a single picture passing from her to him, he had begun to suspect that the long-legged nimble young woman he had left at the peak of her beauty had been traded in for a prematurely aged woman: one who wore her hair tied in a conservative bun, wrapped herself in a white shawl, and carried herself with the same demeanor as the older mothers who spent all but the least precious hours of the day kneeling outside some church in Addis, praying for the dead and salvation. His worst fears had been relieved the moment she stepped off the plane into the waiting terminal where he stood holding a bouquet of flowers, flanked on either side by a photographer and reporter from the town's local newspaper. (The headline three days later in the *Peoria Herald* would declare "True Love Reunited,"

beneath which ran a two-hundred-word article on shrinking prof-
its and impending layoffs at the local tire factory.)

On first seeing her enter through the glass doors of gate A2 of
the Greater Peoria Regional Airport, my father could have said, at
least for a second, that he was ready to fall in love if not all over
again, then for the first time. Mariam, as it turned out, was still
beautiful. She was still young and wore her hair down with the
ends curled just slightly like the peak of a question mark. He
could have never said that this was the same woman he had married on a sunny summer afternoon at St. Stephanos church in
Addis, partly because he had never really known who that girl had
been. Their courtship had been brief and dramatic. Most of it had
occurred under a backdrop of fiery speeches and frequent gunfire
in the last days of a monarchy, a time that those young enough not
to know better declared to be the end of history. It was easy to fall
in love under such circumstances, and in fact, you could have said
that those who weren't busy dying or in jail were busy fucking and
falling in love in cafés and motels all across the capital. Love was
in full bloom, and on the same evening that my father, Yosef Getachew Woldemariam, declared the need for a violent and unre-
lenting upheaval of society to a café crowd of recently radicalized
college students, he promised Mariam that as long as there was
breath in his lungs he would love her. With so much at stake, it was
easy to give yourself over to another person. Declarations of love
were general all over Addis, offered simply, without hesitation.

Here she was now at the foot of the stairs, three years after
they met, her hair still shoulder length but without the curl, a sign
perhaps of a growing maturity and wisdom, a sign perhaps that
there was not that much left to question or wonder over. As Mariam Woldemariam, twenty-eight years old and three months pregnant, lifted the loose door handle of the 1971 red Monte Carlo her

husband had scraped and saved to buy in order to live up to an old black-and-white picture that was itself a lie, my father sat hunched across the steering wheel, thinking to himself over and over, in a voice that rang as true as if the words had been spit from a god, that if he wasn't careful, this woman would surely destroy him.

IV

When I returned home that evening, Angela was already back from her office. She had taken her position at the dining room table where she often worked late into the night on whatever legal memo was due the following day. She seemed genuinely surprised when I entered. Since I had moved in she had never come home from work and found the apartment empty without knowing why in advance; doing so now had awakened a series of old anxieties within her.

"Where were you, Jonas? I called you several times but your phone was off."

"I stayed late at the office to help Bill with a statement," I said.

I could see a faint trace of relief come over her with those few words, which I said as convincingly as if they had been true. Her greatest fear was of abrupt and sudden abandonment, whether it came through death or a simpler form of departure. She tried like most people to never show that, but it was evident even in the way she insisted on always holding hands when crossing a busy street, as if that offered any protection against what she feared.

"Why didn't you call?"

"I'm sorry," I said. "I didn't know that you would be so worried."

"You know that's how my father left us," she said. She kept a perfect, straight face whenever she said that. There were already at least a half-dozen ways this imaginary father of hers had left. She turned to him whenever she felt she needed to prove that she hadn't actually been worried. He'd been arrested multiple times for various petty crimes from which he never returned. Once he'd gone out for milk and vanished, for cigarettes on a different occasion. I tried to detect a pattern in the stories, one that would say more about who Angela was and what she had gone through, but the obfuscation was too great; all I could see were hints of an injury that she had yet to let go of. This alone would have almost been enough to make me love her; the fact that she chose to make a mockery instead of a spectacle out of her past moved me, in part because a deeper damage was implied. On one side was Angela, my girlfriend; on the other, fragments of a child whose wounds from time to time pierced through the skin like the shred of a bone on a broken limb. I understood the reason behind her efforts and the price that she paid to make them as clearly as if they had been my own.

"He never came home from work," she continued. "My mother and I sat up all night waiting for him."

"Was dinner still in the oven?"

"Of course it was. It would have been good too, but we never got to eat it."

"Because your father didn't come home."

"Exactly."

"You told me last month your mom threw him out of the house."

"Did I say that?"

"You also said you never knew him."

"Did I say that too?"

"You want me to continue?"

"You're getting confused," she said. She had trouble keeping track of her stories, which was her way of telling me not to take them too seriously while also asking me to remember every one in case one day the truth came spilling out. When and if that day came I wanted her to know I was ready.

"You didn't understand," she said. "First my mom threw him out of the house. Then another time he didn't come home from work. That's the real story."

When I was leaving the apartment late one night to buy her a pint of ice cream at the grocery store around the corner, her final words to me, shouted over the television, were, "That's how my father left me. He went out to get us ice cream and never came back." I heard her laughing as I walked by the open window.

On occasion she went public with her dark humor. At a party thrown by one of her former roommates during law school, a tall blond woman standing in the center of the small circle we had awkwardly stumbled into was talking, for no apparent reason, about her plans to go to Mexico for Christmas that year. The party was full of people like that—all around the room similar conversations were being shared about trips that had been taken or were being planned, resorts and great restaurants that had been eaten at. Angela later confessed that she found the moment impossible to resist.

"Why did she think that we cared where she was going?"

As soon as the blond woman had finished her sentence, Angela jumped in.

"That's funny," she said. "That's exactly what my father did. He went to Mexico just before Christmas, but then he never came back. I guess he must have really liked it. Maybe you'll see him down there. Tall black guy. Used to have a big afro, but that was the seventies so it's probably gone by now. Tell him his daughter Angela says hi."

We spent the rest of the evening trying to find ways to interject the words "That's the same thing my father said just before he left us" into other people's conversations. Mostly we kept the joke to ourselves, but when someone near the front door announced he was going to buy cigarettes, Angela couldn't help herself. She turned to the four strangers standing closest to us and said, "That's the same thing my father said to me and my mother before he left. 'I'm going to go get some cigarettes,' but then he never came back. Every time someone says that, I remember that night."

We were still laughing when we came home a half hour later. People had begun to stare at us, and Angela suspected that it was only a matter of time before someone came over and offered their apologies, so we left abruptly without saying a single good-bye.

"If I was white, everyone would think I was joking, you know that. They'd laugh and say, Ha, ha, ha, Angela is so funny. Instead everyone thinks it's true."

"It's kind of true."

"There's no such thing as kind of true. If I told you the whole story, you could say that it's true, but you don't know the story. You only know that I don't know where my father is. But you don't know why or how he left. I say I don't have a father and everyone thinks they know the whole story because they saw something like it on television or they read about it in a magazine. To them it's all just one story told over and over. Change the dates and the names but it's the same. Well, that's not true. It's not the same story.

"Believe me, Jonas. Once you leave the room all that sympathy becomes a joke."

I placed the book bag that I carried with me to the center every day on my side of the bed. Inside were the handful of personal items that I had kept at my desk: the collected poems of William Carlos Williams and Hart Crane, along with a framed photograph of my father in Rome that I had taken from my mother's closet the last time I saw her.

"How's Bill doing?"

"He's fine," I said. "Although I think he's having a problem with funding."

Angela would later say that I had deliberately lied to her at that moment.

"You said Bill was fine. You said you stayed late working with him. None of which was true."

But she would be wrong about the deliberate part. At the time I hadn't given much thought to what I was saying. I had returned home and I had found Angela sitting at the table, buried in work but still worried about where I was, and I had thought it almost miraculous that such a thing should occur. Nothing in my life up to that point had quite prepared me for that, neither my parents nor the handful of lovers I had had before then. Everything else I said after that I said with the preservation of that image in mind.

It took two days for Angela to learn that I had lost my job at the center. She always left for work just as I was waking up, and of course when she came home, I was supposed to be there waiting; our schedules had remained unchanged. We didn't talk about my work during those two days, except to speculate once as to what might have happened to one of the clients we had worked with together.

"Do you remember the Kurdish family that came in just before I left?"

"What was their story?"

"Turkish—the father was arrested five times for no real reason. You may have said it was close to a dozen."

"Seven. A dozen would have been too much. He was arrested seven times—beaten and tortured twice. He had to give bribes every week to keep from being arrested again. His family was going broke and hungry as a result."

"Was any of that true?"

"I don't know," I said. "I doubt it. He was smart. He came in lying. I just helped him do it better. My guess is that right now he and his family are doing just fine."

The next day she tried to reach me on my cell. Had I wanted to keep the truth about my job hidden from her, I would have answered my phone when she called. Instead I let it ring for the entire afternoon without even looking at it while I sat on the bench Angela and I had claimed. There I tried to recall just what exactly I had said to her the night before, and how much damage I may have caused as a result. Similar slips with the truth had occurred before, but there was often very little at stake.

At four p.m. she gave in and called the center directly. When Bill answered the phone, she asked him where I was.

"He must have thought I was an idiot," she said later that evening. "Does he know we live together?"

"Yes. I told him as soon as I moved in."

"That's worse," she said. "Honestly, I'd rather be an idiot."

The fact that she had been embarrassed enraged her further; it made her victim to what she assumed would be other people's pity. For the next fifteen minutes she puzzled over what had made me lie to her. "Are you trying to get out of this?" she asked. "If so you don't have to lie. Just get up and leave."

And then later: "Do you want me to be angry at you?" "Are you angry at me?" "Do you want to get back at me for something?" "Did I embarrass you?" "Do you not trust me?" "What else have you lied about?"

And for all of her questions I didn't have a single response. Once found out, I had nothing to counter with in return. Angela yelled, and as her rage grew louder I found myself mentally backing out of the room, not all at once as I had previously done with Bill, but in slow, gradual stages so that it took some time before Angela noticed that all but the obligatory lights had gone out.

"Please tell me you're listening to me, Jonas," she said. "You haven't said anything."

"Of course I'm listening," I told her. "That's what I've been doing. I know you're angry and you have every right to be."

I learned after that to never try to placate her with what she knew to be simple, generic words of comfort.

As angry as Angela may have been that night, she was calm and rational once again a day later. There were other concerns on which she could focus her energy. I had lost my job, and after the following week, when my last paycheck arrived, I would no longer be able to help with the rent or the massive debt that Angela had assumed putting herself through college and law school. Even worse, I now figured into someone's statistic—the twenty-five-to-thirty-five-year-old black male without a job; Angela had come too far in life to bear that for long. She never forgot the heights to which she had ascended, and at every moment she was looking back wondering how easy it would be to fall.

"We need to find you a job," she said. To which I wholeheartedly agreed. Two weeks later Angela came home with what she said was great news.

"I had lunch today with Andrew, one of the senior partners at the firm. Somehow we started talking about you, and I told him you had just lost your job working at the same center where we met. He asked me what you wanted to do, and I said you were going to start applying soon to graduate school to get your Ph.D., but in the meantime you needed a job. He said he knew of one that had just opened up at his old school—a part-time teaching job that might not pay well but would be helpful in the future for the references alone. I think it would be great if you applied."

Even had I wanted to, I couldn't have said no to Angela. While she claimed to have forgiven me for lying to her, the damage remained. Her trust in me, and our relationship, was far from repaired, and I knew that a part of her was constantly on the lookout for any sign of deception. During the weeks I spent at home before I eventually began teaching at the academy, I felt obliged to send her messages several times a day to assure her that I was either at home or diligently searching for a new job. I told her frequently that I loved her, and couldn't have been happier than where I was right now with her. She craved stability and security, and I wanted to give that to her. And while the desire to root myself may not have been as deeply ingrained in me as it was in Angela, I had grown tired by then of floundering and could have easily said, if asked, that I was also looking for something more enduring. Even beyond that I had begun to sense that my place in the world was rapidly shrinking, that this was not an age for idle drifters or starry-eyed dreamers who spoke wonderfully but did little. A time would come soon, I was convinced, when I would be politely asked to step off board the ship that was ferrying the rest of the population, and in particular my generation, forward. If I didn't latch on to something soon, I'd find myself thrown overboard, completely adrift, bobbing out to sea with nothing, not even so much as a life vest of companionship to hold on to.

After three interviews and a background check that involved several phone calls to my former college professors, I was hired at the academy to teach a double course in literature and composition. I had studied English in college, and with the assistance of several friends had landed some temporary work copyediting a couple of obscure academic journals, for which my work was criticized as being mediocre at best. It was enough, however, to qualify me to teach a course at the academy that the other teachers were reluctant to take on, or saw as beneath them, even though a name like mine, Jonas Woldemariam, often failed to inspire linguistic confidence in others.

"Where's that accent of yours from?" the dean of the academy had asked me during our first interview, after I had said all of eight words to him: Hello. It's a pleasure to meet you.

"Peoria," I told him.

He hesitated for a second before moving on, and I could see him wondering if it was possible that there was more than one Peoria in this world, another situated perhaps thousands of miles away from the one he had heard of in the Midwest and therefore completely off his radar. He was clever, though, and worked his way around that.

"Did you spend a lot of time there?"

"I was born and raised there."

"I see," he said, by which he meant to say that he didn't really see at all, and was even more confused than before. Afterward he led me on a personal tour of the academy's four floors, the very last of which offered a view of Upper Manhattan that stretched to the lower end of Central Park, forty blocks south from where we stood. "It's a beautiful building," he said, and it was easy to hear the genuine awe in his voice when he spoke and the invitation for me to share in that awe with him. I had, however, paid scant attention to the details until then. I had been led up and down the stairs and through the hallways, but I had only been thinking of what could still possibly go wrong before the interview was finished. Regardless, I agreed wholeheartedly.

"It's fantastic," I said. "Really."

When the dean called two days later to say that I had the job, I hung up the phone; I felt victorious. I had finally broken through the surface on which I had subsisted and was now going to be a part of real life.

From the beginning I knew that I wasn't going to be hired on as a full-fledged teacher; there were enough full-time faculty members in the English department as it were, and none, even those entering their third decade at the academy, were looking to retire.

"It doesn't mean we won't have a full-time position for you in the future," the dean told me. "In fact, I'm sure that if all goes well, we can all but guarantee that, but for now we can only hire you as half-time, or better yet, say three-quarter time since you'll have plenty of homework to do."

I spent the months before the school year started supported by Angela, who in her relief at seeing me gainfully employed had rather proudly declared that her boyfriend didn't need to serve tables or find another temporary job. "Don't worry," she told me with what was supposed to pass as a sly wink. "I got you. And once you start working we can talk about what you owe me," which of course could not be counted in simply monetary terms since what I owed her extended vastly beyond the remittances she gave me to cover the costs of dinners and grocery bills. I accompanied her more frequently to firm-sponsored events, and when asked what I did I was proud to respond, "I'm a teacher." We began to think of ourselves as a black power couple in a city full of aspirants, the kind who would someday vacation for an entire month in the summer and whose children would attend elite private schools like the academy with the tuition paid full in advance.

A few days before my classes were scheduled to begin, Angela came home from work with a large elaborately wrapped bag that she set on the kitchen table as soon as she entered. She didn't have to tell me that the package was a gift for me. It was obvious from the unrestrained smile on her face when she walked in. Angela was one of those people who took an almost excessive pleasure in see- ing their gifts received, although in her case there was nothing vain or self-serving in it, and if anything, the act of gift-giving as per- formed by her was fraught with danger, which made the genuine looks of surprise and pleasure that much more meaningful when they came.

Before I had finished unwrapping it Angela told me what it was.

"It's a satchel," she said. "You'll need a nice one when you're a teacher. Or at least that's what I hear anyway. Although if you hate it you can tell me. I still have a receipt. It's black so it will go with everything."

The bag was highly polished and elegantly stitched, most likely by hand, around all the edges, and although I made no mention of the price, and almost went out of my way to prove my ignorance of its worth, I knew from the first click of its silver clasps that it had cost multiple times more than what we could have ever hoped to have honestly afforded.

I began teaching at the start of the new year. It was early January and I was heading off once again to school for what felt like the first time. Angela sensed my anxiety, even though I never mentioned it. Without saying anything she woke up earlier than normal with me. We dressed for work standing side by side at the foot of the bed. Afterward we even took the same northbound train to Fourteenth Street, where Angela eventually transferred to the proper line. Her excuse for doing so was that she wanted to make sure I got to work safely.

"You never know," she said. "You could get lost or kidnapped in this city." On a crowded train we pressed ourselves together. I slid my hand under Angela's jacket and held her stomach for support. When it was time for her to get off the train, she leaned back so I could kiss her good-bye, and in parting said, "Don't be afraid of them, Jonas. They're just kids."

When I arrived at the academy and the first of my students entered the class, I understood what Angela had meant. By any standard I had been afraid for too long of anything that I thought might pose a physical or emotional risk, and Angela, in her own way, had always been aware of that. I hardly spoke in the company of strangers, and went out of my way to avoid expressing a contradictory opinion. Until Angela, I had kept my attachments to a minimum.

As soon as I began teaching at the academy I noticed that there was a distinct, almost palpable difference in the general haze through which until then I had conducted my life. Things, objects, people all suddenly appeared sharper, as if I had been wandering through the world with a pair of dirty, poorly cared-for glasses that blurred the lines and washed away distinctions. Angela, who had always struck me as pretty, with her large, wide eyes and equally large head, in which every feature was somehow perfectly exaggerated from her ears down to her lips, was now strikingly and even beyond that alarmingly beautiful. I couldn't help staring often, and not only at her but at so much else throughout the city, from women on the street to men freely urinating in parks. There were vast swaths of both city and normal life that I had failed to notice, if only for the simple reason that none of it, as far as I had understood, concerned me and the quiet discreet life I had been living. I had always suspected that at some early point in my life, while still living with my parents and their daily battles, I had gone numb as a tactical strategy, perhaps at exactly that moment when we're supposed to be waking up to the world and stepping into our own.

With my new job at the academy, I began to see myself as part of that active, breathing world which millions of others claimed membership to. When asked how my day was, I had, if I wanted, more than just a one-word response at hand. I had whole stories now that I often wanted to tell, even if I didn't have the words for them yet.

V

When my mother finally entered the car, she noticed that today the seat belt only half worked. It hung tired and limp from the car ceiling, unable to tighten or relax, its position fixed, permanent, like a dead limb that can only be lifted and dropped and lifted again, vital and useless at the same time. When she slid into the passenger-side seat and buckled the belt into its metal clasp, it took on a second, unintended presence that was more than just physical. The belt, clasped around her stomach, became for her a confirmation of the simple fact that in some places, life did indeed matter, and deserved careful, deliberate protection. The lower half wrapped around her waist and today, the feeling was not that different from the sensation she felt when she wrapped one arm around her stomach and squeezed herself to the point of nausea.

The car didn't roar to life so much as it sputtered, as if waiting to be convinced of the role it still had to play in my parents' marriage. My mother adjusted her weight from one side to the other, and the white vinyl seats squeaked along. The seats had baked throughout the summer, at times becoming too hot to touch, and now, for once, they were cool, almost perfect. In the winter they would freeze, becoming as cold as their color promised, and in six years the vinyl would begin to crack into long, thin, parallel streams that leaked artificial fabrics into the hair of anyone who sat there. She wasn't showing yet but soon enough she would. Her stomach had already started to round just slightly, as if someone had crawled underneath her skin and blown one burst of air, a breath just strong enough to puff the skin into a soft little ball. Her hair had begun to grow damp and limp with constant sweat, making even the slightest curl all but impossible. She had seen this happen before, first with her girlfriends and then one by one with each of her three younger sisters, all of whom had married after her, all of whom had taken a small sadistic pleasure in taunting her with their outstretched stomachs and physically present husbands. One by one she had watched them swell and then burst like balloons, suddenly shocked and disappointed to find that the great surprise hiding in their stomachs was simply just another baby, no greater or worse than the thousands of others who were born and died that day. She, however, was a modern woman, one liberated from the standard burdens of family life. She envied no one, least of all her sisters. With a husband at the time lost to God knows where (perhaps Kenya, perhaps Egypt, she had thought, never suspecting him to be one for jail or cargo ships), and no children to clean or feed or watch over, she was free to take the money she made each month typing letters in the Ministry of Agriculture—"failing crops and historic food shortages are to be expected"—and put them to use in the modern way. She bought shoes: black, brown, tan, red, blue, white, gold, purple, all with heels, straps, and the all-important gold stamp: Made in Italy. She bought cigarettes imported from England, a bottle of scotch to entertain friends with. Mariam took taxis instead of buses home from work when it rained in the winter or when the crowd had swelled to a near-violent breaking point in the summer. At those moments she would step gingerly from the curb just a few feet away from the bus stop and raise one arm (the left one, carrying two gold bracelets and a quarter-carat diamond ring), quietly imagining the jealous stares of the women she worked with, of the dozens of other women she didn't know and had never met but who happened to be standing there at that moment with their children or husband next to them, their heads still wrapped in a shawl, their eyes cast down.

If she had known any English at the time, she would have turned to them and said, To hell with you all.

A s the car slowly slid in reverse out of the driveway, she remembered that she had forgotten something upstairs.

"Wait," she said. It was the first word she had spoken to her husband that morning, and if either one of them had had a penchant or taste for symbolic speculation, one of them would have said, "But isn't that all we've done? Isn't that the only thing we have to offer each other anymore?"

No such taste existed in either of them, however, and that "Wait" was simply uttered and then lost and left for me to interpret.

My mother took her time getting out of the car and walking back up the stairs to the apartment. She slid her hand along the banister as she went up the steps and took account of the dust that gathered around her fingers. Her own house in Addis, she realized, had never been so dirty. There had been a maid to clean and cook; a gardener to tend to the yard; a squadron of neighborhood boys to lift heavy objects, change lightbulbs, and screw in broken locks (three on the front, three on the rear, and one on each window, because a woman living alone could never be too safe, could never trust solely the kindness of strangers). The dust now was her responsibility. It was what she heard the other women at the church talk about: dust and stains and collars that never got clean. Sofas that were ruined by grape juice left to sit too long. Children's pants stained with blood. All of that was supposed to be her charge now.

She took a seat on the bed, and then after a few minutes laid back, allowing herself the luxury of placing her feet on the hand-me-down white duvet given to her by one of the women at the church. There was nothing she needed or had forgotten. She had come back here for purely selfish reasons. In those few minutes between opening the car door and taking her seat next to her husband, she had caught a glimpse of her life as it would have looked to her if she were standing outside of it: the poor woman with the cheap and overstuffed valise being more of a cliché than she was willing to bear. Unlike those stories, however, she was not running from but to, her suitcase packed not in defiance but in submission, with her in no particular rush at all. She should have expected more from herself, the voice she was trying to quell threatened to say. To which she would have agreed wholeheartedly.

Coming back up to this room was just another one of the minor lies my mother told herself to get through each day. There was only this quiet, solitary repose that she sought, and if the world was a kinder and better place, I imagine sometimes, it would have stopped permanently right then and there exclusively for her. Everything else around her could have continued. Neighborhood children could have aged, graduated, and fallen into drugs and love and premature pregnancies. The old women at the church—Agnes, Harriet, and Jean—could have faded away into their deaths one at a time, like summer months ticked off so quickly they hardly seem to have ever happened. Life in general, in other words, need not have ended, just so long as my mother could be granted the small gift of lying endlessly on a bed on an early September afternoon staring at the ceiling while her husband sat parked in the driveway waiting for her. It could have made a picture-perfect scene, supposing the canvas was drawn wide enough to allow for a view of house, bedroom, trees, and car—a scene quiet enough to deserve the merit of being hung in a famous museum. People could have gazed at it in some future era and said to themselves, "So, this was life."

My mother lay on the bed and counted off the minutes in her head one second at a time. Today, she gave herself two hundred and twenty seconds, a record. On other days she needed only twenty or thirty to step back gracefully into life. That was enough time to compensate for a broken dish, for a day and evening of complete silence between her and her husband. The seconds themselves were nothing more than that. They were the smallest fragments of time that she knew how to account for, and she believed that if she could count and accept them, then she could believe again in the hours and days they made up. If she knew how to do it, she would have counted to the tenth or hundredth of each second. She would have gotten to the very bottom of time, and having arrived, stared at it directly and said, "Okay, I can do this. If this is all there is."

Until today the most she had ever needed was one hundred and eighty-four seconds. That had been enough time to make up for getting lost on an afternoon stroll and being told by a young white boy with bright red hair and freckles that if she knew what was good for her, she would turn around and get the fuck back to wherever she had come from. Most of what he said was lost on her, but she understood the intent of violence and threat in his voice, as we almost all always do. Long before we understand anything we know this.

One hundred eighty-four seconds were not enough for her today, however, nor were two hundred ten, or twelve, or eighteen. Two hundred twenty alone were enough, while anything greater would have been too much. The consideration of time in itself was a threat, one no less real than the sneering red-headed boy on a bike.

She checked the seconds off with her eyes closed. When they were all gone, she opened her eyes and planted her feet firmly on the floor. Time had started over just enough so that the woman who rose from the bed and walked quickly down the steps to the waiting car with a random book in hand (in this case, a coverless tan-colored hardback copy of James Baldwin's *If Beale Street Could Talk* that had been bought by her husband at a garage sale for decoration) was not the same one who had gone upstairs. This Mariam was lighter, more prone to smiling and acknowledging the simple beauty of a fall afternoon drenched in solid light and smoothed over by sporadic pollen-filled breezes. Like the other Mariam who preceded her, though, this one knew just as well that a time was approaching when closing your eyes and counting off the seconds would not be enough. What happened when that time finally came remained a mystery to both. Would they flail and tear their hair apart, or simply sink quietly to the bottom of whatever life they had, never to be heard from or seen again?

She opened the car door, slid in, and shut it hard. It was still possible to believe in Nashville at that moment, to think, perhaps, that a honeymoon was not so impossible after all.

She turned to her husband, who appeared not to have moved

a muscle or inch since she left him, and said, with more conviction than anything she had said to him in weeks, if not months, "Okay, I'm ready now."

W hen she returned to the car, my father took note of what my mother had claimed she'd forgotten. Just enough time had passed between her leaving and returning for him to begin to doubt what she had said about forgetting something upstairs. He pictured her in the apartment staring at him with contempt from the window, or perched in front of the bathroom mirror thinking that she had grown far too beautiful for a man like him. The last thing he had wanted that morning was a fight, but it was clear now that it was going to happen anyway. The fights grew out of their own organic, independent force, obliged only to their own rules and standards. They existed independently in the world, just as surely as the oak trees that lined the driveway existed whether he was present to see them or not. He could no more keep the fights from erupting than he could make the trees vanish by an act of will or, say he had the authority, one of mercy.

That morning the fight began as soon as my mother returned to the car with a copy of a book she had never heard of and could hardly read in her hand. In retrospect it's easy for me to say that it was the book that did it, but it could have just as easily been a change in a pair of shoes, earrings, a favorite shade of lipstick that proved to my father that he had waited for nothing, and had there-fore been made, once again, into a fool.

"It seems," my father said to his wife as soon as she sat down in the car, "that you didn't forget anything at all."

Note the words, the first that my father said to his wife that morning, deliberate and in a different context almost polite. They're important here. Of the tens of thousands of ways two people can turn against each other, my mother and father were faithful to a handful of words to provide that final spark, chief among them being "you didn't." As in, "You didn't turn down the heat before you went to bed last night." Or in later years, "You didn't pay the rent last month," and "You didn't find a job, a career, a life, a home we can live in, a school to send our son to." There was always a "you" who had failed to do something and another "you" who never failed to see that. Sometimes I think if they had never learned to use the second person singular their lives could have turned out so much better. They could have turned to that indifferent and guiltless third person the same way they later turned to faith and cardboard boxes to keep death at bay. They could have used it to endure the burden of layoffs, failed spelling tests, and the soaring cost of heating oil, but at least in this way they were like most Americans, saddled with a "you" to blame and the need to see someone hang.

As soon as my father said the last two words of that sentence, he felt the abrupt and dramatic shift in the air that precedes any violent confrontation. Something vibrated, buzzed. If there was a way to narrate it, he would have described it as the tiniest particles that make up the air we breathe becoming suddenly charged and electrified with a palpable life all their own. The world around us is alive, he would have said, with our emotions and thoughts, and the space between any two people contains them all. He had learned early in his life that before any violent gesture there is a moment when the act is born, not as something that can be seen or felt, but by the change it precipitates in the air. Once, at the port in Sudan on his way to work on the loading dock, he had almost rounded a bend on the other side of which a young man from

Kenya or Tanzania (he could no longer be certain which) was being kicked to death by a group of men for reasons no one ever learned. They were all living there in makeshift boardinghouses—refugees and migrant workers—piled on high together, which sometimes made it hard for him to read the air for signs of disturbance. That day, however, Yosef had come to a corner where one goat stood tethered to a pole in the ground, and there, just as he was about to turn, he had felt something that told him to turn away in the other direction and wait until the news of whatever was happening reached him at lunch. He had felt the same thing before in minor and significant ways. His father had once nearly killed him when in a rage he had swung at him with a knife still in his hand. The blade had cut seamlessly through the air, dividing the space Yosef had been standing in less than a second earlier cleanly in two. He was only nine years old at the time, which made him old enough to remember what he had sensed in the moment between his calling his father a bastard and the knife swooshing through the air. At a rally of high school and college students in Addis twenty-four years later, he had been the first to duck as the crowd approached a wall of waiting soldiers, at least one of whom had his sights firmly fixed on him because he had stood in the front, tall and proud and far too arrogant, with a picture of Lenin raised high over his head. That soldier had caught Yosef from more than a yard away, and just as he began to curl his finger around the trigger, Yosef had felt the shift that told him death was near.

The bullet that had been intended for him landed instead squarely in the abdomen of a sixteen-year-old boy who only two weeks earlier had arrived in the capital from a small town in the north. That boy had never heard of Lenin, or the Communist utopia, and unlike Yosef, he had missed the signs completely.

. . .

My father did not want a fight that morning, but one was coming to him nonetheless. He waited to determine its shape, and once he had, he leaned over his wife, locked the door, and threw the car into reverse, his foot pressing hard on the gas as he sped backward out of the driveway, away from the trees that continued to wave their branches obstinately in the breeze. He was not a romantic, or a man given to casual admiration of nature, but as he pulled out of the driveway, his wife's voice just beginning to reach its feverous pitch, he did think that in a different time and place, one better and more forgiving, he would have liked to have spent an afternoon like this sitting quietly under trees similar to the ones that surrounded his house. There he would have played out his fantasies of the lives he could have lived. The trees, in fact, were what had first drawn him to this house. Walking quietly alone on a summer night eight months earlier, he had spotted them from a block away, and compelled by forces he believed to be greater than himself, he rushed forward without pause or question toward them. He had been alone for so long that he had grown used to acting on instinct, and that night instinct had told him to head straight toward a row of trees on a street that was otherwise void of them. Once there he stared up and admired how simple it was to think the world beautiful, and to his surprise he found that perhaps that thought alone was enough to make life bearable.

At least this is how I like to picture him, whether it's accurate or not: as a man in search of a home standing underneath, or perhaps even across from, a row of trees on a summer night. If he was ever happy here, and I doubt he was, it would have been on that evening, which I've only just now invented for him. I can't say that I ever actually saw him stand and stare at the trees, or that I remember him ever mentioning them. He was not that type of man anymore, admiration and reflections on beauty having long since become a thing of the past. More likely than not, the trees, like that apartment, like nearly everything else in his life, was an accident, one that he simply stumbled onto. Regardless, history sometimes deserves a little revision, if not for the sake of the dead, then at least for ourselves. And so I say that on a warm summer night my father, Yosef Getachew Woldemariam, walked with his back straight and his head held high toward a row of trees that, with their massive trunks and sky-piercing branches framed against a clear indigo sky, held the promise of the one thing he wanted more than anything else in his life: protection.

VI

The first real arguments that Angela and I had were sparked by minor things—a gas bill that had been paid late that Angela credited to my general negligence, or an unnecessary expenditure on a pair of three-hundred-dollar shoes that Angela claimed were still cheaper than a therapist. It was easy, as a result, to assume that they didn't portend to touch on anything greater than the strains on our finances and the different ways we had of coping with them. From the beginning it was common for Angela to spend the better part of a Sunday afternoon struggling to add up the numbers that accounted for our daily life. She would add up her salary and my salary, and then deduct for taxes, rent, food, credit card bills, law school debt, and whatever sum she chose that month to wire back home to her mother. When she was finished she would always come to the same conclusion—it was never enough. Regardless of how much she occasionally scrimped on lunches, taxis, and after-work drinks, by her accounting we still came up short.

"I don't know how people live in this city," she told me. "All these people and most of them seem to make it work."

After one particularly long week of late nights at her office,

Angela spent four hours on a Saturday afternoon calculating the cost of our life. She did the numbers repeatedly, accounting for certain future variables such as a promotion or better than usual holiday bonus. When they still failed to amount to something substantial, she put her pencil down on the table and looked up as if she was waiting for me to grab hold of her before she fell. I had seen that look of profound disappointment and frustration on a woman before, although never on her. As soon as it appeared, I began to search for a reason to leave.

"I'm going to go find us something for dinner," I said. "I'll be back soon." I kissed her once on the forehead before walking out, which gave me just enough time to see the incredulous look on her face. Here she was worrying about our survival and I was thinking about dinner, she had wanted to say, neither one of which was true. We were both thinking about the same thing—our fragility, as individuals and now as a couple. Despite Angela's mathematical aerobics, I always believed that we had enough to keep us afloat. I checked our balance every couple of days, and while nothing was being gained, oftentimes very little was lost at the end of the month. For a woman who had grown up deep on the side of poverty, however, that was far from enough. The line that separated the two halves of her life, in her mind, could be moved at any time, and she was convinced that only increasingly larger sums of wealth could protect her from a return to the poor, rootless childhood that she had known. There was little I could say in response. At the time I didn't know what else I could do but run.

When I came back home from the grocery store, our fight began. It continued throughout the rest of the evening. This is what it sounded like.

"Did you find what you wanted at the store?"

"Yes. Everything was there."

"So you're going to make dinner?"

"Unless you want to order in."

"No. Do whatever you want."

And then, for the next four hours.

"_____"

"_____"

The only words we exchanged before falling asleep were questions, polite and meaningless.

"Can I get you something to drink?"

"Do you mind if I watch television?"

After that we turned out the lights in succession, first me and then two hours later Angela, who had spent the latter half of the night back at her table scratching out one by one all the figures she had added up.

You see, at the beginning we weren't fighters. We weren't yellers or throwers, even if we eventually came to be. It would take time and much deeper wounds for us to get to that point.

It was shortly after that Angela and I decided to get married. Having seen some of our weaknesses exposed, we hoped to cover them back up with a small, almost clandestine marriage at city hall. Angela's boss Andrew arranged for a private ceremony in a judge's chamber, even though he couldn't attend. It would be two more years before I ever met him. The only common friend of ours there was Bill, in whose office we had first met and who we credited with having brought us together. He came with a former client of his, a Pakistani woman who now that she was in America was hoping to someday be an accountant.

"Maybe next time it'll be me standing here," Bill told me, even though I could tell he didn't really believe that. He thought he was

saying that for my benefit or for the benefit of the woman standing quietly next to him, but he was the only one who needed to
hear those words. In the end there were six of us gathered in the
judge's chamber, which had none of the oak-paneled walls that I
had expected but was instead poorly dressed in slightly fading
yellow wallpaper adorned with pictures of a much younger man
standing with the various mayors of the city. The whole thing was
done and over with in less than a half hour.

"Is this how you imagined it?" I asked Angela over an elaborate lunch at the Four Seasons that the partners at her firm were
paying for.

"It's better," she said. "By far. We could have been married in
a garage and I would have been happy. For most of my life I've
tried not to imagine much of anything. Or maybe I did once, but
then I got tired of never seeing any of it come true so I eventually
stopped. I never even thought about what I wanted to do when
I grew up or where I wanted to live, much less who I would marry.
You have to believe in better things to come in order to do that. I
don't think I had much of an imagination, which must be why I'm
so fond of you."

Angela leaned awkwardly across the table to kiss me once on
the forehead, and then again on the lips, a gesture that seemed
born as much out of gratitude as love. We raised our glasses of
champagne to toast and looked around curiously to see if anyone
was watching us. It was a Friday afternoon and the restaurant was
crowded with a dozen other couples in suits. Once we realized that
no one was, we searched for other ways to the change the subject.

"Don't look now," Angela said, "but we're the only black people here." She pretended to whisper to me from behind her menu.

"Don't worry," I told her. I covered the left side of my face
with the menu. "I don't think anyone's noticed."

"Someone is probably wondering why they don't see more black people here, especially since we've all supposedly come so far."

"I'm sure then that they're grateful to see us."

"As long as it's just the two of us, trust me. They're delighted."

When we returned home later that evening, we promised ourselves that in a not so distant future, we would do the day all over again in a more elaborate fashion.

"I'd like to do it in Central Park," Angela said.

"Where?"

"You know that little castle in the middle? I want to do it there. We can rent the whole place out."

"And you think that'll be big enough for all our guests?"

"You're right, Jonas."

"I was thinking of something slightly bigger."

Eventually we settled on taking over the grounds surrounding Bethesda Fountain, including the tunnels leading into it and the surrounding pond, a grand affair that only a fairy tale could sustain. And if at the end, behind our idle bedtime chatter, there was something deeply unsatisfying about what we said, there was also at least an underlying belief that what we had done, while far from perfect, was still more than either of us had ever expected.

I was still reveling in the fact of our marriage when I returned to the academy on Monday. A chemistry teacher who had been at the school for fifteen years and still wore on her blouse and skirt stains that appeared to date from her first year in the lab had warned me earlier to never let my students into my personal life. "Once you do," she had told me, "you'll never be able to get them out. They're like viruses. They'll pass anything you tell them along from one year to the next, but it will only get distorted and warped and worse as it goes along."

I had attributed my one-day absence to personal reasons, but of course my students were careful observers of all their teachers, and within ten minutes of my class beginning a hand was raised in the front.

"Is that a wedding ring, Mr. Woldemariam?"

I looked at my hand, as if to confirm the fact that the ring Angela had slipped onto my finger three days earlier was actually there.

"It is," I said.

I had no sooner said that than two other hands went up. When did I get married, and what was my wife's name? When I told them she was a lawyer, there was a general hum of approval; all assumed that I must have married up. Without my considering it, fifteen or twenty minutes passed like this. I went from one-word responses to more elaborate narratives about how we met and how long we had been together. I had to defend the intimate size of our marriage by explaining that neither of us had family nearby and we wanted to make the wedding about us. I took as much pleasure in my divulgences as my students. I had rarely spoken at such length about myself, and never so honestly. When the class ended we had covered only a fraction of what I had planned, but I hardly cared. I could credit the lost morning to a necessary student-teacher bonding.

Something broke after that day. I shed many of the reservations I had around my students and increasingly found myself engaged in short periods of idle chatter with them. I was often inter-rupted by questions of an entirely personal nature that I some-times tried to diffuse quickly and which on other occasions I went to great lengths to respond to. My students soon knew that I lived in the East Village, north of Houston, somewhere between First and Fourteenth streets, in a one-bedroom apartment that got little to almost no light during the mornings, and that before then I had spent time in Brooklyn and Queens. In college I had tried briefly to be a poet—I had a love for the modernists, Bishop, Pound, and Williams being top among them—as did most of the people I knew, but while I had given that up, I still kept my love for certain poets alive. These were only warm-up questions to the greater narrative that they wanted to get ahold of. Near the end of my first semester one of my students—a round, freckled-faced blonde who until then had never spoken in my class—finally asked me where I was from.

"Excuse me, Mr. Woldemariam. Where are you from?"

I had heard the question before, of course. Bill had asked it and then answered it as he saw fit during our first meeting, although with less tact and subtlety.

"Woldemariam? What is that? Eritrean. No, let me guess. Ethiopian. Probably an Amhara name, am I right?"

I had come to an easy agreement with Bill, but I found myself reluctant to do the same with my students.

"I'm from Illinois," I said. "If that's what you mean."

The girl, I think Katherine was her name, fidgeted in her seat until one of her friends whose name I no longer recall came to what she must have thought as being her friend's defense.

"No. I think she means where are you really from."

I had considered saying that I was *really* from Illinois, but then I realized that most if not all of my students knew the answer they were looking for already, whether it was specifically Ethiopia or just Africa in general that they wanted acknowledged. They had heard it, just never from me, and now they wanted a personal confirmation that would elevate their knowledge of who I was beyond the general rumors that swirled around the teachers at the academy. In that way they could mark me as being theirs. At that point, as fond as I may have been of my students, I had no need to give that to them.

When I later told Angela about the questions my students had asked, she laughed and said, "If they can get an answer to that, I'd like to know too."

"Meaning?"

"Meaning sometimes I think you're not from anywhere at all. Your parents are Ethiopian, or I assume they are, because I never met them. The only thing you've ever told me about them is that they didn't like each other, and none of you are close. I don't ask you for more than that because I figure you must have your reasons, but it gives you a cold, sometimes abstract air. You know what Bill told me once about you?"

"What?"

"That when he first met you he thought you might have come here illegally. He was only partly joking. He said there was something about the way you barely spoke in the office that reminded him of the illegal immigrants he used to work with. He was wrong though. Talk to any immigrant long enough and they'll tell you where they came from, and then once they start most of the time they won't really want to stop. Next thing you know you're looking at pictures of someone's grandparents or village, but the most anyone can get out of you is that you were born in the Midwest. Most of the time you don't even say the city. Just the Midwest, as if that means anything."

I had heard something similar before from Angela. Shortly after we started dating she noted what she referred to as my unusual reserve. Friends in college had often told me that I could sometimes come across as indifferent. Rarely was I confided in, but it wasn't trust that I seemed to lack, but empathy, or empathy that could properly express itself as such. People needed to know in tangible and familiar ways that they were being heard; it wasn't enough to say that they were, or to stand in close proximity when called upon, even if you were willing to do so for as long as needed. If there weren't warm feelings, then perhaps there were no feelings at all.

I dismissed most of what Angela said. I still thought of myself as capable of the great displays of affection she seemed to be waiting for, and who knows, maybe with time I may very well have found a way to express them, but there was always another crisis lurking not too far off to which we had to respond. In quick succession Angela lost two important cases that she had spent the better part of the past six months arduously working on. Even though she had no reason for thinking so, she assumed after the first loss that her job was in jeopardy. Other more senior lawyers at her firm were involved in the case as well, but it was Angela who decided she would assume the brunt of the failure. She came home after the first defeat and lay down on the bed in a semi-fetal position. She was worried about her future. "I hate not knowing what happens next," she said.

"Lawyers lose cases all the time," I told her, even though that was hardly what she needed to hear. That cases were lost was evident.

"I know that," she said.

What was less obvious was that for Angela each loss posed as the commencement of a greater disaster that she had always imagined would someday occur, one that she believed wouldn't end until she had been stripped bare of all that she had ac-complished.

"I've never believed that things work out for the best in the end. It's simply not true as far as I can see. Once we learned about the decision Andrew came to my office and told me not to worry about it. 'Don't worry,' he said. I almost laughed when he said that. Don't worry. It's only the people who've never had to worry about shit in their lives who say that."

When a judge handed down the second defeat two months later, Angela was fully convinced that she was going to be fired any day. She spent the later hours of the night worrying about how to pay the debt she had amassed along with her substantial portion of the rent. "We have almost nothing saved," she said. "And there's no family that we can turn to, so what happens then to us?"

The next day she went to a boutique in the West Village and spent several hundred dollars on a single pair of shoes. She threw them down on the living room floor and said, "If I'm going to lose, I might as well have good shoes."

"I thought you were worried about money."

"I needed something to make me feel better." She didn't have to point out that it was because I had failed to do so. On the night she told me she was worried about losing her job, my response had been to rub her shoulders gently for a few seconds before drifting off to sleep. In small but significant ways I had been hiding from Angela's doubts and fears as if they were my own. When she came home defeated, I had to remember to look her in the eyes, which meant that I must have often forgotten to.

Without acknowledging it, we began to draw lines around the apartment. Angela cornered herself off at the dining room table. I kept to the kitchen and bedroom. We both stayed up late working:

Angela on the next set of memos for the newest case, while I took my time grading papers on symbolism in short stories and poems that the school required the students to read. Our greatest failure up to that point was that we were unable to explain to each other the degree to which we were afraid of the same things—suddenly losing whatever minor gains we had made in life and the security that we hoped came with that. We knew our place in the world was far from secure; each defeat, whether it was at work or at home, only reinforced that. We had failed to say that much to each other, so it was only inevitable that soon we would begin to multiply our losses.

VII

The blow that temporarily knocked my mother unconscious came hard and swift and was coupled with the crash of her head against the passenger-side window. She didn't see it coming, which is not to say that she didn't expect it to happen. The blow, she knew, was inevitable from the moment her husband spoke, because in doing so, he had crossed a line that not even she was aware of having made.

Like a courteous guest, the blow had announced itself ahead of time, and like any good hostess, she had prepared herself in advance, turning her head just slightly to the right to protect the delicate spots—eyes and nose—in the seconds between her husband locking the door and raising his hand. The only thing that had yet to be determined in those remaining seconds was how hard and where he would hit her. Over the course of the past six months there had been a few full-forced, closed-fisted punches, dozens or perhaps even hundreds of open-handed slaps, some minor, some not. There had been an irrational childlike kick to the shin that made it difficult to walk, and two days later a flashlight that upon hitting her just above her left brow had temporarily darkened the world in that one eye. ("Imagine," she would say to me thirty years later in an obvious attempt to impress me with how well she knew English, "the irony of that.") No two blows were ever the same, even if they were delivered to the same spot within seconds of each other. Each had its own force and logic. As a general rule, however, the first punch, kick, slap, or push was the hardest; the rest, when and if they came, being generally milder, softer—a concession to both their bodies' ability to endure pain.

The blow that knocked her unconscious today was a first. Neither a punch nor slap but a simple, deliberate shove to the head. A push, open-handed, with all five fingers spread open as if her head was a ball that could be palmed and then tossed at will. In the end, though, it was the passenger window that did it. It was the glass that took her narrow face and diffused the force with which it came through millions of tiny particles of sand; and in the end, it was the glass that decided that there was nowhere else for her head to go but back to the white vinyl seat from which it came. You could almost imagine the side of her head leaving an impression on the window, a haunting daguerreotype portrait that would have forever captured the right side of my mother's face, with its high cheekbone and pointed chin, the side she liked to show off in pictures because she knew it was the prettiest side she had.

The last thing she recalled was reaching for the door handle as the car began to reverse far too fast out of the driveway. It was an instinctive gesture, born no doubt out of the secret conviction that all she had to do in order to right the world to her expectations was get away. Did she actually expect to make it out of the car, however? I doubt it. She should have realized by then that an escape was impossible. The car was moving too quickly, and the passenger door was already locked, and then there was the matter of her

husband's arm stretched over her body like a guardrail—one that
at any moment was prepared to fight to bring her back. Had she
gotten away she would have gone crashing into the driveway, the
concrete being far less generous than the glass that had absorbed
her head. Escape anyway was never really more than just a fantasy.
After all, how many times did I watch her pack and unpack her
suitcases: dozens, at least, which I alone can recall. We were always
supposedly on the move, to St. Louis, Kansas, Chicago, and Des
Moines, ready to disappear but somehow rarely getting any farther than one of a half-dozen motels on the outskirts of town, or
on occasion, when the situation demanded it, to a shelter for the
battered and homeless. Life, for my mother and me, was lived in
the spaces between attempted departures.

　　During the twelve minutes and thirty-two seconds that she was
unconscious my mother's mind wandered off into a gray area that
I like to think of as the future conditional: the "will" and "would"
that are simultaneously built on the past and yet foolish enough
to imagine that what happens next is simply a matter of will and
hope. And so there was this dream: of Mariam sitting alone on a
couch in a house with dark wooden floors and whitewashed walls,
a child asleep in a corner bedroom painted orange just as hers
had been. The house was a near-perfect replica of the one she had
grown up in, with arched doorways leading to the kitchen and
bathrooms, along with windows every few feet opening out onto
a grassy banana-tree-filled courtyard. The differences here lay in
the furniture, sleek, low-slung, and thoroughly modern, just like
the city the house in her dreams inhabited—let's say a place somewhere along a coast, New York, Los Angeles, Seattle. What matters most, however, is the stillness, the sheer absence of sound that
is otherwise impossible to find except in dreams. Here then is the

place where no harm can happen: sanctuary that even the dead would be envious of.

B y the time she woke up, the 1971 red Monte Carlo her husband was driving was halfway over the bridge spanning the Illinois River. She came to just in time to catch sight of a barge heading south along the river, its minor wake washing up along the abandoned shoreline littered with recently defunct brick warehouses that, she would say to me in a future time and city, seemed like the perfect metaphors for modern life—long, neglected, and relatively empty. It was not a beautiful view from the bridge, but it was an honest one, and for that she respected it. Even on a clear, sunny afternoon it carried with it a tinge of gray, as if sorrow were automatically built into this town and its recent decline. Ahead of them was a factory known for its tractors and earth-busting machinery. In two months it would be roughly two thousand souls and feet lighter—her husband's being just one pair—while behind them, my mother knew, was a downtown whose finest days she had arrived far too late to see. She was not a spiteful person, except in her worst moments, but like anyone, she took a measure of comfort in knowing that recent disappointments in life were not hers alone.

She touched the side of her head just as the bridge came to an end. A small knot had already grown and in an hour would begin to throb as if the blood pressing against the grain of her scalp were seeking a way out.

I'm swelling in two places, she thought to herself.

She always did have a thing for pairs. While most people lived content with individual moments, my mother was constantly on the lookout for the twin event, the correlation that proved nothing happened by accident, and by extension, that none of us was ever really alone. I remember once coming home from school and finding her standing in front of the living room window with a plastic bag filled with ice wrapped around her hand. I was ten or eleven at the time. I knew enough by then to expect the worst—a temporary arrest, or her rendered into a ball of flesh huddled in a corner, but no one was home except her, and the visible signs of struggle— pillows on the floor, a TV blaring loudly, or a torn bra left dangling on the edge of a chair—were absent.

She actually looked serene that afternoon. Her body was pressed against the window, a distant but faint smile on her face, the kind we employ when remembering something deep and personal, something that no one else would ever understand.

"I burned my hand making tea," she said when I came through the doors and asked her what she was doing and what had happened to her hand.

"And just by chance," she asked me a few seconds later, "did you hear the news this afternoon? Two women, just a few blocks away from where we live, were burned to death in an apartment fire this morning."

Up ahead a sign offering a room for $29.99 per night loomed, came, and then went. It was three thirty in the afternoon on a Wednesday and they were only twenty miles outside of the city, which meant that they were still one hundred and forty-three miles away from the fort Jean-Patrice Laconte had built in 1687 when first settling this land for the French. The remains of Laconte's fort were historical landmark number one along the road to Nashville and, with the exception of a potential detour to Springfield to see Lincoln's home, were at the top of my father's list of the important places in history he wanted to see on this trip.

He had made a list of at least a dozen such places that he planned to someday visit, most of them scattered around the Midwest where less notable bits of history were easy to stumble upon. He hadn't mentioned wanting to stop anywhere to his wife before they left. He was afraid of what the explanation would have sounded like, having already tried a couple of variations in his head.

There are some places I want to stop at before we get to Nashville.

There is an important historical landmark on the way to Nashville.

He had given up after that, confident that his desire to delve into the obscure parts of the country's history made sense only to him. Since arriving in America, he had tried to come up with a series of standards by which he could judge his assimilation. He gave himself points for knowing answers to certain questions, like which teams were playing football that Monday night, or which television actresses he would most want to sleep with and which ones he wouldn't. If while at the plant one of his coworkers said, "Hey, Yosef, who's that playing on the radio?" and he responded correctly by saying Ray Charles, then at least one, sometimes two points were added to the poorly tracked column in which these things were supposed to matter.

It had been almost a year since he had begun keeping track, but there still weren't enough points in his column to satisfy him, and undoubtedly he failed by almost any measure to appear as a real American. Unlike the other men at the plant, he spoke very little while he was at work. He knew that too many words and sentences strung together on his part were an open invitation to be mocked. If he said anything more than "Mr. Henderson, I have finished with the task you have given me," he could expect to hear his words echoed back to him in a comical but perhaps not so far from the truth accent, and so he kept his mouth shut and spoke in grunts or, better yet, gestures when he could.

He wanted other inroads into America, and his list of historical landmarks was his most recent one. By his reckoning, the more obscure the landmark the better. Anyone in the world could claim to have laid eyes on the country's more famous or important monuments. There were plenty of immigrants in D.C., New York, and Boston who could see towering skyscrapers or marble monuments out their living room windows, but where did that get them? Nowhere, he thought. It meant nothing to stand in the shadows of such buildings if you didn't know the history that preceded them, and if you didn't believe that as a result of that knowledge they belonged to you as well.

My father planned on rectifying some of that that afternoon. He had read about Laconte's fort in a small pamphlet at the immigration office in Chicago where he had declared his intentions to someday be a citizen of the United States. The pamphlet, titled "A Brief History of Our Great State," concerned itself mostly with facts about Lincoln and the post–Civil War years. Only one paragraph at the beginning had mentioned Laconte and a few other early explorers. "Pioneers of the American wilderness," it had called them, with Laconte as chief among them; this had been enough to convince him of the path he needed to seek out. Afterward he could say, "This is very similar to an early American landmark . . ." or "This reminds me of an old American fort that I visited," and anyone who heard him would be impressed and would think, Look how far he has come.

He understood that he wouldn't get there all at once. It would take time and patience to become the kind of man he dreamed of. This visit to Laconte's fort was merely the start. Perhaps he wouldn't get all the way into the heart of America just yet, but surely in the end he would feel closer to it. He'd stand in the center of one of the country's first ruined forts, and if he had to, he promised himself, he would drag his wife, kicking and screaming if need be, to bask with him in the light.

While my father drove lost in his thoughts of history and Nashville, my mother was missing mountains. They had always been there, holding down all four corners of the city she had been born and raised in, neither imposing nor protective but significant nonetheless. They weren't the type of mountains that inspired awe or wonder. Uneven, stunted, and without the requisite snow-capped peaks, they rose around the edges of the city in clusters of threes and fours, and in the morning and evening drew the clouds into them. It's baffling to realize sometimes what we miss and in fact have always loved, she thought. Whether it's a particular view of green-and-brown-clad mountains or a voice we assumed we had long since put to rest. They come back and find us whether we want them to or not. On that morning she missed the mountains, even though in the twenty-eight years she had spent in Addis, she had never once deliberately considered their existence. She had never stared at them because they were simply and irrevocably there. That alone had been reason enough to believe they were always destined to be.

She picked up on their absence just as the red Monte Carlo approached sixty-five, a respectable but not reckless speed above the limit, and as she did so, she realized she had no idea or reason

for being here in this car on this day in this country. The entire
sequence of events, as it turned out, had been a mistake. There
was never supposed to be a husband she hardly knew, much less
loved, or a child whose existence she had hidden for first one, and
then two, and now three months. The facts of her life had crept
up on her, had asserted themselves one at a time—first a plane
ticket, then a middle-aged man, who had at once grown slightly
heavier and more diminished than she remembered, standing in
an airport with a cheap bouquet of flowers. That in turn had been
followed by a few nights of rough, mediocre sex with that same
man pushing away inside her with an urgency born more out of
desperation than love or attraction. Taken together, those facts
had accumulated enough mass and force to assert themselves, in-
controvertibly and without doubt, as the sum total of her existence.
It was no different from adding up cans of peas and cartons of
milk in a grocery store. Take one town, one man, one apartment,
and one unborn child and add them all up together and what do
you have if not the definition of a life?

She almost pressed her hand against the window, as if there
were something on the other side of the glass that she could touch,
and in doing so would save her from the irrepressible fear that
she was lost and would never find herself again. That gesture,
however, would have made the longing that much more difficult
to bear. It was better, she believed, not to translate emotions into
actions, to let them lie dormant, because once they were expressed,
there was no drawing them back. They enter the world and having
done so become greater than us. Of all the lessons I learned from
my mother, this was the first. It was conducted on the steps of a
brick Catholic school with two angels guarding the doorway, neither of whom had the power to comfort or protect, despite what
their roles suggested. I remember there was something resem-

bling a bruise beneath her right eye that morning. The night before had been rough, although I can't say I recall the details as to
how or why. What I can say is that that morning she put on a
light blue dress and for an hour curled her hair so that the ends
turned in toward her neck. She put on lipstick and pressed her
eyebrows down and stretched her eyelashes up, and before leaving the house she sprayed herself with a quick burst of the only
perfume she ever wore, the same one I continue to smell after all
these years regardless of where I am, because every time I think
of her, I breathe her in.

It was my first day of school, and taking me there was the only
social outing she had had in months. She treated it with all the
pomp and circumstance that other women bring to more significant affairs—a dinner party here, a first date there—since while
she had had these things in the past, they belonged to a different
Mariam, one utterly unrecognizable from the one who stood in
front of a mirror worrying about whether her neckline revealed
too much for an early Monday morning.

We walked the six blocks to my school together, hand in hand,
and I remember thinking, or maybe I'm just saying this now because there are few children in the world who do not want to
remember their mothers as being beautiful beyond imagination,
that there could be nothing better in the world than this. I had
never seen my mother smile or walk that way before. She literally
seemed to glow as she walked down the street, heels clicking and
the inverted curls of her hair bouncing in sync, her beauty rising
out of her in cone-shaped beams that I'm sure would have had the
power to pierce any heart they touched. It was the most memo-
rable walk I've ever had.

It wasn't until we arrived at the school that her mood changed.
It was almost possible at that moment to breathe in the confu-

sion and anxiety that came with her seeing herself surrounded by women as young as or younger than she was, but without the bruises and uncertainty of language she carried. Those women wore jeans and shirts with logos advertising baseball teams and hardware stores, their hair unkempt, their lips naked. They walked their kids to the top of the steps and shook hands with the teacher and then banded together in circles that seemed almost preordained, as if their gatherings were reflections of a natural law that grouped women together by the size of their bodies and the color of their hair and the year and model of the cars they drove.

She left me just a few feet away from the school, kneeling down on the curb behind a rusted red van so she could hide in its shadow and see me clearly as she told me the first in a series of lessons that she later referred to simply as Things You Must Never Forget. She told me dozens of such lessons throughout my childhood, each delivered with the same insistent wide-eyed stare and stern voice that seemed to say on every occasion, you will never hear anything as important as this again, even if the point she had to make concerned utterly trivial matters: the proper way to break a clove of garlic; the necessity of keeping your socks dry. That first lesson went like this:

Jonas, I want you to remember what I say now. Are you listening? You must listen. This is important. There are things that you must not ever tell anyone. Is that correct? Must not? It's okay. It doesn't matter. You know what I mean. You are good. Say that after me.

Good.

No. Say, I am good.

I am good.

Yes, you are. And so you will listen. If someone asks you what's wrong, you say nothing. Say this, Nothing is wrong.

Nothing is wrong.

Good. Say it again.

Nothing is wrong.

Perfect.

She kissed me once on both cheeks before safely crossing the street, where a row of identical two-story brick houses with small front porches and unguarded front lawns stood ready to hide her. With a few quick flutters of her hands, the kind generally used to shoo away dogs, pigeons, and the empty-handed poor, she waved me up the school's steps, where I stopped and stared until she disappeared around the corner, because she knew that I would never leave until she was gone. A piece of dark blue fabric from the end of her dress trailed her for a fraction of a second and remained fluttering in space even after she had rounded the bend. It could have just as easily been a patch of blue stolen from the sky and delivered to earth for all the consideration I put into it. Imagined or not, that last patch of blue stayed floating in the air, and I could still see it even after she was gone just as clearly as I could see the stop sign on the corner and the maple tree that shaded the sign and intersection. That patch of blue was no less real for not having technically been there, just as my mother was no less real for being out of sight. We persist and linger longer than we think, leaving traces of ourselves wherever we go. If you take that away, then we all simply vanish.

It took the firm grasp of a teacher to pull me into the school, the bells having made their last call.

I said earlier that I couldn't remember what happened to my mother the night before she took me to school, and perhaps that is true. Perhaps I can't remember, neither then nor now. At the time I did know, however, that it was easy for terrible things to happen to women when they were out of sight. They took hard hits, and then later slept in your bed where you could protect them.

VIII

As Angela and I began to withdraw from each other, I found myself increasingly taken with my teaching; each new class was an opportunity to step farther away from what I thought of as my slightly bruised and sequestered self. Even if it was only for an hour and a half, after my first year at the academy was over, I knew that it was important to seize every chance to do so. I gradually began to transform myself from a quiet, seemingly sullen teacher, known primarily for my expensive black leather briefcase and the brown-bag lunches I carried to work, to a fully engaged and often dynamic lecturer who sometimes filled in his daily lessons with small digressions and slightly fanciful tales.

From the beginning I loved my job at the academy, but at that point it wasn't because I was attached to teaching or to my students, to the late-nineteenth-century classroom with the stained-glass windows I taught in or to any of my colleagues, who were generally at least a decade older than I was and looked at me as a curious but nonetheless interesting intruder. I wouldn't form any deep attachments to my students or to the building until much later, until I was certain that I was leaving. Only then would I recognize them. What made me happiest when I began were the

simple tools of my trade: my chalkboard, my attendance notebook, my grade book, and the top drawer in my desk that came
stocked with a month's supply of pens, chalk, staples, paper clips,
white-out, tape, and glue.

There was more to it than just this, however. Shortly after I
began teaching at the academy, I began to think of English as my
subject and then my discipline in a way I had never done before,
not even in college when I stayed up late writing essays on Robert
Browning and the emphasis on light in Hart Crane's poems. Having grown up in the shadows of my parents' high-pitched accents
and broken grammar, I had always hesitated before I spoke and
often whispered my words in case they failed to properly impress
whatever audience was before me. What I didn't understand until
I began teaching was that knowledge, or perhaps intimate knowledge I should say, was the first step toward possessing anything. I
knew every corner and inch of my apartment and the house I had
grown up in. I knew Angela and large fragments of her sad history
from when she was born until we separated, and I can say that
each in some way was mine. Angela was my girlfriend and for
three years my wife, and until I moved out of the basement apartment, with its secondhand furniture and low ceiling, it was mine
as well. I had a more intimate knowledge of each, and therefore a
greater claim on each, than anyone else living on this planet. Often
when I went home from work on the subway at the end of each
day, I thought to myself, I am going home to my wife. I am leaving
for my home. The *my* was everything. Take that away and what
did you have beyond a series of meaningless nouns—home, wife,
car, dog, child. After one year at the academy, I began to think of
English in the same way. First it was my class, and then it was my
subject, and then my discipline, until inevitably I had finally
claimed the entire language as my own.

I rewrote newspaper articles in my head, and at night ran through my collection of books for fragments of novels that I could bring to class the next day. I graded my students' essays with a dark red pen whose ink I spread liberally across the page so that entire paragraphs were often rendered almost illegible. Unlike most people who stake their claims on a particular field or discipline, however, I wore my ownership lightly. I rarely corrected my students when they misspoke, and not simply out of decorum or consideration, but because I had come to believe that true ownership did not have to be announced, much less fought over. Mistakes and assaults on the English language were made by the millions every hour of every day, and yet not even those infinite errors had the power to take away what I thought of as truly being mine.

My classes ended early each morning, and yet I often stayed throughout the afternoon in order to prepare my lessons. I had a list of standard texts that were supposed to be covered—a Faulkner short story, some pieces by Poe, and a handful of nineteenth- and twentieth-century poems, many of which I committed to memory so I could recite them to my students as I strolled through the aisles. There was the familiar "Let us go then . . ." and "I heard a fly buzz . . ." and of course the singing songs of myself; to these I added some of my own, slightly exotic favorites—a page from Rilke and selected bits from Rimbaud, Bishop's "One Art"—all of which I imagined gave my class a more personalized, global feel. While many of the other teachers seem to have merely stumbled into the courses they taught, I began to think of myself as having been born or almost preordained for my course. The economics teacher was also the football coach, while our history teacher had been, until just four years earlier, an aspiring Broadway actor. No one seemed to complain, though, not the teachers or the students, despite the academy's reputation and motto of being an "institution of exceptional scholarship."

My syllabus had an intuitive, logical arc to it. We began with familiar domestic narratives, essays, and poems, before moving on to more modern and slightly obtuse pieces, several of which were read in competing translations. I explained it to Angela as being a part of the same pattern in which life was lived. As babies and young children we know and understand only what is immediate and before us, I told her. We accumulate memories and in doing so begin to make our first tentative steps backward in time, to say things such as "I remember when I was." And from there our lives grow into multiple dimensions until eventually we learn to regret and finally to imagine.

While it was common even among the most disciplined teachers to allow for small fabrications, from the beginning the stories I told my students existed on a more ambitious plane. Now when asked for details about my life, I indulged myself. When one of my students wanted to know what I did before I began teaching at the academy, I told him that I had spent years working in a coal mine and had the blackened lungs to prove it. To another I was the captain of a Japanese trawler, and then a few days later a pimp and hustler. The more outlandish my responses were, the more my students wanted to know the truth, which had been the point all along.

Not only was I good at these inventions, I was grateful for them; only in fiction could I step outside of myself long enough to feel fully at ease. The stories all came naturally, just as I had shown myself more than capable of coming up with last-minute narrative fillers for the asylum applications I once worked on. I thought of this as a distinctly American trait—this ability to unwind whatever ties supposedly bind you to the past and to invent new ones as you went along. While most of it was frivolous—these stories of imaginary childhood deprivations and absurd careers were never more than an easy laugh for my students—I strayed on occasion into darker ground, if only to make sure that I held their interest.

"My family," I told my students once after having been asked why we came to America, "had to leave their home abruptly. That's why we ended up here."

They fell hard for anything that sounded like that, and were quick to imagine the missing details on their own. They assumed war first, hunger and poverty second; despite their best intentions, and how many times they had recently heard someone say that Africa was more than just the sum of that, I knew these were the only images they had. Africa was everywhere in the news and the pity for it and its inhabitants had spiked a thousandfold as a result. There were rallies in Central Park for the dead of Sudan, and protests outside the UN and several different African consulates against more general crimes ranging from corruption to blanket oppression. The news at night showed throngs of people gathered around a stage wearing the names of the dead, while at the same time celebrities across the country thoughtfully called for an end to genocide.

My students were naturally infected. Some of the first ones I had taught at the academy were organizing a Save Africa Now campaign, which they asked me to be a part of, assuming, however naively, that they had a natural ally in me. Two years later I hardly remembered them; they had been shy to the point of invisibility in my class, but they had grown into themselves, and with one year left at the academy before college, they stood taller than me, with matching dark brown shaggy hair that dipped just below their eyebrows as if they were still afraid of being taken too seriously. I asked them what they wanted to save Africa from.

"Violence," one of them said. And if that wasn't enough, the second one followed up by adding, "Millions are dying, Mr. Woldemariam."

I never asked them how they planned on ending the violence that had recently upset them; letters and more rallies were somewhere in the plan, money would surely be raised and sent—the fact that action was being taken was enough to ensure that whatever they did was right. I had already heard all I needed. They were visibly disappointed and I'm sure later full of contempt when I refused.

"My family's Irish," I told them. "I'd feel like a fraud if I joined."

I shared little of my life at the academy with Angela, and so she never heard anything about those early stories, any one of which would have given her a moment's pause. When she asked me how the job was going, all I could tell her was that it was fine, in part because I suspected she no longer cared.

"What about going back to school?" she finally asked me. "You've been there for two years. I thought you wanted to get your Ph.D."

The idea of me with a doctorate still held sway over Angela, even if I had quietly placed it on the same shelf where numerous other ambitions of mine now rested. It was part of her faith that this was one of the only ways that we could secure a bright and happy future, and in that regard she was no different from the immigrant parents I had known at the center who were convinced that the only thing that would save and protect their children in America were advanced, specialized degrees.

"I don't think I'm ready yet," I told her. "I still have a lot more reading I need to do. And more experience teaching can only help."

"And for how long are you going to do that. Two more years? Five, six? It's just a part-time job, Jonas. It's not supposed to become your life."

And that was at the heart of what worried Angela—that despite our being married we had yet to form a life as commonly prescribed by others. In life, one made steady but consistent progress. Capital was raised, furnishings and homes were purchased and then later resold for a double-digit profit. More than two years into our marriage and we were nowhere near that. Angela's concerns over money and stability had yet to diminish. As time passed she needed more pillars to keep her fully propped. Her law degree had been the first, and now she wanted to know where the second was.

A few weeks later Angela told me I lacked a clear sense of identity. We were sitting at opposite corners of the apartment on a Sunday afternoon in late or early April, both of us supposedly busy with work, when Angela called out across the room to me, "You don't have any idea who you are, do you, Jonas."

It wasn't the full-on frontal attack that I had been expecting. Instead, Angela tried to soothe her frustration and disappointment with me by naming its origins. If I didn't know who I really was, then I could hardly be held accountable for not facing life head-on as she expected me to. I was innocent if there was no person behind the skin that could be charged.

Had I defended myself at that moment, we might have reached some sort of an accord. I might have been able to explain to Angela that she was, in fact, partly correct in her statement, but not in the way she presumed. I may not have had a solid definition of who I was, but that was only because for so long I had concentrated my efforts on trying to appear to be almost nothing at all—neither nameless nor invisible, just obscure enough to blend into the background and be quickly forgotten. It had begun with my father, who I had always hoped would never notice me. It was in his company that I first learned how to occupy a room without disturbing it. Whenever he came home from work, I'd sit in different parts of the living room—in the center of the couch, on the floor, or next to the coffee table in order to see how he acknowledged me. On several occasions I came too close and was told to get out of his way, on others I was either grunted at or quizzed about my progress in school that day. Eventually one evening he came home from work and didn't notice me at all. I was sitting near the end of the couch, with my knees lifted to my chest and the lamp next to me deliberately turned off, and I realized then that all I had to do to avoid him was blend into the background. That knowledge followed me from there so that eventually I thought of my obscurity as being essential to my survival. Whoever can't see you can't hurt you. That was the reigning philosophy of my days.

Learned instincts, however, are hard to wean oneself off, and so I offered no meaningful defense to Angela, just a sly, hostile retort.

"I'm sorry you feel that way. It must be very hard on you."

After that, who I really *was* became a source of constant debate between us.

"Are you an illegal alien, Jonas? If so you know you can tell me. I love refugees, remember."

We were in a taxi heading north on First Avenue to a Christmas party being thrown by Angela's firm when she said that. Our driver was from The Gambia—Angela had asked him where he was from as a way of instigating this conversation. She had pressed her head directly against the partition and asked, "Excuse me, sir. Where are you originally from?" She had often claimed to hate it when people asked cabdrivers this question. She and Bill had once loudly debated it in the center's conference room just before she left and began her career as a lawyer.

"Leave them alone," she had argued. "Why do they have to tell you where they're from or why they left their countries? So they can get an extra dollar tip from people? No one asks the old black cabdriver where he's from or what's happened to him in his life, because they would think that was rude and crazy. Unless he has an accent. Then it's free rein. Then it's, tell us why you came here and how hard it must be."

She hated it, but like most of us was susceptible to her own curiosities and couldn't help wondering over things that were foreign. I often suspected that when she was alone she asked every cabdriver that question.

"My husband's African too," she said, and at that point I still expected an attempt at humor, something along the lines of "My husband's African too. Maybe you know each other."

The cabdriver had played this game before and knew enough to ask, as if he genuinely cared, "Really, where from?"

"We're not sure," Angela said. "Someplace on the east coast. He doesn't like to talk about it."

It was then that she turned her attention back to me with a standard, slightly mocking quip that under almost any other circumstance I would have had an easy, lighthearted response to.

This was how we avoided saying what our true intentions were, a status quo that until then I was generally happy to keep.

"So what is it, Jonas? Illegal immigrant or not?"

"Sorry. Born and raised here," I said.

Angela fell quiet for five and then ten blocks. We were almost at the party when she asked me, while staring straight ahead at what could have been her reflection, in what was almost a whisper, "Then why don't you act like it?"

"And how do you act like it?"

"Talking would help."

"I talk all the time."

"Not about anything that matters. You come home from work and then sit there so quietly that sometimes I begin to think that maybe you don't really know English at all."

"I have a degree in it."

"That's what you say, but how do I know if you don't act like it."

Later that same evening at the firm's Christmas party, after three glasses of wine and a grand total of about one hundred words said on my part, Angela began to introduce me as her husband who had just arrived from—

"He just came here from Sierra Leone a few months ago. He's still traumatized by the war, which is why he doesn't speak much."

I pulled her to the side and told her that wasn't funny. She apologized and said she wouldn't say it again. The next time we were introduced to someone Angela said,

"This is my husband, Jonas. He doesn't look it, but he's from Japan."

The joke was lost on everyone but her. When we returned to

our apartment, both of us drunk after having spent hours standing side by side while hardly speaking, Angela tried to explain her
intentions to me.

"I see you standing there smiling and nodding at everything
everyone says and at first I think, maybe he doesn't understand
what they're saying. Maybe he's going deaf and I should tell someone to call him ugly to see if it gets a response out of him, but then
I see you laugh, or pretend to laugh, at what has to be one of the
dumbest jokes I've ever heard, and I think he's not deaf, he just
doesn't care. He's not really here listening to anything anyone
says. I've concluded that you're an alien, and not the legal or illegal kind, but a real alien who's decided that the easiest way to
get by in life is not to say or do anything that might blow your
cover."

I wanted to but could hardly disagree with what she said. I
sought out peace wherever I could and often earned it with my
silence. She on the other hand seemed to almost thrive when given
the chance to express a contradictory opinion, her seven favorite
words in the world being, "I don't think that's true at all."

Angela began to spend more time away from home after that.
She said she had made a New Year's resolution to try to find
happiness wherever she could. It was the type of statement that I
thought I would never hear her make, even as she tried to cloud it
over with a tinge of irony.

"Laugh," she said, "if you want to. But I'm serious about this.
I think it's time I found out what this happiness thing is all
about."

She left for work before eight a.m. and often wouldn't return
until close to midnight. Many nights she claimed to have passed

diligently working in her office. When she finally came home one night more than just slightly drunk, I asked her if she wanted to try to tell me now where she had actually been.

"I was at a bar," she said. "With some clients and some of the partners from work."

It was a plausible but barely disguised lie, and she all but dared me to name it as such.

"Does that bother you, Jonas?"

"No. It doesn't bother me at all."

"I didn't think it would."

That was the first important step away from me that she made, and I knew that there would be others, and that many of them would be small, hardly even perceptible, which is the way distance between two people normally grows—in baby-step-sized increments. By the end of their life together my mother and father were no longer able to stand being in the same room with each other for more than a few minutes. If one walked into the living room, the other soon left for the kitchen. My father slept and read on the couch. My mother took most of her meals in her bedroom. I used to wonder if there was a space large enough on earth for them to inhabit at the same time. I pictured dining rooms the size of football fields and bedrooms as cavernous as an airport hangar— spaces that were large enough to reduce the person standing at the opposite end to little more than a speck on the horizon. They had always had personal boundaries for as long as I'd known them, and over the years those boundaries had become distended to such a ridiculous size that their sense of hurt and damage at the hands of the other preceded them by miles.

Had we managed to keep that tension throughout our days as well as our nights, we might have ended even sooner than we did, but there was a shared desire to try to retain the last vestiges of the best parts of our marriage. Where we failed in the evenings we tried to make up for during the brief time we had together in the mornings. A new routine sprang up between us. Angela woke up before me as normal, but rather than rush to assemble herself for work she would wake me up with a string of small, barely palpable kisses that ran down the side of my face, behind my ears, and down my neck, and maybe because she thought I was still sleeping and couldn't hear her, or maybe because she thought I could hear her better because I was still sleeping, she would say one of two things: "I'm sorry. I love you." Or, "I love you, and let's not fight again."

"You look angelic when you're sleeping," she used to say. "Why can't you always be like that?"

We were both suckers for wishful thinking, and each morning, regardless of how quiet and tense we were the night before, there would seem to be the possibility that it had all just been a stupid mistake, and that whatever was wrong between us could be righted come morning by the sheer force of will and love.

Our morning routine was something to marvel over. We floated around our little apartment, picking out clothes, showering, dressing, and drinking coffee as if we had been choreographed to do so, stopping every now and then at perfectly timed intervals to kiss each other on the cheeks or lips. Those moments after waking up were the best thirty minutes of the day and seemed to pass in a dreamlike state all their own, one in which Angela and I were both only partially clothed, so there was always a private piece of bare skin that could be touched or observed—a belly button, a birthmark on the lower half of a back, or the hard smooth space between Angela's breasts. And while it's true that I may have been at least partially aware of the guilt that fueled the change in our morning routine, it's also true that I remained wholeheartedly grateful for it nonetheless. So long as I didn't have to stare at anything difficult too directly, I thought I was happy to try to forget where Angela had been or what she had looked like when she came home the night before, if it meant that I could find even a modicum of comfort in exchange.

Angela and I learned to live two separate but simultaneous lives. Several nights a week she vanished into what she claimed to be work while I continued with my classes. We sometimes raised our voices at each other over small, petty things. I remember Angela asking me why it looked like there was piss on the bathroom floor when she came home, and I remember saying that unless she thought I was deaf she could try taking off her heels when she came through the door at night. But more often than not we simply stared at each other from a great distance even when we were in the same room. In the morning we tried to begin all over again. Sometimes we made love before leaving for work. We always made sure to kiss as we said good-bye.

What finally brought that time to an end was a phone call, which in retrospect I can hardly blame Angela for having made. All boundaries are there to be tested, and Angela, having crossed several, could have never retreated slowly back into the woman she had been just one year back, even though I often told myself she would. I managed her absence and the growing distance between us the way I imagined my mother must have managed many of the years she spent with my father—by telling herself incessantly that this too shall pass. Eventually I had to understand that it wouldn't.

It was the second week in April when Angela called me from her office to say that tonight she would be home exceptionally late.

There was something simultaneously callous and tired in her voice, as if she had been forced to make this call after a long, strenuous debate.

"I'm going to be very late tonight," she said.

"A lot of work at the office."

"Are you asking me that or telling me that?"

"I'm assuming that," I said.

"Okay then," she said. "If that's what you want to assume. Then yes. I have a lot of work to do tonight. We have a big case. Huge, in fact. Thank you for asking."

She hung up the phone before I could respond, and while I had thought about calling back, I had also thought that there was nothing to be gained by doing so.

I often went to bed early, but on that night I found it impossible to sleep. I stayed awake until well past midnight when Angela finally came home more exhausted than I had seen her before. She dropped her bag next to the door and slipped straight into the shower. She didn't see me watching her until she came to bed.

"You're awake," she said.

"I couldn't sleep."

"That's a first."

"I have to wake up early to get to work."

"Don't you want to ask me how my night was?"

"Difficult, I imagine."

"And that's the best you can do?" she said.

"No," I replied. "It's not. But right now I'm too tired to try to do any better."

Rather than continue, I pretended to drift off to sleep, leaving Angela to hover over me. When we woke up we tried halfheartedly to continue our morning ballad. Angela kissed me once on the cheek and apologized for coming home so late.

"I'm sorry," she said. "I didn't realize what time it was. I had a drink after work and must have been a bit tipsy when I came home."

We showered and then dressed. As we were getting ready to leave, Angela leaned over to straighten my tie, and as I remember it, a warm, almost blinding sensation swept over me. I can't say that I did or did not raise my voice. I'd like to believe I didn't, but if I did, I can't think of what I might have possibly said. I do know that at some point I grabbed Angela's hand firmly by the wrist, before she could pull it completely away from me, and that I may have even begun to twist it. I know that my fingers encircled her wrist completely and I could feel the bones underneath, which surprised me because I had never held Angela like that before. At some point shortly after that, maybe three to four seconds maximum, I thought to myself that despite what I may have ever wondered about my own strength, it was more than enough to hurt her. Once I was certain of that, I let her go.

Had I wanted to apologize, I never had a chance. Angela grabbed her purse off a chair and left the apartment without a word, which led me to think as I walked out the door fifteen minutes later that perhaps what had happened hadn't been serious at all. By the time I reached the academy I had convinced myself of that. "It was nothing," I said. "And it will be completely forgotten soon." I was still thinking that when my students entered and sat down—that nothing of any import had actually occurred, and what I thought might have been a transgression of an important boundary that I had long ago placed on myself was nothing more than a slight deviation from the norm, which explains in part why I was so distracted when my class began, and why, according to one of my students, it looked as if I was talking to myself before the morning bell rang.

. . .

Angela left work early and was already at home by the time I returned. It had been more than a year since that had last happened, and even then it was only because she had become sick at her office and had left with a fever. And while I knew she wasn't ill that afternoon, I did understand that she was hurting. In both cases, she tried her hardest to deny that. Before I could ask her what she was doing back, she told me.

"I decided to finish up my work from home today," she said. "They're doing some renovations in the office so there's noise everywhere. I told Andrew about it and he said there were no meetings planned for this afternoon, and as long as I had my cell phone and checked in with my secretary, I might as well go home and finish the day here."

"Is it working?"

"So far no. I can't seem to get anything done."

I was ready to volunteer to leave the apartment so Angela could have the space to work, but she knew that was coming and had prepared accordingly.

"I bought some groceries," she said. "I thought we'd stay in and that maybe you'd make us dinner?"

There may have been no romance to it, but there was also no hostility or tension either. It had been weeks since we'd had an evening where we were both home together for the entire night. Angela watched me closely throughout dinner, as if we had just met and she was waiting to catch a telltale sign that revealed a personal deficiency—a tendency to blink too often or to chew with my mouth open. She had assumed until that morning that she knew these things already. Briefly there was a shared pleasure in thinking that we still had significant parts of each other left to uncover, and by the time dinner was over I had begun to think that was enough to count the evening a success. We'd fall asleep and peel back another layer. As we were beginning to prepare for bed, she stopped me in the bathroom. Her eyes were slightly glazed; when she caught her reflection in the mirror behind me, she turned away so I could no longer see them.

"Can you sleep on the couch tonight?" she asked me.

"Of course," I said. "I was going to stay up late reading anyway."

Which was precisely what I did. I read and graded papers until the sun came up, always hoping that I would hear Angela mumble a few words in her sleep that would call me back to her, or at least hint at that desire. When the morning came we stumbled around each other, our grace completely gone.

PART II

IX

It was somewhere near here, along this relatively empty stretch of Interstate 155, roughly forty miles southwest of the Greater Peoria Regional Airport, between the towns of Fayette and Tupelo, Illinois, that my parents made the first unplanned stop of their trip. There isn't much here now and I doubt that there was more than thirty years ago when they first drove down this road. Little, if anything, changes on the surface around here, and even less does underneath. I wouldn't be surprised if the billboards advertising lunch and dinnertime buffet specials were the same ones that were here back then.

I've been on this road before, on several occasions as a child with my father, and then again later with my mother just before she gave this land up for good and headed out east for the modern city and apartment of her dreams. I didn't know it at the time but two completely different versions of history were being offered to me in preparation for my inevitable role as both advocate and judge over what happened between my parents during this trip, the events of which would determine nearly every aspect of their relationship from that point on, from the varying times that each went to bed to the odd glances I often caught them casting toward each other in the presence of strangers.

There are hardly any cars along the road at this time of day, which would be roughly, give or take an hour or two, around the same time my parents would have passed through, the only great difference being that of the seasons, fall for them and the early weeks of spring for me. Still, I imagine the days would have looked much the same—mild, pleasant days and a sun that rose and fell at roughly the same time. More important, however, is the shared sense that you can get at the start and close of each season—the tumult and confusion that comes when the air holds the distinct memories of two different times at once. On several occasions over the past week I've stood outside my rental car on a warm, slightly humid evening and found myself drifting back into memories that belonged to late September, the rush and fear of the start of a new cycle of classes and students blurring into my own childhood memories of taking back roads to school so as to avoid being caught alone on the sidewalk by any one of a dozen students and adults I feared. On those occasions, when the wind is warm and smells vaguely of a rain that has recently fallen or is about to do so, I've found it better to simply pull my car off the side of the road, or if I'm walking, to cease and temporarily forget wherever it is I'm going in order to submit to the confusion of time and memory carried in by the breeze. Within a single breath I can jump across decades. I can recall sprinting at full speed toward the relative safety of my elementary school doors, and what it felt like to hide in an empty classroom for an hour after the school day had ended, because only then could I trust that the path to my house was safe, that the streets were once again clogged with rush-hour traffic and people waiting in line to get on buses. And yet it's only after I've fully recalled the sights and sounds of my own students twenty years later spilling into the arched-stone gates at the start of each morning, and the ensuing panic that their voices—loud and breaking with emotion—always aroused in me, that I'll remember this is not September at all but May, that I've lost the one career I've had, and that I'll never experience that same rush of panic and affection that came with hearing my students laugh and curse at one another again.

The brown historical signpost on the side of the road says there are four miles between here and Fort Jean-Patrice Laconte. It's the first and only sign like it, and I'm sure that if I hadn't pinpointed the fort's location on my atlas beforehand, I would have missed it entirely. There are signs for gas stations, fast-food restaurants, picnic spots, and scenic views that are neither scenic nor interesting that are more obvious than this. I have the feeling that the sign is not supposed to be noticed at all, that it was placed there strictly out of obligation, or as a concession to some group of historically minded citizens who believe all of American history is worthy of preservation. I name them fondly in my head: the Guardians of America's Forgotten History, picturing gray-haired old men in responsible dark suits with forest-green sweater vests underneath. Surely they would deserve a name as grand as that, a title that could stand up there with the Daughters of the American Revolution and the Mayflower Society. Their task no less noble than the committees assigned to preserve trees, houses, and former Civil War battle sites. I've looked in the history books. There is almost nothing out there about Fort Laconte. In the large green and white textbooks assigned to my students there wasn't even a single mention of Jean-Patrice, much less his fort and the role it played in the founding of America. I would have never known

about it had it not been for a conversation my mother and I had
years ago.

"Your father took me once to see some leftover fort on our way
to Nashville."

She was living at that time in a coastal village an hour outside
of Providence, Rhode Island.

"It'd be nice if I could see the ocean from here," was her only
complaint, if it could even be called that. She had enough memories of the ocean by that time to get her through, and a view of
the ocean would have simply served as a nice but unnecessary prop
for her memories. While my father had chosen to plant himself
firmly in the middle of the country, she had opted for a series of
small eastern towns, moving up and down the coast, from Boston
to Virginia. I visited her rarely. The two of us went to dinners and
movies together, more like an old tired couple who had nothing
left to say than a mother and son who saw each other no more
than once a year. I never visited her unannounced, and would have
been unable to had I tried.

She wouldn't have remembered the name of the fort, and at the
time I hadn't thought to ask her. There were hundreds if not thousands of things that she had never forgiven my father for, and
taking her to that fort could have easily been one of the minor
ones, on par with his tendency to fall asleep with the lights on and
to leave his fingernail clippings on the bathroom floor. But perhaps it's because that conversation was one of the last I had with
my mother before we lost touch for several years, or perhaps it's
because when I was younger I had a special love for forts that the
image of my parents standing outside the ruined remains of one
somewhere along the road to Nashville stayed with me. As a child
I built dozens of forts in my bedroom, in corners around the
house, and on a few occasions in the garage when either my

mother or father had left with the car with promises never to return. None of the forts were especially sturdy. I was never a craftsman; even at my most diligent the rules of geometry failed me. My forts were often too tall or short on one side. They were always crooked and looked as if they would break at the slightest touch. Nonetheless, there was a gradual development in size from one to the next. The first ones had been made of small rocks and twigs, no longer or taller than a book lying flat on its back. I built them from pieces scavenged from the driveway and held them together with tape and glue when I could find them. Those forts housed nothing, or nothing that was tangible. They were built under my bed, out of sight and therefore protected. I suppose I imagined that even if they were too small to hold little more than a paper clip and a few scraps of paper, they still represented at least one sanctuary that could not be broached. On more than one occasion I prayed for the ability to shrink down into a thumb-sized version of myself so I could enter the fort's stone and wood walls and discover that there was nothing there that could find me. In later years I studied how-to books written for children. How to build an igloo, a tepee, a birdhouse, a tree house. The books carried full-page diagrams with numbered instructions at the bottom. They told you how to build the walls and the roof separately, and how to create a proper foundation to hold them together. All you needed to know according to those books was how to put each piece together, and this was, inevitably, where I always failed. My walls were always too weak and my roofs had a tendency to slope at odd, irregular angles, too fragile to carry anything but the smallest weight.

For seven years I tried to construct as many versions of home as I could find. By the time I was twelve I had probably tried them all, but always with one distinct variation that was of my own making. I built each, regardless of how poorly it may have been constructed, as far as possible out of anyone's general line of vision. I put the birdhouse in the closet and kept a small circle of rocks near the head of my bed. There were no back- or front-yard forts for me. I didn't build protective cocoons to fight from or to defend. I built mine to hide in because I always knew an attack would come, and that even at their best, the most my forts could do was soften the blows when they came.

It's nearly one p.m. by the time I arrive at the single wooden barrier and guard's post that mark the entrance to Laconte's failed fort. From the highway exit, after a few quick turns, the route becomes a narrow dirt and gravel road, wide enough for only one car at a time. The sun is high and shining bright, casting its full force down on the large open green meadow, in the middle of which sits what looks from a distance to be a small pile of building blocks, the kind a child would use to arrange towers and squares in the middle of a playpen. Most of the trees surrounding the edge of the meadow have bloomed but not yet fully matured, so there is still a mix of white petals and green palm-sized leaves along the branches. I've arrived a few hours later than my parents would have, but on a clear day such as today, I don't imagine it makes much of a difference. The leaves would have begun to turn for them, and the grass I imagine would not have the same shimmering green effect it has now, but otherwise nearly everything else is surely the same. The lone guard gate, the absence of any other cars or people, the arrangement of stones lying scattered on the ground—I can say with confidence that we all shared this.

I park immediately in front of the entrance, in a space designated for the handicapped. It's a touch I admire, this desire to make every part of America seemingly accessible to anyone who wants it. The fact that few want or care for this particular part is beside the point entirely. Here is proof of our largesse and our generosity, freely given, with nothing expected in return.

The noise from the highway and the main road leading into a town of only a few hundred residents is hardly audible. It's the first time in almost a week that I've been beyond the sound of traffic, and getting out of the car, I can't help feeling that there is something missing to the air, that it's the silence and not the sounds of horns and shifting gears that is the real intrusion. The guard steps out of his little wooden compound, a man-sized shoe box if ever there were one, and takes note of my out-of-town license plates and clothes, suspecting, I suppose, a madman of some sort. He has a bored but wary look to him as he carries his clipboard and pen, his face hidden under a dark green park ranger's hat that seems to have been lifted from an advertisement for Boy Scout paraphernalia. He is clean-cut and wholesome, no doubt born and raised not too far from here. I don't hold his suspicions against him, even as he stands in front of my car pretending to note the year and make of the model I'm driving while secretly eyeing me for any odd behavior from underneath the brim of his hat. I suppose like most of us he's seen too many horror films about what happens when a stranger comes into town. His sort never fares too well, always the first to die and with the least to say.

I play my role perfectly, standing nonchalantly to the side while he takes his notes. I know that we're all supposed to be wary these days, of strangers and strange bags and especially of strangers carrying strange bags, and I want to do my part in easing some of the collective tension as best I can. In the past I've held back a few seconds before revealing my last name, and have been quick to offer my support or condemnation of violence and war, whichever one was needed to ensure that everyone around me felt well, and that all was well indeed. Today, however, I'm guilty on both counts, with my clothes wrinkled from a week of travel, my face unshaven, and my black leather attaché case strapped around my neck. I want to make reassuring small talk with the guard. I want to discuss the weather, the rising cost of gas, a baseball team that I know nothing and could care less about. I wonder if this would be enough to put his mind and pen at ease. I know it would be too much to say, "Don't worry, I come in peace," or to offer him, without asking, a peek inside my bag, or into the trunk and backseat of my car, where he would find the remains of three days' worth of fast food eaten while driving. I could tell him that yes, I understand, it's a dangerous world, but he need not worry, at least not about me, and if he wanted I would even go so far as to put a reassuring arm around his shoulder, a sign of camaraderie that I'm sure he could use. I say and do nothing, however, hoping as I always do for the best—that perhaps he will find a measure of comfort in my prep-school uniform of khaki pants and dark blue shirt, of which I have a suitcase full, one for each and every day of the week, and that he has a large house and dog to turn to at the end of the day.

After a few more minutes of careful observation, and a quick glance at a stopwatch he keeps tucked inside his pants pocket, the guard looks up at me and says, "The park closes in about an hour. You'll have to leave soon."

I nod my head. I smile at him. Don't worry, I want to tell him, these days I always do.

X

After that night Angela and I had only the semblance of a marriage left, even as we appeared to draw closer. She spent less time at the office, and never had a reason to call again to say she would be late. We began to take long walks throughout the city in search of some minor and relatively obsolete object that Angela had suddenly declared she needed. It was her way of trying to salvage or, at the very least, make the most out of what was left of our marriage. There was a deliberate, almost childish quality behind the effort. Angela had taken my hand while I was still in bed on a Saturday morning and had pretended to drag me out using all her strength.

"Come on," she said. "It's beautiful outside and I want you to help me find some things."

We lived our weekend lives for the next several months as if they were scenes plucked from a movie made to convince one that there was nothing more charming than being young and in love in New York. One weekend we went searching for an old record player, the next an appropriate stack of classic records to go with it. We searched for vintage dresses and matching hats in the East Village, and made Saturday and Sunday markets in Union Square and Chelsea a habit. We busied ourselves with the city in a way that we hadn't done since we first started dating, and at least in that regard New York seemed endlessly generous to us. The sheer density of the city, which at times we had both claimed to hate, was buying us time.

Those late spring and early summer ventures across Manhattan, and on one occasion Brooklyn, were often riddled with nostalgia, small-pocketed bursts that left holes in our day. During one trip we went to a coffee shop on Bleecker Street that had been closed for at least a year; it was where Angela had passed her first afternoon in New York waiting to meet her future roommates. The coffee shop may have been gone, but it was hard to declare its absence a loss for any reason other than a personal one.

"The coffee was terrible," Angela noted. "And the bathroom was full of shit." Still, we went back to it on a rainy Sunday afternoon in May because Angela wanted to be reminded not so much of that first afternoon in particular but of who she was on that day, a young stranger to the city with vast stretches of her life still open before her. A couple of weeks later I took her deep into Brooklyn to stand outside the last apartment that I had lived in before we moved in together. I had been too embarrassed to show it to her, even though I suspected she would have found the building and the neighborhood charming and closer to her own heart than the apartment she had moved into. It was a four-story brown-brick building, squat and half a block long, its sides covered in seemingly meaningless graffiti. Most of the people who lived there were Bangladeshi or from somewhere in Central America, and the building carried on its walls traces of both—a bit of Bengali and Spanish speaking together. We took a shortcut through a large cemetery to get there. A hard winter had meant that half the trees had yet to bloom, and only scattered patches of grass were green, which made the entire grounds seem unbalanced, as if the grass and trees were changing sides as we walked. Angela thought that it made the cemetery, with its angel-crested obelisks and granite mausoleums, look a bit psychotic.

"It's like it can't make up its mind whether it wants to live or die," she said. "It's unhealthy."

When we reached the apartment, we spent a good five minutes standing outside watching a few kids ride their bicycles up and down the same block.

"We should have lived here," Angela said. "There are no kids on bikes where we live."

"It's not too late," I noted. "There's probably an empty apartment right now."

Angela seemed to consider the thought seriously, and she might have even tried to picture us setting up camp on this block and eventually having children of our own, but there was a stale, false note in that image that she couldn't get past.

If these trips sound like the beginning of reparations, they weren't. We both sensed that they were the prelude to what might be a long, slow good-bye even if we never acknowledged it as such. When my classes ended for the year, Angela found her temporary way out.

"They asked me at work today if I want to spend the summer in L.A. It's an important case. I'd be working with another firm out there who's also involved in the suit, but I'd be the only one from our offices there all the time."

It didn't matter whether or not it was an important opportunity for her. She wanted or needed to get away, but despite her bluntness and her training as a lawyer, she couldn't say that to me directly. We went to the airport together in June. I promised Angela I'd come see her in a few weeks, and she promised me that she was going to do the same. We talked every night for the first ten days, but after that we gradually began to skip a day here and there for reasons that we attributed to the difference in time and Angela's busy schedule. When two weeks had passed, neither one of us had bought a plane ticket yet, and I was convinced that neither of us was going to. I'd be lying, then, if I didn't admit to being somewhat grateful for the phone call that came in July telling me that my father had died. I announced the news to Angela early the next morning before she left for work. "I'm going to come," she said. "I don't want you to be alone," and before she hung up the phone, "I'm sorry that I'm not with you there now." By lunch she had a return ticket back to New York for the following night. I met her at the airport; we took a taxi back home, holding hands all along the way while not saying much of anything. When we were finally settled in the apartment, Angela crawled into bed and invited me to join her. We fell asleep partly out of exhaustion, partly out of relief at finding ourselves together again. There was no blame, hurt, or disappointment to be shared or stifled. It was simply us.

The next morning Angela asked me what she could do to help. "I can handle the arrangements," she said. "You shouldn't have to do that."

The thought of arranging anything had never crossed my mind.

"The funeral," she said, after I had stared at her silently long enough. "And if there's a will or anything else that needs to be taken care of."

"We don't have to do anything," I told her. "He's going to be cremated. They can send his ashes by mail if we want them, but I don't think I do."

"His ashes by mail?"

"That's what they said."

"And what about your mother?"

"I'm sure she knows already."

A part of Angela assumed that it was grief that had so efficiently reduced my father's death for me, and so for two days she said nothing more about it. She thought she could console me with a nice dinner out and frequent, spontaneous bursts of affection, and because I was greedy, I took every one of them. After two days, though, she wanted more evidence of mourning. She would often stop and ask me how I was holding up if there was a prolonged silence between us.

"I'm fine," I told her on each occasion.

"This has to be difficult for you," she said. "Even if you were never close."

"If it is," I said, "I'm not quite sure just how."

That was when she told me that she hated what I was doing, and that I was "acting as if nothing happened," although it was the "You're doing it again" that struck me the most. She returned to Los Angeles three days later.

"There's nothing that I can do for you here," she said. "You seem to be doing just fine. And the case is almost finished now. It'll be all over by September at the latest."

Those were not the last words Angela said before she left, but they were the ones that remained. After she was gone I spent a week debating whether there was a not so subtle intention buried within them, and when I failed to come up with a definite response, I called Bill and asked him if I could return to the center as a volunteer for the last month of the summer, if only to avoid the long emptiness that stretched out before me each morning.

There was very little left of the center when I showed up on the first day in August. Two of the three old but still functioning Xerox machines that had taken up the bulk of the front entrance were gone, as were several plants that even in the best of times had never fared well at the office. A gray steel filing cabinet was missing from the hallway. Two desks that sat in the center had been completely cleared but were still facing each other for no apparent reason. Above it all I could clearly hear, without any interruption, the rush of traffic coming from Canal Street and the jackhammers on the Bowery and the trucks idling as they waited to get over the Manhattan Bridge. There was nothing left in the office to absorb that noise.

The same woman Bill was with at our wedding was now sitting at my former desk answering the phone, which rang only twice while I was there. She barely looked at me when I entered, and I wondered if she was embarrassed for or because of me. Bill greeted me at the door with a long extended handshake, although I had the feeling that had we known each other better, or seen each other more than a few times in the years since I had left, he would have preferred to hug. He had that worn, battered look you often see on people after they've come from a hospital visit, or from the funeral of someone they were once close to.

"As you can see," he said, "it's not the same around here anymore. We have a couple of interns from Columbia, a couple of part-time lawyers who work pro bono, but really it's just me and Nasreen."

In the judge's chamber, Angela and I had both cast cynical looks at each other when Bill arrived with Nasreen. When we discussed it later we didn't even remember her name. We called her that "poor woman," as in, "I feel sorry for that poor woman." All we saw was that Bill had taken someone into his bed who, while perhaps not much younger, we assumed to be in no position to claim control over her life.

"It's probably not the first time he's done this," Angela noted, and while I had no evidence to the contrary, I assumed she was right. Bill, with his concern for all things foreign and misplaced, seemed like the type.

"I'm the only full-time lawyer left," Bill continued. "One quit six months after we let you go. The rest left a few months later. Since then it's just been me, but to be honest I don't think we're going to last much longer."

"It'll change," I said. "You'll be fine eventually."

"You're right, it will. But the damage will have been done by then. We've lost almost every case we've taken for the past six months. It was my fault. I didn't 'diversify' enough. I had too many difficult cases. I fucked up. I would have never done that a few years ago, but I thought, fine, fuck it. Why not, right? How long can one country keep up all this suspicion? Soon, I thought, there would be something more than just terror behind our policies, but I was wrong.

"Let me tell you, Jonas. I didn't even need you to make up their stories. They were good enough on their own. They were perfect. Absolutely perfect."

Bill gave me one of the empty offices to work in. It had previously belonged to another lawyer, Sam, who had bright red hair and pale freckled skin that most of the clients couldn't stop staring at when they first arrived. The children especially looked as if they could stand there forever and gaze up at this strange red-haired wonder.

"See what you can do with these," he said.

He handed me a manila folder with a half-dozen one-to-two-page statements that had been typed according to a format that Bill had prescribed. I read through them quickly, but in each case I could have stopped after the first couple of paragraphs. The rest was familiar, and had already been spoken or written hundreds of times before in this office. I felt tired suddenly reading them again, and I knew that this was how much of the country felt as well. We were straining to break our hearts. My students had all but admitted as much when they said they wanted to save Africa and that millions were dying. Without such a grand scale it was impossible to be moved.

For Bill's sake I put my best effort forward. I spent a substantial amount of time correcting the grammar in each of the statements, and then went back and filled in the color. Imaginary prison sentences were added. Threats more severe than the ones that had actually been spoken were issued. One man, instead of having just a brick thrown through his bedroom window, had his house burned down while he was at work. By the time I finished with my revisions the day was over; it was summer, the sun had almost set, and I was certain that there was no one else left in the building besides us. For my day's worth of labor Bill and Nasreen invited me to join them for dinner. Neither asked where Angela was, and I realized that like Bill, I must have worn my troubles where anyone could see them.

"I'm cooking," Bill said, as if to deliberately further upset the equation he knew I had made about his relationship. He must have had dozens of similar lines that served as proof that his relationship with Nasreen was based on two equals' meeting. Others would have shed the spotlight on Nasreen and the accomplishments she had had in her previous life and what she was doing now to save him. Bill was smart and considerate like that.

"I'm sorry," I told them. "I have dinner plans with friends in the city already."

When I didn't return to the center the next morning, Bill was hardly surprised. He told me as much when I called him two days later to say I wouldn't be coming back.

"Classes are starting soon," I said. "And I'm just realizing how much work I have to do."

"You don't have to tell me, Jonas. I understand."

In previous times the guilt would have gotten the best of me. I would have apologized and eventually returned, but I knew this time I would do no such thing. For the next few weeks I sought other distractions. I spent many hours on a bench in Tompkins Square Park watching a group of homeless teenagers play guitar. I dug through used bookstores for early editions of collected poems that I had claimed to love while I was in college. And all along I told myself that I was fine and not in the least bothered by anything in life, even as I sometimes felt a gentle, almost palpable hum of danger. I had often felt something similar as a child, and I thought that I had buried that feeling as deep inside me as it could possibly go so that I would never know it again, but still it returned at the oddest hours—while waiting for the light to change at Seventy-second and Madison on a trip to watch the opera in Central Park, or while ordering coffee at a diner on Second Avenue. When the last week of August finally arrived, I entered my classroom literally humming.

I told my students as much on the first day of class, after they had nervously shuffled their way in and taken their seats according to a self-selecting order that would take me several weeks to understand.

"It's great to be here," I said. "I'm very excited about this semester." Which was not how I normally began the first day of classes, with such a high-hearted enthusiastic tone, but in this case I thought an exception was in order. Angela, by design or coincidence, was coming back home that night.

XI

There is almost nothing left of Laconte's fort these days. What was once here has either slowly eroded with time or since been picked off piece by piece by bored kids or scavengers of American history, who have carted away what little remains to homes and workshops where the past is minutely and painstakingly re-created. The large stones that once served as the fort's first line of defense against attack are fortunately still relatively intact, being far too large and heavy to be lifted away in the night. To some degree they are the real reasons I'm here—these large, unpolished stones, carried here block by block by teams of horses. After the gun they are the first real signs of modern warfare in America, and speak to the old European tendency to draw boundaries and solidify ownership. These stones say unequivocally, This is mine, and everything that I can see beyond these walls is mine as well.

The battle that was fought here must have been a remarkable, vicious sight: long and meticulously planned to draw out the forts' inhabitants one wave at a time for the slaughter. The stones had served their purpose well. No one as it turns out was killed behind their walls, and all who died here did so outside in the open field, either running for their lives or pleading for mercy.

These are just some of the facts that I've since picked up about Fort Laconte and the battle in 1687 that brought it to an end. There are other facts as well, although none as personally relevant. For example, the fort had a prison inside its walls, even though it never at any point had more than one hundred inhabitants, all of whom knew each other well and had traveled for months and years up and down the Mississippi coastline together, exploring and claiming the new frontier for France. The prison was used only once against a member of the expedition as punishment for hoarding food in the winter when rations were scarce. It was used on multiple occasions to hold captured Tamora Indians who had remained from the beginning hostile to the presence of Jean-Patrice Laconte and his men. The men who were held here were often tortured. Their wrists and ankles were bound together for days at a time. They were hung upside down, beaten, flayed, and almost always starved. They died quickly from hunger or disease.

The fort took five months to construct. The outer walls were approximately fifteen feet high and nearly a foot thick. There was a storage shed for munitions and another for food. Jean-Patrice Laconte had his own private stable built inside the fort's walls for his two favorite mares to make sure they would never be slaughtered if there was ever a food shortage.

One great difference between the fort as it stands today and as it appeared to my father and mother thirty years earlier is the wooden fence built around the remains. The fence is minor, and if it had not been for the "Do Not Enter" signs posted every couple of feet along its wall, I would have probably walked around it in search of the entrance gate. As it stands, there is no gate, or if there is one it is surely locked and would be as difficult to get through as the fence itself.

The guard has returned to his shoebox. From where I'm standing I can see him clearly through the side window. His body is perched over the day's newspaper, his hat lying harmless inches away. His vigilance has tired itself out and he's gone back to being just another ordinary man, concerned with the day's sports news and politics. I don't know if I have the right to feel a certain pride at having been able to put him to rest, but I do anyway. It's just as I had hoped. I am not a man to be feared or worried over; I have a face that even a skeptical stranger could learn to trust.

I take the long way around the perimeter of the fence, ducking into the shade cast by a nearby copse of trees—white elms with glistening, almost translucent trunks. Near one I find a spot almost completely hidden from view. I place my hands on top of the fence and hurl my body smoothly over to the other side where the shade is even thicker, the grass still damp with dew. It's been said that the only way to truly know any history is to walk in its footsteps. People the world over make pilgrimages to this or that historical landmark to do precisely that. They congregate on Civil War battlefields, at grave sites, and at the homes of the dead to get a glimpse of the past as it must have looked a century or millennium ago. I can't say that my aims here are quite so grand, and even if they were, there isn't much left here for me to imagine. This place is an historical landmark in only the strictest sense of the phrase, to the degree that almost any piece of land on this earth could be said to be of significance to someone.

What happened here between my parents late on a September

afternoon thirty years earlier is, I have to admit, largely a matter of wild and perhaps even errant speculation. The events of 1687 are shrouded in less mystery than those of that day. In effect, 1687 has more going for it than 1977, and I don't think it would be wrong to say that I can see clearer the causes and effects of a battle more than three hundred years old, along with the lives that fought and died in it, than I can understand my parents, who for their part always remained strangers to me.

Looking at the remains of the fort—its size and scope, its proximity to the forest and to the spring that runs alongside it—I don't think anyone who came here did so expecting or wanting to fight. Laconte's fort is more defensive than anything else—an extra precautionary measure for a man who knew he was on hostile ground. After most of the men here were killed, a nearby garrison of French soldiers was sent in to investigate and if possible capture or kill the Tamora warriors who had raided the fort. In the official report written by Captain Pierre-Henri Scipion, a simple, rhetorical question is asked, almost as if by accident, near the end of the last paragraph. Why, Pierre-Henri wanted to know, didn't Laconte equip the fort's walls to defend against an attack? I can see what he means now. There are hardly any cracks or holes along the fort's wall to defend from. When the fort was attacked the men inside had to either shoot blind from over the top or risk their heads. You could say this was an accident, or an oversight, or a criminally stupid thing to do on the part of Laconte, but that would fly against the facts, in defiance of all reason and logic. Laconte was a decorated and well-known soldier of two different wars. He had lost his right hand in one battle and had been injured on multiple occasions both before and after. He was not a man who took risks lightly. He knew how to defend. This I imagine is why Scipion asked his question, which would be better served if it were rephrased to say, What could make a man like Jean-Patrice Laconte, citizen of France, battle-scarred veteran of two wars, father of six, and friend of Robert de la Salle, construct a fort where it was all but impossible to kill your enemy as he advanced?

The answer is simple, and if Scipion saw this place as I see it today, I wonder if he wouldn't rethink his question, or if he wouldn't perhaps refrain from asking it at all. Arriving as he did so shortly after the battle, he could still see bloodstains on the grass and on the white bark of the trees where men caught trying to escape were bound and then executed. There were broken weapons, axes, muskets, discarded bits of ammunition, unpaired shoes lost while running, bits of torn cloth from shirts, pants caught on branches, and the sense of a great, heaving tragedy lingering in the air. Looked upon like that, it would be impossible to see this meadow as anything other than a graveyard in the waiting—a spot designated if not by divine providence, then at least by history for bloodshed and massacre.

It would have been different, though, when Jean-Patrice first arrived. It would have looked more like it does right now—a tranquil meadow on the edge of a forest within a short hike of a stream. It's the kind of place that you want to lie down in the middle of and stare up into the sky with your head resting on the grass without thought or worry for this life or the next.

If Laconte had had more time, I'm sure he would have eventually gotten around to securing the fort better. Posts would have been built, a second interior defense would have been constructed, holes for guns and cannons would have been bored through those beautiful stone walls, and I'm sure no one who lived here would have slept so well again.

.   .   .

Stopping here at Fort Laconte was my father's idea, but I'm certain that it was my mother who made the most of it. She had a way of lingering around objects, of fixing them in her gaze as if she could see into the very atoms of which they were made, and once having done so, come to a definitive answer as to their nature and their history. A couch, a wine glass, or a coffee table was merely the form that an object took—its visible public form, free and open to all. When I was a child my mother would sit in the living room for hours and stare at the furniture. She noticed a room in a way no one I have known since has. There were few things to consider—the green-and-brown-striped couch that my father often slept on, a dark brown reclining armchair that seemed to resemble an old, tired basset hound, complete with wrinkles and folds, and an Impressionist-like painting of what looked to be a wide old boulevard somewhere in Europe in the middle of a storm, which hung opposite the couch, on a wall that got little to no light during the day. These were her companions, and she knew them well. When I came home from school, more often than not I found her there, sitting quietly with her legs curled up underneath her, enmeshed in the silence and comfort of objects that she had neither bought nor chosen for herself. She had theories about who the previous owners of each object may have been, and they would come to her in visions that kept her company in ways both my father and I failed to.

"I think someone very fat used to own this couch," she said to me once. She ran her hand along the middle cushion. "You see. Look here. See that." That was how she spoke when excited by an idea—in short, declarative bursts, the tried-and-true pattern of immigrant speech.

"Only a very fat person could make it soft like that." And she was right, the middle cushion was softer and did sag more than the rest, and if you looked closely, as she asked me to do, there was still the impression of a body sitting on it, or so she led me to believe.

"They must have been very old," she added, and as a matter not of opinion but of fact, incontrovertible and without doubt.

I noticed afterward that she never sat in the middle of the couch, and that when on occasion a guest or two came to visit, she would wince, almost in pain, to see someone sitting there, particularly if they were heavyset, which most of the older women in our church who came to visit every now and then tended to be. She worried over the poor knees of the ghost of the middle cushion, who for her continued to feel the weight of this world even in death.

And so on the afternoon that my parents arrived at Fort Laconte, while my father slowly circled the fort, stopping carefully to read the historical notices nailed to the posts in the ground, my mother would have lingered around the edges, closer to the forest than to the fort, in order to get a more complete view of the scene before her. She would have searched out a quiet place to sit, somewhere near here, along the back walls, where a few of the stones have fallen, creating what appears to be a little network of benches to sit on. A stone like this one would have been perfect for her. Roughly three feet high with a relatively even, flat top—the lone stray of the broken wall. Someone, not her, of course, must have moved it here to this corner of the meadow. It seems to not belong to the fort at all, an accidental product of nature, sprung out of the ground like an errant tooth breaking through the surface. It's the perfect place to sit. From here I can see the entire arrangement of the fort: its slightly less than perfect ninety-degree angles, its few remaining walls and the empty spaces where a stable and sleeping quarters were. You can make out the edges of the guard's booth, and if you had a husband you were trying to hide from, you could see him coming from all sides. If all is quiet, and you strain your ears, you can make out the faint trickle of the spring that runs inside the forest.

Coming here she knew nothing about Fort Laconte—its creation or its bloody demise, which is not to say that she did not sense that something tragic had happened here. As she sat on the stone she tried to imagine what it might have been, running through a catalogue of seismic tragedies that seemed to occur somewhere every day. Her first instinct had been war, and while she knew that to be the proper answer, she indulged herself a bit longer and tried to picture the former inhabitants of Fort Laconte as victims of plague, famine, and then finally a tornado—a natural event that she had witnessed on television for the first time a few weeks ago. There had been flattened houses, uprooted trees lying in the middle of the road, and a few grainy images of a swirling dark gray mass descending from the sky like a finger pointing, in what seemed to be an almost godlike gesture, at what would survive and what would be tossed away. As she watched the footage on the news that evening, she thought she could almost hear the voice of the tornado as it leapt from roof to roof saying, "I'll take you, and you, and yes, even you."

She tried to imagine such a tornado descending down on this place hundreds of years ago but the thought failed to inspire. She tried again with a famine and did better. The images came quickly but in the end fell short. The inhabitants of Fort Laconte, as she knew well enough, had all been European, and there was no stretch of her imagination that could allow her to conceive of hungry white faces, not in this day and age, or in any age for that matter. She was certain that even four hundred years ago the world would have conspired to prevent such a sight, and so she shaded in the faces, broadened out the lips and noses, and came up with a picture more suitable for a slow, hunger-pained death.

At this point my mother felt a sudden uptick of emotion and energy brought about by a nice soft breeze, one that shook the leaves hanging above her, sending a flock of black-winged birds fluttering into the air. Or maybe it was just that she had grown tired of sitting on that stone, that her legs and back ached from its rough surface, which pressed into her skin, leaving a lattice of lines engraved on the back of her thighs, and that this was why she stood up, stretched her arms, and headed in the direction of the forest behind her. The reasons for her getting up don't really matter, at least not in the way they would if this were one of those childhood fairy tales in which the young maiden is called upon to enter the woods, from which she may not ever return. If it was that kind of story there would have to be a voice, something deep and slightly ominous, or the temptation of a miraculous treat, which would serve as the bait to ensnare her into a trap from which only her wits or a prince could save her. In either case, her folly or her greed would serve as her downfall, and anyone hearing the story would understand the lesson clearly: Stick to what you know.

My mother walked to the edge of the forest, where already it was notably cooler, the sun all but completely absent with the exception of a few errant rays of light that struggled to break through the canopy of leaves that would vanish over the course of the next few weeks. The air smelled different here—dead, damp leaves, mud, even the trees gave off a scent of their own. She walked a few steps farther, until she was more in the forest than out, and looked back at the spot she had just left. How completely different it seemed from this perspective. The stone that she had been resting on wasn't that large or rough after all. Sitting there she had felt briefly like a queen perched on a throne surveying her old ruined kingdom. From here, though, the stone looked almost suitable for a child to play on, kick, and tumble over. Even the meadow, which was flooded in light and appeared to literally glow from within, seemed hardly to be of any consequence. Perhaps, she thought, this was the way everything in America actually was—all smoke and mirrors, with only illusions of grandeur. It was hard if not impossible to really know anything when you were stuck in the middle of it, and that was precisely where she was, right in the middle of the country, with no clue, much less knowledge, of what lay on either side. She promised herself that if she ever got away, it would be to one of the coasts, someplace where she could have a view of the ocean, from which she could look back west or east and see all of this as clearly as she saw it now.

Somewhere in the middle of that thought my father entered the scene with his pocket notebook in one hand and a pen twirling in between the fingers of the other. My mother didn't notice him until he had entered the picture completely and was standing near the middle of the meadow, just a few yards away from the stone she had been sitting on earlier. They were only a hundred feet apart, but my mother felt as if miles separated them. My father walked across the meadow, stopping once to take a few notes on the arrangement of the wall at this end of the fort. It was a theatrical gesture, performed as if he knew someone was watching him from somewhere. It was meant to say, "Look at how closely I observe. How thoughtful I am of my surroundings, what a bright and intelligent man I truly am." He stopped just inches away from the spot where my mother had been sitting earlier, and looked to the left, and then to the right, and then directly into the forest. My mother stepped back slowly, hiding most of her body behind a tree, while leaving just enough of her head off to the side to see him staring back directly at her.

There are two directions the story can go in at this point. I can either see my mother peering from behind a tree, preparing to take flight into the forest, where she wouldn't get far, the distance from here to the brook being only a matter of a few hundred yards, or I can let her stand her ground and remain exactly as she is. The temptation to set her loose makes for a stronger narrative. I can let her dash past bushes and branches. I can give her scrapes on her arms, let a little blood trickle down her legs over her knee, where it dries and hardens into a firm dark blotch. When she arrives at the brook she'll have to decide whether or not she has the courage to ford it in her shoes and in her dress. Looking back, she decides that she does and takes the first leap into the water, which is cold and instantly shrivels the skin around her feet, causing them to swell with blood. She loses a shoe in the brook, bends down to pick it up, and drenches the bottom of her dress in the water. The dress clings to her tightly, hugging her calves as if pleading not to be forgotten. She stubs her bare toe on a stone, holds back her cry, and scrambles up the bank onto dry land. There is no discernible path so she runs straight, or in a direction that appears to be straight. As she runs she grows more confident in her footing. She stumbles less and quickly learns to spot the clearings ahead. Leaves rush by, and as she runs she can't help thinking to herself there is no stopping her now. She is an athlete, a long-distance gold-medal-winning Ethiopian runner, capable of heroic feats of endurance and strength, and soon the world will know her name. If there were barriers before her, she would hurdle them in one long, clean stride—a gazelle in disguise. An army of men couldn't catch her. Their bullets, arrows, and rocks, along with their violent, angry words—all would sail harmlessly by or fall uselessly to the ground in her dust.

And how long could she keep this up—this twenty-eight-year-old soon to be mother of one, dressed in a comfortable but ill-suited-for-marathon-running dress and flat-soled canvas shoes that easily slip off? The obvious answer is, not long at all, five, or let me be generous because this is my mother and it's hard not to be, and say ten minutes at most. And then what? Exhaustion. Confusion. And then looming up ahead, the end of the forest, which as I can clearly see is not a forest, just an uncultivated field of trees left behind by the state to keep the roaring highway at bay. And here it is—the overpass that leads down to the interstate—a road busy with semi-trucks and sedans coming off or returning to the highway after a pit stop at the nearby gas station. There is nowhere to go then but back, which is precisely where she and I are headed now, but God, what a beautiful run we might have had.

XII

After having spent the better part of the past three months apart, Angela and I made the mistake of treating our reunion as if it were inevitable. We opted out of the usual welcome-home affair; there were no elaborate homemade dinners or even small presents to speak of. Instead I waited for Angela at the airport with a bouquet of flowers, which she seemed strained to receive. On the train ride back to our apartment she said, "Let's just try to be normal. We shouldn't make a big deal out of my coming back home. Right."

For several weeks we did just that. Angela went back to work; at night we took up our usual positions around the apartment and waited for one of us to fall asleep first. It wasn't until September was almost over that I asked her why she still hadn't unpacked one of her suitcases. She had tucked it in the back of the closet; I had tried a couple of days after she arrived to put it on the shelf and found that it was still full of clothes, many of which were new and had been bought in Los Angeles.

"I don't know why," she said. "Maybe I forgot about it."

"There's not much space back there. It'd be easier if I could put the suitcase away."

That was as close as I could come at that point to forcing her hand, and a part of me expected her to say that she had no plans on unpacking anything, and that it was only a matter of time before I came home one day and found all of her belongings gone. And even though she may have decided already that that was where we were heading, she still hadn't accepted it.

"Don't worry," she said. "I'll get around to it soon. I have enough to worry about right now."

It was some time shortly after Angela and I had that conversation that the box with the last of my father's belongings finally arrived from the boardinghouse he had been staying in when he died. There had been, or so I had been told when news of his death reached me, administrative issues that needed to be taken care of before his belongings could be sent to me. There was no will, and very few items to begin with, but nonetheless they had said that it would take some time before they arrived. I had promised myself not to think about them again until they did.

The box came on a Wednesday afternoon, shortly after I came home from work. I was there when the delivery truck arrived and watched as a young man roughly the same age as myself unloaded it from the hold with very little effort. I signed for the box and then placed it at the foot of the bed, next to a stack of old magazines that Angela had promised for weeks to throw out. It came with a letter that had been poorly taped to the top.

Dear Mr. Jonas Woldemariam—

    On behalf of the entire staff of the YMCA please accept our deepest condolence at the passing of your father. In accordance with our own regulations and we hope your father's wishes, we have enclosed the items left behind in his room.

Even before my father died we had no claims left on each other, neither he to me as a father nor me to him as a son, but here was one now. Whereas in most cases the break in the family is precipitated by some large, unforgivable event, or a sudden realization of neglect, my father and I had simply drifted off into different corners of the country and had ceased to think often about each other since. I did return to visit him on several occasions over the course of the roughly thirteen years that had passed between the time I had left and the time he died. I drove down from Chicago, where I had gone to visit friends while I was still in college. He had finally moved out of the house we had lived in and into the boardinghouse where he would spend the rest of his life living off his factory pension. He spent most of the morning and afternoon getting dressed while I waited for him across the street in the parking lot for registered guests of the YMCA. After more than an hour I went inside to check on him. The door to his one room was still unlocked, and when I walked in I found everything almost exactly as I had left it sixty-four minutes earlier. The only difference was that instead of sitting in his robe, my father had donned a pair of black socks and spread out neatly on the bed next to him a dark brown suit with the coat resting above the pants, so that it was possible to believe that what I was staring at was not my father, but his ghost, and that the suit lying neatly on the bed was there to serve the memory of the man who had once worn it. When I asked him if he needed any help, if everything was okay, he simply smiled and asked what time it was.

"It's almost eleven," I told him.

"Then we still have time," he said. "Just give me a few more minutes."

And that was precisely what I did. I gave him eighty-three more minutes to slip into his suit, which had never fit him properly, and which now looked even worse dangling from the folds in his neck, as lacking in definition as if it had still been hanging in a closet. When he finally came out, he saw me from across the street, and perhaps because he knew that I was watching, he refused to take hold of the arm rail that led down the half-flight of stairs to the sidewalk. Instead he took each step one at a time, one foot landing a few seconds after the first so that each step taken became an event entirely unto itself. It wasn't the energy to walk any faster that he lacked, however. It was the courage to do so that was missing. He had come to the conclusion that the world was full of danger, both visible and invisible, and as he explained to me later that morning over a plate of cold scrambled eggs and half-eaten bacon, something terrible and awful was lurking just around the corner.

"I'm certain of it," he said, some of the missing life and energy having returned as he spoke in between long alternating sips of coffee and water. "I tried to protect you and your mother from it, but I can't any longer. Have you been paying attention? The signs are all there." His eyes trailed off, and the "it" that was threatening us all remained unnamed, and given how vast and unending it must have seemed to him, I can understand why. At the time I thought it was only the fear of growing old and dying that held him captive. I can see now that death was only the start of the terror—the first and easiest thing to name. Better then to move slowly, to brace yourself for the final fall.

When the end for my father did come, it was not as soon, nor did it look anything like I had expected. He had a type of frontal lobe dementia that normally claimed its victims after a couple of years. With nothing to live for I assumed that it would be even less, but instead he shuffled on through life for five and then eight more years, all inside his spare, white-tiled room in a three-story brick YMCA built just opposite the Illinois River. The last four years of his life he spent thinking about the years between 1974 and 1976 and what he had gone through to get here, with dozens of cardboard boxes as his companions through the past. I saw him once during that time, and only for a single afternoon. After I left I promised myself I would never return, and had remained true to my word until the box arrived. His English by that point was increasingly broken—half-phrases shouted out quickly when remembered, or clichés repeated over and over. He struggled to answer the few questions I put to him. He told me simply, on more than one occasion when I asked him how he was feeling, "I am tired yesterday," a phrase he must have repeated often and without meaning to the social worker and doctor who were occasionally brought in to treat the old indigent residents in the building. It was only when I was convinced that his actions and speech were genuine that I offered him a few simple phrases in Amharic. His body did not rise to attention as I had expected, but instead sank down even farther into the one plastic chair he kept in his room. I'll never know the range of confusion that ran through him. If anyone knows what it's like to feel the world around you collapse in its entirety, to fully know that everything that stands before you is a mere illusion, and that the so-called fabric of life is in fact riddled with gaping holes through which you can fall and still be said to be alive, then it was my father at that moment. I realized after I had left and was flying some thirty-five thousand feet above the earth, happily bound to my new relationship with Angela, that this was how my father must have sounded thirty years earlier, when he first arrived in America with less than a hundred words to his name and no past or future tense to speak of.

When I saw him that final time, nothing about his appearance suggested delusion. He still kept himself neatly shaven. He still picked away at his neat, trim gray afro, and even the deep grooves around the sides of his mouth made him look more like an old, varnished wooden puppet than a man in his early sixties living out the last years of his life alone. He still wore button-down shirts that while perhaps worse for wear around the edges nonetheless maintained with a simple sweater or jacket an air of casual dignity. I don't know how long it must have taken for him to dress himself by that stage in his life. I wouldn't have been surprised if he woke up early each morning just so he could make it out of his room for dinner. And why not? If the last thing a man has to hold on to is his sense of pride and accompanying dignity, then more likely than not he will expend every last trace of energy doing so. The appearance my father had created had formed a veneer of survival and graceful aging. He was half out of his mind, and probably had been for decades and no one knew it.

Once I had the few remaining objects of my father's life in front of me, I knew that I would eventually open the box and plunge into what had been the quiet madness of his last years. Knowing that, I held off for as long as possible. I made myself a cup of tea, after which I checked the hallway to see if my neighbor had picked up his newspaper for the day. He hadn't, and so I brought it inside and read quickly through the headlines while sipping my tea. I had never done it before and had no reason for doing so now, but I checked as well the daily index of stocks, bonds, and commodities on the back pages of the business section. I said out loud, to no one in particular since I was alone, "Look at that. Gold has gone up again." I tried again a few seconds later with a stock listed as WSK, which had posted yesterday a rather significant—and I'm sure to many people disappointing—loss. For a few more seconds I became one of them.

"Come on, WSK," I said. "You're killing me here."

And while I still couldn't quite see myself as one of those severely tailored men in suits who marched around Manhattan, I did begin to think that perhaps the differences between us weren't so great after all. We all had fathers, and some of us even had dead fathers, and speaking of dead fathers, here was what was left of mine, sitting just a few feet away in a cardboard box—the only true and proper resting place for a man like that.

That was the only way I could think of approaching my father's belongings—through indirect, oblique angles, as if I had just stumbled upon them at a party, long-lost friends I hadn't thought of in years and whose names I was struggling to remember. I had to walk around them, ignore them, and pretend as if they were all just part of another normal day for someone like myself—a stockbroker, or analyst-in-training.

I didn't expect to find any letters or a journal that my father had kept. He was hardly the type for sentimental preservation and was never one to state his thoughts directly. What I did find, however, could be considered a record of events, or a loose journal of thoughts. My father as it turned out was a drawer. Not a particularly talented one, but a drawer nonetheless. Of the hundreds of pieces of loose paper floating around the bottom of the box, almost all contained sketches of boats of various shapes and sizes that he had made. There were sailboats, tugboats, and freight ships; speedboats and a few ocean liners that appeared to be sketched from a catalogue. There were boats hovering alone in the middle of a blank white page, and others that were drawn out at sea, complete with waves and a stretch of land in the corner. A few were barely larger than the corners of the pages they occupied, while some nearly stretched across all four and were intricately designed with portholes, anchors, and flags blowing in the wind. There were dozens of sketches of three-dimensional boxes floating around them, as if my father were trying to find a way of fitting those boxes inside the boats themselves. This was what he saw and thought of every day. Boats coming and going, unloading their goods or bringing new ones on board. Some of the more detailed ones must have been drawn up close, perhaps from only a few feet away, or maybe from on the boats themselves. It was an easy walk, entirely downhill, from the YMCA to the piers. He must have made it often while he was still able to. The pictures nearest the top were barely sketches—spare, with only the general outline of a ship near the bottom left-hand corner. They have the air of having been drawn from a distance, both physical and emotional, that speaks to the way my father must have lived those last few years.

There were a number of ways of looking at those drawings. The first and easiest would be to say that they were pictures of things he saw every day, and perhaps the last and most sentimental would be to say that they expressed some deep eternal longing to be carried away, some profound private knowledge of death, which was just around the corner, an echo of the River Styx and the final passage we all must make out of life. I knew at that time that I would make of them what I wanted depending on the mood and occasion, and on that particular day they were signs that my father had never ceased to try to recapture the moment everything in his life seemed to go wrong.

Besides the pictures that box contained one last interesting memento: a small bundle of photographs of him in front of various monuments taken all over the world. There he is in Rome, outside the Colosseum; and in Athens, next to the Parthenon; and in Paris, with the Eiffel Tower looming large in the background. In each picture he's wearing almost the exact same outfit—dark brown slacks with a beige button-down shirt with a brown vest over it. He looks something like a cowboy—one misplaced and lost in time. The pictures must cover at least a year, maybe even two. In one he's holding a small suitcase as he stands next to a cot, which explains in part why his outfits over the years hardly varied. It was the one decent set of clothes he had, and if a picture of him was going to be taken, then it had to be taken in the best possible light, with the finest clothes he still owned.

What surprised me most about the contents was how little they revealed in the end. If my father was a stranger before, he seemed even more so now that I had caught a glimpse of his final thoughts. It wasn't supposed to have worked out like this. According to the stories, children who opened boxes containing the last precious items of their parents were always granted some vital, significant revelation, or at the very least, a dark secret uncovered. Family histories are supposed to be riddled with such things, for without them how do we achieve that much-needed catharsis we're all supposedly longing for? But then I thought that was the problem all along, that before a family secret or past can be revealed there has to be a family to begin with, and what we were was something closer to a jazz trio than a family—a performance group that got together every now and then to play a few familiar notes before dispersing back to their real, private lives.

By this time it was nearing eight p.m. I knew Angela would be home from work soon. If I stayed home, we would have sat through another dinner, straining at all times to pretend as if something horrible wasn't happening to our marriage. I had no extra energy to expend, and so rather than wait for her, I tucked about a dozen or so of my father's boat sketches into my pocket and headed west out the door, in the direction of the piers along the Hudson River; it didn't matter particularly which one, so long as I could stand as close as possible to the river's edge. The idea had struck me that it was time to see if my father's boats were seaworthy. I wanted to know if they could float. I know that I'm saying that somewhat disingenuously, which was how I said it to myself back then as well, but I needed a premise to begin with, something to justify my walking out of the apartment alone toward the piers on a dark November night. I felt that I couldn't say to someone if asked, "I'm going to take a walk along the Hudson," without somehow implying that I was up to something mysterious or perverted, even though the piers had recently shed their transvestite prostitutes and their little gangs of effeminate boys who had no money and nowhere else to go. Nor could I casually say, "I'm going to go walk along the piers now so I can be closer to my father, whose life and death I've been ignoring for too long. If you don't mind, I'd like to be alone." I needed an emotional cover, and those boat sketches provided it.

For the third straight day the unseasonably warm temperature had held, and even though it was November, for the second time in as many nights I walked with my jacket slung over my shoulder, both mildly surprised and delighted to see that tables and chairs had been set up outside, that people were dining and smoking, and that since night came early, many were already drunk. It was simultaneously festive and panicked. Car radios and boom boxes were playing loudly; there were more than a dozen kids standing outside the steps of the old tenement houses. Since we knew it wouldn't last much longer we seemed to be trying that much harder to hold on to these last traces of summer and fall, and there was something about our collective efforts that was ultimately frustrating and futile. I noticed that as I walked I was breathing in deeper, trying to concentrate inadvertently on the smell of the air while at the same time making sure to take note of every mild breeze that blew my way. By the time I had reached the pier I was tempted to almost yell out, Enough of this already! Let's get back to our normal everyday lives, but then I reached the water, and even with the lights from New Jersey streaming in from across the river and the blare of traffic behind me, I thought that this was a beautiful, magical place, this island that despite its massive numbers and seemingly crushing density still let you reach its borders so easily, almost as a consolation prize for enduring the brute force with which it could sometimes bear down on you, as if to remind you that you always have the option to leave and at the same time come back should you care to.

I found a place along one of the more run-down stretches of the waterfront, which was being rebuilt for the city's growing leisure class. I had hoped to stand immediately next to the water, able, if I cared, to dip my toes into it, but the best I could find was a slightly elevated spot with a short metal fence for a barrier. I thought of taking the sketches out of my pocket and seeing if I couldn't twist them into some sort of paper boat, the kind that kids supposedly sailed along the curb into sewers in a more wholesome time. I also thought that I could just as easily crumple those papers into tight little balls and cast them out into the river, where they would surely bob and float for a while before sinking, but in the end I chose instead to stand there and stare at the water as it occasionally lapped against the rotting wooden piers that probably hadn't held a boat in years. I stood for twenty or thirty minutes, long enough to finally get the courage to ask my father, now that he was dead and I was here trying to remember him, if he was finally happy.

When I came back home that night, I found Angela already in bed, sitting propped up with all the pillows on her side and a dense legal text in front of her. She didn't say anything when I walked through the door and neither did I. When did we become like this? Looking back now, I would have to say it was sometime shortly after we had gotten married and had supposedly settled onto the smooth track of our lives and careers. Of course, it's not our jobs that I blame. We had each wanted to varying degrees settled, stable lives that would serve as a counterweight to our own panicked childhoods and the wanderings of our parents. That was one of the first things that had brought us together—a shared vow, as sacred as if not more so than our wedding vows, that we would never be like the people who brought us into this world. We had promised each other as much as soon as we moved in together. There on that bed on which she now sat pretending to read, oblivious and indifferent to me, we had said things like "I never want to raise my voice in anger at you," and "We'll make this into the happiest smallest apartment in the city," and "I fight every day at work. I don't want to with you."

Which one of us said what hardly mattered anymore since we had failed on all accounts, and perhaps that was the greatest source of our disappointment with each other—that despite what we may have said we were finding that we were still perhaps only a few degrees away from what came before.

In hindsight it makes perfect sense that that should have been the night we finally began to talk about bringing our relationship to an end. The evening was already full of attempted closure, and so why not add one more.

Shortly after I got into bed, Angela, without ever looking up from her book or taking off her reading glasses, said, "You know, we don't have to stay like this." And at first I thought by "this" she meant the cold, silent treatment we were giving each other, but then I noticed that she hadn't looked at me and clearly wasn't planning to, at which point I understood the true intent of her words.

"No," I said. "We don't have to do anything."

"What does that even mean. 'We don't have to do anything.' That's what you come up with. I say we can end this marriage and you say, 'We don't have to do anything.'"

It was one of Angela's specialties to repeat my words back to me twice—the first time to prove how little they meant, the second time to show how obvious they were compared to hers. Years ago, in a moment of good humor, she told me that she would someday compile the Jonas Woldemariam Book of Clichés.

"I have them all here in my head," she said, "beginning with the very first one you told me on our first date. 'God, it's hot in here.' You actually said that at the restaurant when the waiter told you it was cash only. What were you trying to pay with—a Discover card, Diners Club?"

"A MasterCard."

"Are you sure? I remember a Discover card"—the Discover card being one of the great running jokes between us; the imaginary card that we used to pay for awful, tacky things that no one else would ever want to buy. We walked into animal gift shops and stores that specialized in embroidered pillows with the faces of "loved ones" just so we could ask the clerk behind the counter, "Do you take the Discover card?"

"You actually looked over at me then and said in all honesty,

'God, it's hot in here.' I wanted to laugh, but you looked like such a little boy that I was afraid you'd cry if I did."

To the "God, it's hot in here" line she added, "I can't believe someone would do that," and "It's really been a pleasure meeting you."

"You say that to everyone. 'It's really been a pleasure meeting you.' Serial killers, street vendors. I think if someone robbed you the last thing you would say to them as they walked away with all your money would be, 'It's really been a pleasure meeting you.'"

And now that night she added one more to her list: "We don't have to do anything," a statement that was intended to express a vast array of possibilities, from leaving each other to staying together until the bitter end, but that failed to convey either extremes or anything in the middle.

"Did you go to work today?" she asked me.

"Yes."

"Did you go see someone else tonight?"

"No."

"Are you lying to me?"

"Of course not."

While normally Angela could interrogate for hours, we stopped short that night after those few questions. If you've ever lived in close confines with someone you love, then you know what I mean when I say that our words became a part of that apartment that night. In larger apartments, in greater spaces, what's said in one room has a way of staying there. Bedrooms can be avoided. Kitchens, living rooms—these can be walked around if the space permits, but in our cramped little apartment what was said once stayed hovering over everything. Angela stood up and went to the bathroom to prepare for bed. I could see her through the crack in the bathroom door with a toothbrush sticking out of her mouth, and I imagined her saying to that toothbrush, We don't have to stay like this. I extended that sentiment to every object in sight— the couch, the television, the hand-me-down stereo system given to us by a richer friend, the duvet cover, which was hers, along with the one chest of drawers we had space for and then finally the three pots, two pans, and half-dozen plates and cups that formed the whole of our kitchen supplies. To all of them I said that night, We don't have to stay like this anymore.

XIII

Regardless of how hard I try, I can't imagine my mother waiting for my father to come find her in the woods. It would have been too coy a gesture for her, a halfhearted, poorly played game of hide-and-seek. Instead, she would have gone to him, picking the nettles off her clothes as she emerged out of the forest into the harsh bright light of the meadow. My father knew better than to ask her direct questions about her motives. Simple inquiries, particularly those involving the words "Why did you?" were always fraught, and he had learned to avoid them. This time, however, he felt he couldn't resist, and when he found her, he told himself he'd put the question to her directly and take whatever came next. "Why did you leave?" he was going to ask. Not "Where did you go?" or "Where have you been?" The destination hardly mattered. It was only the reason for leaving that counted.

Standing there looking for her he had maintained his composure while secretly beginning to fear that he had been suddenly abandoned. They had been the only two visitors at the fort. No one had arrived since and no one would come after. When my father came to the spot where he thought my mother had been waiting for him and found no one, he had instinctively turned back to the parking lot to see if the 1971 red Monte Carlo was still there. It was. He turned then to the guard's booth, but from where he was standing he couldn't see if it was empty or occupied. He considered running over and saying something like "My wife is missing." Or maybe something less dramatic and urgent such as "Excuse me, sir, have you seen my wife? I think it's time we left now." He suspected then that perhaps even the guard was gone. He had abandoned him as well. For much of his life he had believed such a moment was possible, and for several years after his mother's death he had been convinced that the entire known world would someday pick up and vanish without a trace and never tell him. It was easy for him to picture as a child. His father, cousins, uncles, and aunts all waking up in the middle of the night and deciding that they had someplace else they would rather be. He learned to sleep lightly, for no more than four hours at a time, always alert and vigilant, half awake and expecting even in his dreams to see his father tiptoeing across the living room with a tightly bundled cloth sack tied to the end of a stick. He had once attributed this fear of abandonment to losing his mother at such a young age, but he realized later, after he had seen more of the world than the countryside village he had grown up in, that it was not so irrational a thought at all. It was something that could be expected to happen at some point or another, just as one expected to someday marry or have children. There were abandoned thatched-roof huts all over the countryside in Ethiopia and again in Sudan, with people taking off and disappearing in both directions, everyone in flight. He had seen makeshift Sudanese refugee camps sprouting up along the desert terrain just before he had left. At least a thousand people were there, with most of them crammed into white tents propped up with a few pieces of wood. He had heard rumors of similar ones being built for Ethiopians in Sudan but had told himself that regardless of what happened, he would never go. The total effect was one of mass confusion punctured by silence, with deserted villages everywhere he went. He was sure that there were hundreds more now, and that more likely than not, there would be hundreds more again in the near future. Hiding in the bed of the pickup truck that had carried him all the way to the port in Sudan, he had spent entire days staring at them from underneath the blue tarp that protected him from the sun—one empty village after another, and by his rough estimate forty-three in all. Each had been made up of relatively the same size and structure—fifteen to twenty round thatched-roof homes, with a few brick structures lying farther on the edge. Some were still almost completely intact, others had been thoroughly looted—one town nothing more than a shell of empty boxes, suitcases, and metal safes, with everything that had once housed them burned cleanly to the ground.

They had stopped at what was left of one village to rest and found a handful of old men who had chosen to stay behind to wait out their last days. Over a cup of tea one of the men had pointed to a mat of straw and brick lying just a few hundred feet away. He spoke in a language my father didn't understand and so the man clasped his two hands together in the shape of a triangle to tell him that this was where his house once stood. A second later he swiped the air clean, as if decapitating it. Whether the houses stood completely upright or in ashes, the sense of emptiness that hovered over them was always the same.

This forgotten fort was America's version of a similar event—three hundred years earlier but a similar event nonetheless. My father knew for certain that this was why he had come here. He never said it to anyone, but he knew that in one of those villages, just as here in this fort, a child, a boy, had been accidentally or deliberately abandoned and that he was wandering out there in the savannah-turned-desert or in the forest searching for whoever it was that had left him behind.

When my mother came walking out of the forest, my father's first unmediated response had been to hold out his hand as if beckoning her to join him. He was relieved, almost delighted to see her, and there was something edifying in watching her emerge from the shadows, as if she were coming to rescue him. She caught the gesture from the other side of the meadow and rather than continue to walk forward came to an abrupt halt. He held his hand out for a few seconds longer, expecting her to take it at any moment, or for her to at least take a few steps in his direction as an acknowledgment that a sort of truce was being offered. When she failed to do so, he promised himself that he would never reach out to her again.

Let her stand there for the rest of her fucking life, he thought. Let her fall down, drown, sink into a pit, and die. She'll never have my hand to help her up again.

PART III

XIV

I called in sick to the Academy the next day. The dean of students
when I spoke to him laughed affably enough at my attempt to
sound ill over the phone and concluded by saying, "We all like you
very much here, Jonas. Let's not make this a habit now." I wondered precisely what the "this" he was talking about referred to.
Was it the getting sick, or the pretending to be sick, or the calling
in at the last minute when it would be impossible to find a substi-
tute in time, leaving him to fill the role, or was it the fact that I
had openly lied, and not with that much effort or conviction, and
why if it was any of these things, or all of them at the same time,
he should worry about it becoming a habit since I had never done
it before and at the time as far as I could see would never do
it again.

When I left for work the following day, I was still carrying
traces of my father with me. His boat sketches were in my pocket,
and as I walked to the subway and again on the train, I occasionally ran my hand over the images without taking them out. Appropriately enough, I thought of this time together as being the
closest we had ever been, and whether I wanted to or not, I had to
take advantage of the situation.

On an uptown-bound local train stuck just a few feet shy of Forty-second Street, I began to explain to my father all the reasons why he would have hated New York, had he ever dared to see it. We never had a conversation like that before—one in which I talked and he listened. Until then I didn't think of it as something that haunted me.

"These trains alone," I told him, "would have killed you. You never had much patience. Anything could make you angry. Five minutes of waiting on one of these platforms for a train would have been too much for you. The crowds would have only made it worse, especially in the morning and after work. Remember you hated tight, enclosed spaces. As you got older, even too much time in a car could make you upset."

Had he actually been there he would have agreed. It was like traveling with a tourist who understood nothing about the world you inhabited and was discovering himself through it. If I knew something about the history of the train lines that ran under New York, I would have shared that as well. The one thing he liked was man-made history—the story of planes, buildings, anything that had been constructed against nature. At the Seventy-second Street stop I pointed out to him that we were now firmly on the Upper West Side. "Which can say a lot about who you are," I explained. "It can be a good or bad thing. It depends on how you see it."

I decided to get off the subway a few stops early. We exited on Eighty-sixth Street. I continued the conversation once we were walking north on Amsterdam Avenue toward the academy.

"That's the academy right there," I told him. "You can see the top of the bell tower through the trees. I'm the only one who calls it the academy. That's not its real name. I stole it from a short story by Kafka that I read in college—a monkey who's been trained to talk gives a report to an academy. That's the title of the story: 'A Report to an Academy.' I used to think of that story every day when I first started teaching. I never told anyone that, not even my wife, Angela. I used to wonder if that was how my students and the other teachers, even with all their liberal, cultured learning, saw me—as a monkey trying to teach their language back to them. Do you remember how you spoke? I hated it. You used those short, broken sentences that sounded as if you were spitting out the words, as if you had just learned them but already despised them, even the simplest ones. 'Take this.' 'Don't touch.' 'Leave now.' That was how you talked. I never wanted to sound like that. I've lived here my whole life, and even with all my education, I'm still afraid I do."

When we reached the gates of the academy, I pointed out to him that this stroll we had taken from home to school on a bright, warm fall morning, with broken leaves scattered on the ground and what a poet once described as slanted light that one could almost walk on, was one of the most important things in my life that he had missed out on.

"This was the best part of the day for me," I told him. "I'm probably the only child in history who woke up each morning looking forward to his walk to school. I loved leaving that house, and I should tell you that on many mornings I hoped my mother and I would never return. Sometimes we came close, and even though we always came back, because I was young I never stopped believing that it was possible that someday we wouldn't. After two blocks I'd find myself thinking that at any moment now we were going to head off in a different direction. I imagined cars and helicopters coming to pick us up, and I would have had my mother entirely to myself. I wonder if it surprised you that we didn't disappear."

We parted at the school's front doors with a promise that I

would see him later. I arrived in my classroom ten minutes before
the first bell rang. In my first days of teaching I had always arrived
at least thirty or forty minutes early, in large part to gape in wonder at my classroom and my place in it. Other teachers used the
room later in the afternoon, but it was mine at the beginning of
the day; those were the best hours to claim it. As the sun rose
higher, I would watch the light stream in through the windows and
spread across the darkly polished wooden floors and the desks
that in previous decades had been bolted to them. For the first
couple of years it had always struck me as a remarkable sight, one
worth waking up a little bit earlier to witness and for which I
would often remain grateful throughout the day. Recently I had
stopped doing this, and generally arrived only minutes before the
morning bell.

I took my place behind my desk and waited for my students. I
hadn't done that since my first year at the academy, when every
day was full of a punishing anxiety. I needed those thirty minutes
behind my desk to remind myself that I did indeed know what I
was doing, and had every right to be there. Angela had caught
hold of that anxiety as well, and for nine months had woken up
early and made breakfast for the both of us. On numerous occasions I'd run part of my lecture by her.

"Pastoral poems," I told her, "are almost as old as poetry itself. Some of the first poems written were pastoral. Even if they
don't seem like it initially."

She would sit at the table and pretend to take notes on what I
was saying, and in more mischievous moments would raise her
hand and ask questions to which she knew I had the answer.

"I'm sorry," she asked, "but what exactly does pastoral
mean?"

. . .

The first of my students trickled in a few minutes before the bell. They were the smartest of the group and took their seats near the center. The rest arrived in no discernible order, but I noticed that all of them, smart and stupid alike, seemed to hardly talk, or, if they talked, it was only in whispers. Most said hello as they entered, but their voices were more hesitant than usual, as if they weren't sure that it was really me they were addressing.

I watched them as they filed past my desk. They were an attractive group, and several of the girls in the class of mainly boys would undoubtedly grow up to be described by both men and women as striking, if not beautiful, a fact most had already begun to prepare themselves for with their year-round tans and delicately applied streaks of blush and mascara. I waited until they had all taken their seats, and when I looked at them, I saw something approaching a hint of wonder on their faces, which may very well have always been there but which I was just recognizing.

"I'm sorry for having missed class the other day," I began, and because I felt obliged to explain my absence, I told them what I thought was the next closest thing to the truth.

"My father passed away recently. I had to attend to his affairs."

And yet because I had just finished talking to him, I felt that didn't say enough. So I continued.

"He was sixty-seven when he died. He was born in a small village in northern Ethiopia. He was thirty-two when he left his home for a port town in Sudan in order to come here."

And while I could have ended there I had no desire to. I needed a history more complete than the strangled bits that he had owned and passed on to me—the short brutal tale of having been trapped as a stowaway on a ship was all he had to explain himself. It made for such a tragic and bitter man, and as he got older it must have been even worse. I imagine the past died multiple times within him as his memory faded and whatever words he had left to describe it disappeared alongside. And so I continued with my father's story, knowing that I could make up the missing details as I went, just as I had once done for Bill and his brood of migrants at the center.

"He was an engineer before he left Ethiopia," I told my students, "but after spending several months in prison for attending a political rally banned by the government, he was reduced to nothing. He knew that if he returned home he would eventually be arrested again, and that this time he wouldn't survive, so he took what little he had left and followed a group of men who told him that they were heading to Sudan, because it was the only way out.

"For one week he walked west. He had never been in this part of the country before. The mountains that surrounded the city had disappeared, and after several days on foot he realized he was going to miss them. Everything was flat, from the land to the horizon, one uninterrupted view that not even a cloud dared to break. The fields were thick with wild green grass and bursts of yellow flowers. Eventually he found a ride on the back of a pickup truck already crowded with refugees heading toward the border. Every few hours, they passed a village each one of thatched-roof huts a cluster with a dirt road carved down the middle, where children eagerly waved as the refugees passed, as if the simple fact that they were traveling in a truck meant they were off to someplace better. He had done the same as a child; cars were rare and precious back then and even the adults would have chased them on their horses if they hadn't considered it beneath them. He thought about how terrible it was going to be for some of those children when they realized how much misery leaving often entailed.

"When he finally arrived at the port town in Sudan, he had already lost a dozen pounds. His slightly bulbous nose stood in stark contrast to the sunken cheeks and wide eyes that seemed to have been buried deep above them. His clothes fit him poorly. His hands looked larger; the bones were more visible. He thought his fingers were growing.

"This was the farthest from home he had ever traveled, but he knew that he couldn't stay there. He wanted to leave the entire continent far behind, for Europe or America, where life was rumored to be better. He didn't really care where, as long as he could find work and sleep peacefully at night.

"It was the oldest port in Sudan and one of the oldest cities in the country. It was originally built by the English in 1875 after they had taken the country, although at that time it was mainly used to bring in weapons from Europe because there were constant uprisings. At its peak hundreds of thousands of people lived there, but now only a fraction of that population was left. Several wars had been fought nearby, the last one in 1970, between a small group of rebels and the government, but things had been quiet since then. He could still see the remains of those wars all over the country. There were burned-out tanks and cars on the edge of town and dozens of half-destroyed abandoned houses. There was sand and dust everywhere and on most days the temperature came close to a hundred degrees. The people who lived there were desperately poor. Some worked as fishermen but most spent their days by the docks looking for work. My father was told that he could find a job here, and that if he was patient and earned enough money he could even buy his way out of the country on one of the boats.

"On his first day in the town he walked down to the docks

where hundreds of men were already waiting. Most of them were Sudanese, but there were plenty of migrants from different corners of Africa. The whole continent seemed to be at war and those who weren't seemed to have converged on this town. Some of the men were busy unloading crates from the dozens of small freight ships in the harbor. Many more were idly standing by watching or sitting on their haunches in the shade. He had never seen anything like it, and his first instinct was to try to find a way to get out of there as fast as possible, but it had taken him weeks to get there and he was tired and almost out of money. He had only one small bag, which held a few days' worth of clothes and a picture of himself at home that had been taken six weeks before he left."

The bell for the end of first period rang then. My students waited before gathering their bags and leaving; they were either compelled or baffled by what I had told them. For a brief moment I was afraid of knowing. Quickly, though, I looked straight ahead and I tried to see them all in one long glance before they were gone. They had always been just bodies to me, a prescribed number that came and went each day of the semester until they were replaced by others who would do the same. For a second, though, I saw them clearly—the deliberately rumpled hair of the boys and the neat, tidy composure of the girls in opposition. They were still in the making, each and every one of them. Somehow I had missed that. As it turned out, I had nothing to fear. None of them looked away or averted their gaze from mine, which I took as confirmation that I could continue.

XV

Normally at this time in the afternoon I would be standing by the windows in my classroom, watching as the four hundred fifty-six students of the academy stripped themselves free of their uniforms, ran their hands through their hair, and lit up cigarettes concealed in the bottom of their book bags. This daily ritual always had a calm, soothing effect on me—the lives played out on the corner, from my vantage point, having the somewhat surreal effect of feeling like a special, private performance of adolescent rituals being screened solely for my benefit. At their age I was so deeply invested in my own solitary world that not even my parents, with their relentless arguments and theatrics, could broach the shell I had formed around myself. I failed to notice most of what was happening around me, and later grew to believe that there was some culturally important film that I had failed to watch at the right age, and could therefore never fully understand. In college and even after college friends had shown me pictures of high-school dances, proms, pictures of their first cars and dates. I heard stories of having sex in bedrooms while parents stayed downstairs watching television, and other stories of suspensions, runaways, and failing grades. I knew of course that these things had also happened during my own childhood, but they had no relation to my life at the time. My concerns back then were more private; they primarily involved finding new ways of numbing myself so nothing my parents, or by extension the outside world, did could touch me. Within two years of my leaving home most of what had occurred there had already begun to seem like a long-distant dream whose edges were funny and whose details had been washed away. And while it's obviously true that you can never go back in time and make up for what was lost, you can at the very least spy on it to get a sense of where you might have fit in had you been around to play the game. We think our personalities are solid, definitive bodies, but watching the students at the academy has led me to believe otherwise. In fact, there is nothing so easily remade as our definitions of ourselves. I could, on good days, see myself as one of those boys who stood in the center of the crowds, confident, mildly amusing, and otherwise completely harmless, while on other days I saw myself as better suited to the fringes, with one or two piercings beyond convention, or to the groups that sat on the edge of the parking lot, scorning the spectacle in front of them as they would surely do later in their lives. To label what I did while standing at my classroom window an act of voyeurism is to miss the point entirely. Even the simplest of fools can watch and fantasize. It takes more, however, to really put yourself in the center of things, to watch yourself as you would have looked had you been that age at that time, as if you were witnessing different screen-test versions of yourself in which you were called upon to play all the various roles of adolescence, from the lonely child, to the popular socialite or star athlete, or simply just one of the general majority. For an hour or so on many afternoons I graded and judged my various performances, just as I graded my students' papers and worksheets with a cold, unsparing, critical eye. At the end of the day I returned home and waited for Angela so I could tell her some of the things that I had discovered about myself. A common complaint of hers during the early months of our relationship was how little I revealed about my life before her.

"What were you like in high school?" she had asked me. "Cool. Smart, stupid. Friends, no friends."

"I'm not sure."

"Which means what?"

"Which means I can hardly remember. That whole time seems like one big gray fog in the back of my mind so I never think about it."

To the extent that was true, Angela assented, prying only occasionally for extra details while at the same time happy to hold on to whatever I revealed. There were plenty of memories from that time, but I found it difficult to trust if they were real or not. I know that I read encyclopedia-sized anthologies of poems and stories that I borrowed from the library, and that on many nights I fell asleep in front of the thirteen-inch television that was perched in front of my bed, but these images, like so many others, fell into a vast, indistinguishable corner in which I hardly existed. Where was I on my sixteenth birthday, or what had I done during my long, boring summer vacations while my classmates were drinking their parents' beer on porches or groping each other in empty parking lots at night? To be honest, I couldn't have said much more beyond the general—that I was either alone in my bedroom or sitting out by myself near the river's edge, close to where the cargo boats docked. Violence had made, and to an equal degree when I was older and separated from it, unmade, my world.

· · ·

My students were windows, if not into the life I actually lived, then into the one I might have had had a different set of odds been cast in my favor. I told Angela things such as "I think I would have been on the soccer team. I was very fast when I was young."

"Did you have a soccer team?"

"I'm not sure. I think so."

"Okay, then let's say you were on it."

"Was I any good?"

"Were you any good? Jonas, you were the best. You once scored three goals in a single game."

"How do you know?"

"I remember."

"Were you there?"

"Of course I was. I was sitting at the top of the bleachers watching you. I always thought you were beautiful in your shorts."

Our inventions, you see, worked both ways, and in whatever false histories I created, there was always room enough for Angela to join me when and if she cared to—

"What happened after graduation?"

"You picked me up in your father's car."

"What kind of car was it?"

"A 1972 black BMW."

"Really?

"Yes. It was your graduation gift, remember?"

"That's right. He bought it used from a friend."

"Exactly."

"And where did we go?"

"We drove all the way to Chicago."

"Just the two of us."

"Yes. It was just you and me. We had dinner at a restaurant right on the lake."

"Was it good?"

"It was one of the best meals we've ever had."

Because the truth, of course, was that she needed these fanta-sies as much as and perhaps more than I did. What few stories Angela shared with me about her own childhood consisted almost solely of private adventures that she had taken while left alone, which was nearly always. Angela was never a teenager so much as a premature adult assigned to watch over herself. Her mother, she told me once, "had a bad habit of disappearing sometimes. She always came back after a day or two, and after the third or fourth time I got used to it. She always left a little money."

Inevitably some of the false memories we indulged in had nothing to do with me, even if I was supposedly the one at the center of the story. These narratives were reflections of her own past, the parts she was reluctant but needed to tell me about and most likely had tried to forget, like the time she asked me if I remembered my first "sexual encounter," which was how she phrased it, in cold, clinical terms that were lifted right out of a textbook. I lied and said no so I could listen to what she came up with.

"Well, it wasn't with me," she said, which was when I under-stood that this was her story. "We didn't know each other yet. You were only twelve, or thirteen. There was this person who lived near your house who was a fair amount older whom you'd known for years. She waited for you after school one day and you both started walking home, but when you got near your houses you turned in a different direction and just kept walking. Eventually you came to an open field where there was no one around. Since she was older she led the way. She told you where to put your bag down, and when you did she told you to lie on your back and close your eyes. You couldn't see her face but you knew it was there because suddenly you couldn't see anything at all anymore, not even a little light from the sun. She gave you just a little peck first, and then when you didn't run away, she kissed you harder."

"Did I enjoy it?"

"Let's just say that at the time you thought you did."

When it came to these stories we never sorted out which details were false and which ones may have been true. To have done so even once would have destroyed the whole enterprise we had created from the foundation up, and so we always diligently avoided any prodding that could be construed as a search for verisimilitude. The imagined memories had to have as much weight as the real, or we had to at least pretend they did to such a degree that they just very well might have. And so I never questioned Angela about that particular story, or about all the troubling things that it pointed to, content to believe that at least in this version things worked out for her better than they did in the one I never heard.

If Angela were driving with me, she would say that this is exactly where I belong, somewhere here in the middle of the country, a man unsuitable or ill-made for coastlines, more at home in flat terrain that bears no hint of ending and that strives at all times to be as evenhanded and uncomplicated as possible. I've never lost my affection for this place; many times over the intervening years I've thought that it would be wonderful to stand alone in the middle of any of the fields on the other side of the car windows. Shortly after my mother left my father, I thought of coming back here to commemorate the event. This was the only context in which I knew her, and I understood even then that once she was gone from here we would grow increasingly distant from each other, until eventually someday we were completely estranged. It was a fair price to pay for her tarried freedom.

Her departure in the end wasn't the dramatic event that it had promised to be during the nineteen years my mother and father lived together. There was no furious packing or preceding arguments. They were, if anything, at a relatively tranquil moment in their lives—their fights and arguments having all but ceased, to the point where they hardly spoke at all to each other. It was peace through a policy of détente, with occasional violent skirmishes that flared up from time to time on the side. Two weeks after I had left home for college she left too, packing her clothes in the middle of the afternoon while he was at work, calling a cab to take her to the bus station, and then taking a bus to Chicago, and from Chicago a flight out east to Washington, D.C., where a few old friends from the private school she had attended in Ethiopia had recently resettled. She called me shortly after I arrived at my dorm room in New York.

"I'm in D.C.," she said.

"What are you doing there?"

"I'm staying here for a while with my friend Aster. You don't know her." Nor would I ever.

I understood even with those few words that she would never return to my father again. Washington, D.C., at just over seven hundred miles away, was the farthest she had ever been from home since she came to America, and if there was any one rule to her departures, it was that once you get far enough away, you never go back. What I hadn't known at the time was just how little of her I would see afterward. She lived four hours away from me by car, and yet over the course of the next three years we only saw each other twice, both times at cold, impersonal cafés outside the city, in one of the suburban mini-malls that had taken the place of the northern Virginia farmland. When we did see each other, we talked around whatever we were supposed to have said. She asked me on every occasion if I was happy.

"Are you happy, Jonas?" she asked, much in the same way she had asked me as a child if I was hungry or tired, both states of being that she could easily remedy by either giving me a plate of food or offering me a place to sleep on the couch next to her. What could I say to her except "Yes. I'm happy," which put her mind at ease and allowed us to continue sitting at our table, picking apart whatever pastries she had chosen to buy that day.

M y mother chose a diner similar to the ones we used to meet at to make her first stop of the trip, less than an hour from Fort Laconte and still more than five hours from Nashville. She had kept a cheap little souvenir from it on top of her chest of drawers for years afterward—a palm-sized aluminum pig with a wide-brimming smile and a napkin wrapped around its neck that read "Eat at Frank's." Her excuse for stopping was a simple one: "I have to use the bathroom," she said, and my father, sensing that this time she was indeed telling the truth, and that regardless it was easier to oblige her than to argue, pulled off at the next exit, at least two hours sooner than he would have preferred to stop again.

Inside the diner cold blasts of refrigerated air seemed to hold the people sitting at the counters and at the booths in place, frozen and lifeless, as if they had been sculpted out of the same dough that had been used to make the pies sitting on display in the glass counter next to the entrance. My mother walked in and wrapped her hands around her arms, trying to quell the little bumps that had sprung up as soon as she entered. No one looked at her when she came in—not the girl sitting behind the cash register and not any of the dozen or so patrons who were eating at this odd hour of the day, and yet she still felt as if all eyes were secretly trained on her, and that if she could only turn her head fast enough to the right she would catch them measuring her every step and taking size of the neat little bulge below her waist that could have just as easily been a few extra pounds put on since her conversion to a nearly all-American diet.

She didn't ask where the bathrooms were. The signs were obvious enough and plus she had learned that only the guilty and the frightened asked for things that were otherwise evident.

"The first step to being an American," a friend of her father's had told her shortly before she left Ethiopia, "is to act as if you know everything. The two most important words in the English language are 'of course.'"

Gashe Berhane Getachew was one of the few Ethiopians she knew who had actually lived in the United States, a scholarship child of the former emperor, sent abroad to study agriculture in Kansas; his words, as far as she and everyone in the family were concerned, were nearly sacrosanct when it came to America.

"They didn't know what to do with me," he told her. "When I got there I asked them where their peasants were. All that land and no peasants. My teacher told me, 'I don't know how it is where you come from, but we don't have peasants here.' Liar. They had plenty of them, everywhere. They just kept them far away from the university so I couldn't see them. Please, when you get to America, find the peasants for me."

That became his running joke with her until the day she left. "The peasants, Mariam. Remember me to them." If someone new was present, he would exclaim, "Soon our young lady here will be leaving to find the United Peasants of America."

If Gashe Berhane were here with her now, he would say, "At last, Mariam, you've found them."

The bathrooms were located at the back of the restaurant, just off the kitchen. The only two stalls were empty and the room smelled of a mixture of ammonia and fried chicken that made her both nauseous and hungry. For the past few weeks she hadn't been eating nearly half as much as she wanted. She was afraid that if she gained weight too quickly the barely noticeable bulge would swell and become all but impossible to deny, and so she had kept herself hungry to the point where she often had to sleep once if not twice in the middle of the day to quell the hunger pains in her stomach and the slight dizzy spells that were becoming more frequent.

She stood in front of the mirror and noticed that her eyes were developing dark purple sacks underneath them, and that the knot on the side of her head had now taken a distinctly egg-shaped form. She clucked once, like a chicken, at her reflection. The noise sounded hollow, echoing back to her off the cold white-tiled walls. She heard what she thought were footsteps shuffling behind one of the closed stall doors, and for a few seconds she stood there frozen, afraid someone had heard her and her barnyard imitation. She looked at the floor and saw nothing. She turned back to the door, hoping to find a lock that would ensure her privacy, but there was nothing there as well. She entered the stall farthest from the door and locked it, checking once to make sure that the bolt was secure so no one could walk in on her by purpose or accident. As she sat down on the rim of the toilet, she wondered if this was what giving birth would feel like—the hard-rimmed edge of the toilet seat serving as the delivery table, and the general noise of strangers on the other side of the bathroom door serving as both the hospital waiting room and cafeteria. The delivery room would have to be white, just like this one, and at some point, Mariam thought, she would close her eyes and search for a darkness so complete that not even a hint of light could be seen.

She peed with her eyes closed, and as she did so she thought to herself, *I wish you were this easy to get rid of.* It wasn't the pain that she particularly feared. Even as a young girl she was nearly indifferent when it came to the scrapes, bruises, scratches, and occasional punches and kicks of childhood. If you were injured you suffered but eventually recovered. Time took care of the scars and slow, deliberate movements eased the rest, but it was the exact opposite with having a child. Once you opened up and delivered you would never fully heal again. The wound was permanent, and for all the days of your life there would be another part of you that could break or die over which you could do little but console. She had been told that babies in America were sung lullabies at night to help them fall asleep. Mariam didn't know the words to any lullabies yet, but she had a sense of the tone and rhythm in which they were sung. She tried out one now, humming a tune that was soft and gentle but came from nowhere. It masked the sound of her urine splashing in the toilet, and when she was finished she stopped humming and left the stall.

In the nine and a half minutes that she had spent in the bathroom, the crowd inside the diner nearly seemed to double in size. When she came out, she searched for her husband's face in one of the booths and then at the counter, but there was no one who looked even remotely like him, or her for that matter. The faces here were decidedly uniform in color, shape, and by and large, size as well. They all seemed to be related, distant cousins, aunts, uncles, brothers, all gathered together for a sullen family reunion at Frank's Diner, located just a half-mile off the interstate highway. She walked toward the door, but this time she stopped just short of the exit, as if told to pause by command. This time all eyes in the diner really did turn on her, and for once she turned hers back on them.

That meeting of strangers' eyes is something I've thought about often since—the confused, bewildered stares heading in both directions, passing one another along the way like two cars driving past each other on a highway, headed for similar but opposite destinations. The people on the other end of my mother's glare must have wondered what she was staring at so intently, if perhaps she was mad or in some sort of desperate trouble and searching for a friendly face to rescue her. I have a hard time picturing any cruelty on their part. At that age my mother was too slight and pretty to have inspired any real hostility, but there was no doubt in anyone's eyes that she didn't belong here, and that, at least, is one point on which everyone in the diner could agree. If they shared anything, it was the common sense of relief that came when she opened the door and finally left.

XVI

When I was finished with my class, more than just my mood had visibly changed. I decided to walk back home, and for one hundred and two glorious blocks I was on my own, left to puzzle over the events of that morning and what I had said to my students in the crowded rush of a large metropolitan city at the close of what was for the millions of other people around me just another average working day, no greater or less than any other. It was halfway through the semester and the first signs of winter had yet to be felt. By this time some of the trees should have been bare—scarves and jackets should have been standard, but fall had dragged itself out longer than normal. Everyone was grateful for the delay—the sidewalk cafés were once again crowded with people and talk of global warming and the earth's demise, in which we couldn't help reveling.

As I walked home that night I was aware of a growing vortex of e-mails and text messages being passed among my students. I could almost see the messages moving in the air—tiny encrypted notes carrying word of my breakdown from one phone or computer to the next. They would have been written in a descriptive shorthand—Wht the fck?—that I never fully understood. Millions

of invisible bits of data were being transmitted through underground cable wires and satellite networks, and I was their sole
subject and object of concern. I don't know why I found so much
comfort in that thought, but it nearly lifted me off the ground, and
suddenly, everywhere, I felt embraced. It's often said that a city,
especially one as vast and dense as New York, can be a terribly
lonely and isolating place. I had felt that before, even at the happiest points of my marriage to Angela, even when we deliberately
hid ourselves nearly underground in the five-hundred-square-foot
confines of our apartment, just the two of us, alone and with
nowhere to go for days at a time. I felt none of those lost, lonely
sentiments that night, not once as I walked down Riverside Drive,
with the Hudson River and the rush of traffic pouring up and
down the West Side Highway to my right. Here the tight control
on neighborhood borders and divisions hardly mattered. From my
vantage point the city stood alone, all of its buildings, whether
they were made of glass and steel or old brick, were gathered together in unison.

I waited outside our building for Angela to arrive. I wanted to
convince her of important changes that I was going to make in
order to save our marriage. I knew what I could say and do to
evince that, and was prepared to do so. I had to speak to her,
however, before we entered the apartment and found ourselves
surrounded by the couch and chairs on which we had spent many
nights and afternoons avoiding each other. All it would take was
a quick glance into a closet full of barely worn expensive shoes or
the recent absence of a photograph on a windowsill to remind
either one of us of who we had become. After that it would be
difficult but not impossible to say anything that could convince
Angela that large, substantial adjustments could be made to a
person's character.

I saw Angela from half a block away and gathered my coat and bag so I could meet her on the corner, at a distance safe from home. Before she could say anything I took hold of her one free hand and led her in the opposite direction.

"I'm starving," I told her. "Let's get something to eat before we go inside."

She was too tired to resist, which was what I had hoped for. There was a window of time between leaving work and settling in for the evening where Angela's defenses were weakened and there was an air of almost visible vulnerability around her. I had often caught sight of that and been grateful that it never lasted too long. It was there as we turned the corner and headed south on Avenue A, especially when she asked me how my day had been.

"How was it?" she asked.

"It was wonderful," I told her. "I'll tell you why as soon as we get back home."

Angela and I picked up dinner from the last takeout Puerto Rican restaurant left on our block. There had once been, or so we were told, close to a half-dozen such places in the neighborhood, a fact conveyed to us with great, passionate interest by one of the few remaining longtime tenants of our building, an old, semi-decrepit woman who had otherwise never had anything to say to us. Unlike Angela, who took the news as further proof of a widespread cultural loss happening throughout New York, I considered the disappearance of such places entirely irrelevant, given that something similar could be said of almost any block in this corner of the city, where change was not only constant but inevitable, and without which one could imagine the buildings and the trees that stood facing them slowly withering, as if it was the relentless process of renewal that had kept them standing in the first place.

On our walk back, with our plastic bag of food tucked under my arm, Angela asked me what had been so wonderful about my day. We were only three blocks away from the intersection where we had met. If ever there was a perfect place and time to reinvent oneself, this was most likely it. On some days it seemed as if half the tenements surrounding us were being taken down and replaced with something new that, at least on the surface, promised to be significantly better.

"I had a meeting with the dean this afternoon," I told her. "After my class was over. He called me into his office and said he wanted to talk about my future at the school. I thought he was going to fire me at first. I can't remember the last time we talked in his office, maybe two years ago when one of my students had their parents complain about their grade. He asked me if I was happy with my class, and I told him yes, I was happy, but I wanted to do more. He said that's what he wanted to talk to me about. One of the other English teachers is retiring after the semester, and the dean told me that they wanted me to teach his classes. He already talked it over with the faculty committee and the board. They all agreed that I'd be perfect. It would be full-time, and after two years I would have tenure. He said my salary by then would more than double.

"As he told me that, though, I was thinking about what you had said once about this being just a temporary job, and how I was supposed to go on someday to get my Ph.D. That was always the plan but somehow I forgot that. I became so concerned about just holding on to what we had that I didn't want to take any chances. For so long I lived on almost nothing and I was afraid of going back to that. It's been three years now, and look at us, we're worse off than before. We hardly talk anymore, and I know I'm to blame for that. I didn't want to hear that you were unhappy, and so I did what I did best: I ignored it. I just kept hoping that with time it would eventually pass.

"I told the dean that I would take the job, but only for one more semester because after that I was going to go to graduate school. He said he thought it was a great idea—something I should definitely do, and that when it came time to apply he'd offer me his full support."

I spoke with the conviction of a man who believed every word he said. I could picture the conversation with the dean as if it had actually happened—and had Angela asked me to describe the scene I could have told her in great detail about how he and I had sat together in his wood-paneled office with the arched windows that looked out onto the edge of Central Park after the last bell of the day had rung and most of the students had departed; however imagined that conversation may have been, the effect was nonetheless real. I was going to move forward in life.

Angela, a skeptic at heart, tried to remain unaffected. I thought, If she's ever had an addict in her life, this is what he must have sounded like. Always this promise of renewal. I figured somewhere in that past of hers, between uncles, cousins, and her mother's boyfriends, she must have; the fact that she was grinding down hard on her teeth while blinking rapidly all but confirmed that.

When she finally spoke all she said was, "I'm happy to hear that, Jonas. Happy for you and maybe even for us."

Later that evening, while we were sitting at the table over a half-eaten plate of paella and plantains, we talked about numbers and the things we would like to have someday, nothing lavish this time—we had learned that lesson already—a few extra square feet of living space, more sunlight, and a vacation or two out of the city.

"Let's be conservative," Angela said, "and say that your pay doubles. We'd have enough extra money, after everything is paid, to get a better place. Something that doesn't feel like a basement."

That was the extent of her wishful thinking.

The next day at the academy I continued from where I had left off. The only interruption to the story was when I told my students at the start of class that they could put their anthologies and notebooks away. "We won't be needing them for now," I said. I didn't bother to notice whether any of them looked at me surprised.

"My father's first job at the port," I began, "was bringing tea to the dock workers, a job for which he was paid only in tips—a few cents here and there that gradually added up. On an average day he would serve anywhere between three and five hundred cups of tea. He could carry as many as ten at a time on a large wooden platter that he learned to balance on his forearm. He always had to be alert while doing so in case someone tried to steal the tray from him, or knock him over as a joke because he was clearly a foreigner and could speak only a few words of Arabic. He learned to tie a piece of cloth around his forehead to keep the sweat from dripping into his eyes as he walked. He had never had steady hands before. As a child he had been clumsy; his father would often yell at him for breaking a glass or for being unable to bring him a cup of coffee without spilling. He learned to cure himself of that in Sudan. So as soon as he got this job he began practicing at night with a tray full of stones that were as light as the cups of tea. If the stones moved he knew he had failed and would try again until eventually he probably could have walked several miles without once spilling a drop of tea or shifting a single stone.

"He hid his earnings in a pocket sewn into the inside of his pants. When he had enough loose change to turn into a bill, he would exchange each time at a different store. The one friend he had in the town, a man by the name of Abrahim, had told him to never let anyone know how much money he had.

" 'If someone sees you have two dollars, he will think you have twenty. If someone sees you with twenty, he will think you have two hundred. It's always better to make people think you have nothing at all.'

"Abrahim was the one who found him the job carrying tea. He met my father on his third day in town and he knew immediately that he was a foreigner. He went up to him and said, in perfect English, 'Hello. My name is Abrahim, like the prophet. Let me help you while you're in this town.'

"He was several inches shorter and better dressed than most of the other men that my father had seen there. His head was bald with the exception of two graying tufts of hair that arced between his ears. The last two fingers on his right hand looked as if they had been crushed and then tied together. He bowed his head slightly when he introduced himself and walked with what might have been a small limp, which in my father's mind made trusting him easier.

"At first my father slept outside, near the harbor, where hundreds of other men also camped out, most of them refugees like him. They huddled together in small groups, and as he passed them, he often thought he heard them laughing at him. He was the only one out there who slept alone. Abrahim had told him that it was dangerous to do so, but he had also told him that if he slept in the town he was certain to be beaten and arrested by the police.

" 'They'll take one look at you and know you're not from here,' he told him, 'and then, if you're lucky, they'll put you in jail, but more likely they'll simply beat you and take everything you have.'

"After a week out there he heard footsteps near his head just as he was falling asleep. He kept a large rock next to him and before opening his eyes quickly slid one hand behind his back to where he kept it hidden. When he opened his eyes and looked up he saw three men standing nearby, their backs all slightly turned to him, so that he couldn't see any of their faces, just their long white djellabas, dirty but not nearly as filthy as some of the others that he had recently seen. As he watched, one of the men lifted his hands into the air slowly, as if he were struggling to pass something over his head. He recited a prayer that my father was already familiar with. He had heard it several times on his way to Sudan and on multiple occasions in Ethiopia at the homes of Muslim friends. The man repeated it a second and then a third time, and when he was finished, the two other men who bent down and picked up what at first appeared to be a sack of grain but which he realized, a second later, was clearly a body. The man had been lying there when my father went to sleep. There had been nothing to indicate that he was dead or even injured, which somehow made it even worse to him. He stayed awake for the rest of that night and the next day hardly had enough strength to get through work. When my father told Abrahim later that evening, his response was a simple one: 'Don't think about it too much,' he told him. 'It's easy to die around here and have no one notice.'

"He promised to find my father a better place to sleep, and the next day he did. He found my father preparing his mat near his stretch of the harbor and told him to follow him. 'I have a surprise for you,' he said.

"The owner of the boardinghouse where he was going to stay from now on was a business associate of Abrahim's. 'We've worked together many times over the years,' he told my father, although he never explained what they did. When my father finally asked him how he could repay his kindness, Abrahim waved the question away.

"'Don't worry,' he told him. 'You can do something for me later.'"

XVII

When my mother came out of the diner she found, to her great and unending surprise, that she was not only relieved but grateful to see the 1971 red Monte Carlo waiting for her exactly where she had last seen it, a few feet to the right of the diner's entrance, in a space that wasn't reserved for cars but that was occupied by one nonetheless. For the first time she sensed that she could have stayed inside that restaurant for hours—ordered food for one or two meals, lingered over dessert, and that still she could have come outside and found that car waiting for her in exactly the same spot as it stood in now—a red rock of unwavering conviction in which feet were firmly planted and never budged. She admired this fact about her husband. His persistent, blind, nearly doglike devotion to certain principles. Her father had tried to tell her before she got married that such men were better suited to plowing fields like donkeys than raising families, but she rejected that judgment on the grounds that their world was already changing fast enough, and that it was better to be tied to a donkey than to nothing at all.

She opened the passenger door and took her seat next to her husband, placing her hand gently on top of his. Even though the

car was an automatic he continued to drive with his hand next
to the emergency brake, an imaginary gearshift that gave him a
greater sense of control over his actions.

"Thank you for stopping," she said.

My father was never an exceptionally cruel man, despite so
much of what he said and did in his life, and here is further proof
of that. A simple thank-you set his heart briefly racing, although
he wouldn't have known how to say in which direction. Let me
explain it like this. No one thanked Yosef Woldemariam for anything. Not his boss at work and not any of the casual strangers he
encountered day in and day out. He heard dozens of expressions
of gratitude uttered every day, at restaurants where he ate, at the
gas stations he visited, but none ever seemed to be directed at
him. He considered himself nearly invisible in that regard, a man
who, even in his most decent and polite gestures, passed through
unnoticed, and so when my mother said, "Thank you," merely for
pulling the car off the road so she could use the restroom, he saw
himself as briefly belonging to that legion of polite, good-natured
men whose smallest act of consideration never went unnoticed,
whose wives, children, and coworkers fell over themselves to compliment on the quality of their manners. He armed himself with
those two simple words. He donned them like a knight, confident
in the knowledge that at least for now there were few things that
could touch him. He lifted his hand off the imaginary gear stick,
slid the car into reverse, and headed toward the highway, the few
rural clapboard houses nearby, long since decayed, slipping away
into the background along with their acres of untended fields and
the bright neon signs of the gas stations. A song came to him—
one that he hadn't heard or thought of in years. It was one of
Mahmoud's more mournful ballads—a song dedicated to love
lost, a favorite not only of his father's but of all the young men he

had once known in Addis who despite their seemingly carefree, braggart ways when it came to women were all looking to be coddled like children. He wondered briefly what had happened to them, and for a few seconds he took the risk of remembering some of their faces, bodiless of course, just as they would have been had he seen them hanging framed on a wall in their mother's home now that they were dead or missing. He began to whistle the song, slowly at first, and then with greater confidence, the tune swelling and slowly filling the car with a melancholic tone that brought a smile to the face of anyone who heard it.

He whistled louder and with more passion than before. He was wonderful at it, and he knew that as well. His voice was never made for singing—too coarse around the edges—but when it came to whistling he could sing like a bird, and he did precisely that, until his lungs began to ache and all four verses of the song had been completed. He turned to look at his wife, vaguely aware as he was doing so that he had already passed the exit for the highway and was on a road that seemed to lead in the wrong direction. She was watching him too, and not out of the corner of her eye as she normally did but head-on, with something resembling a tear swelling in her eye for this man she hardly understood, much less loved, but who she knew would try to hold on to her with every last trembling breath.

L ess than an hour later they were completely lost. The two-lane country road they had been driving on had forked, and not knowing what else to do my father turned and followed another. He suspected that at any moment now they would come back upon the highway, see its glimmering headlight-lit lanes from

either above or from the side, but no such thing occurred and all
that was around them were corn and soy fields dotted from time
to time by a solitary oak tree that served as a resting spot for a
group of cows who sat indolent underneath them. For now neither
of them was particularly worried. You could even say both were
slightly relieved to have been freed from the straight and narrow
pressure of highway driving, which allowed little time to slow
down. Here my father drove with only one hand on the steering
wheel, his body slightly slumped as if he could fall asleep at any
moment, if only it weren't for this business of driving.

My mother noticed the first traces of colors on some of the
leaves. My father saw the few scattered clapboard houses and
wondered what they went for in today's market. They could have
said any number of a hundred significant things to each other
during this carefree part of the trip. My mother could have told
my father about how at one point during her flight from Addis to
London to Chicago the plane had suddenly taken a dramatic drop
toward the earth, sending up a loud, nearly unanimous shout of
panic among the passengers, but that she, unlike the rest, had gone
on flipping through the pages of the in-flight magazine, because
what she already felt, up in the air three thousand and then four
thousand miles away from home, was, she was positive, not so
different from death and the cold, detached gaze with which the
deceased, angels, and gods must look down upon us. My father,
for his part, could have shared with her some anecdote about his
time in Europe before coming to America, about the long, lonely
afternoons he had spent wandering in Rome with another Ethiopian refugee, about how after they had visited all the important
historical sights, they found that there was nothing they wanted
to do so much as sleep, sometimes for three or four hours at a time

in the middle of the day, as if all that history had personally weighed upon them with a force even greater than that of the city's traffic-clogged streets, and so they would walk until they found a park or a large patch of grass, or they went down to the Tiber, where they slept with their clothes on, like all the rest of the homeless men in the world.

Other more personal things could have also been said.

Mariam, for instance: I've never told you this, Yosef, but you were not the first or last man I slept with. After you left there were so many young boys wandering around the city. It was full of them, and I found several to briefly take your place.

Yosef: I used to wish sometimes that you would forget about me completely. That I'd come home one day and find a letter from your father saying not to worry anymore about finding a way to bring you here.

Mariam: When you go to work I imagine terrible things happening to you or me. I sit by the window in the living room and look out at the street and I think, What if there was an earthquake right now that swallowed up this entire block. I can see the houses falling down and I know if they did I'd stay right where I was the entire time.

Yosef: I still have the worst dreams at night. Sometimes there's someone standing above me with a bag ready to place over my head. I know that once he does I'll die. I wake up just in time and there you are sleeping and I hate you for that.

Mariam: If you stopped the car right now and told me to get out I would. I wouldn't even take my clothes with me. I always thought this was an ugly place. I could never understand why you liked it. I can almost see why now. If you started to run there would be nothing to stop you. It's almost like the ocean that way.

Yosef: You have no idea what I've been through.

Mariam: You don't even know that you're going to be a father yet, do you?

Yosef: If I could start all over again I would. I'd go back to my father's house and I'd stay there forever. I'd become a farmer. I'd die in the same place as I was born.

Mariam: I have no idea how you've gone on living like this.

And when they were finished they could have pulled off the road, into one of the small, half-dead towns that are a fixture in this part of the country, and parted amicably enough, my mother taking a room in a motel for the night, where after unpacking a few days' worth of clothes she would have laid out her plans for the future, beginning first and foremost with figuring out a way to leave these flat Midwestern plains and the people who populated them, while my father would have continued on alone to Nashville, determined as ever to see the place where country music was born, his head already full of images of modern-day cowboys singing songs with their guitars strapped over their shoulders, as alone as or perhaps even lonelier than he was. But of course they still weren't finished with each other, and so remained obligated to see this story through to its end, which had they had even a remote inkling of would have called their attention to all the obvious signs of trouble lying ahead.

First there is the path they're driving on. They're heading west instead of east and have been doing so for nearly an hour. The sun is blazing on directly in front of them, creating what will soon be a more brilliant than normal sunset, complete with thick, heavy clouds that bring out the purple and pink shades in the sky. There's the condition of the road they're driving on to consider as well. A heavier than normal summer rainfall has created large cracks and holes all along the concrete, which are easy to avoid now but will be all but impossible to see come nightfall. A few of the holes are deep enough to potentially damage a car. There are the names of the neighboring towns: Mount Zion, Athens, Monticello— towns whose names point to a false ancestry and grandeur that they never possessed and are now more than certain to never even approach with their dwindling populations. There is the overpowering smell of pig feces carried in by the wind from a nearby hog farm, and the absence of nearly any other cars on this road. There are global events to consider as well. There is a shortage of oil right now. Gas prices are threatening to cripple the economy. There is the slightly nauseated feeling in my mother's stomach, and the fact that my father has needed glasses for years but has refused to acknowledge it.

Almost any one of these on its own should have been enough to tell my father that there was something wrong gradually accumulating weight, the same way a storm sometimes slowly pulls together its forces, calling upon distant clouds to join together before unleashing its fury. Taken all together, the sound of trouble lying ahead should have been nearly deafening to a man who had reportedly spent his adult life paying close attention to the subtle vibrations that alert us to the danger up ahead. How did he miss them, then? Simple. He closed his eyes. He shut his ears and tried harder than ever to be happy. He looked at himself from afar and saw only a man behind the wheel of a relatively nice car with a beautiful wife next to him on an early fall afternoon in the middle of a country that promised freedom, democracy, and opportunity, choosing therefore to forgo the difficult process of zooming in to get a closer look at the details, any one of which could have pointed him to the fact that something was destined to go wrong. Had he done so he would have stopped immediately and turned around. He would have driven straight back to Peoria at a speed recklessly above the limit and he wouldn't have said a word to his wife about why he was doing so. Not knowing any better, however, he drove on, foolish enough to think that a better day was finally at hand.

XVIII

I knew after the first time I told my father's story that it was important to come down from the almost delirious heights I had reached before returning home. After the second time, the only way I could think of doing that was to ride the subway into a far-off corner of New York, one that I had rarely if ever seen before, and stay there for hours, long after the sun had set and Angela had returned home from work. The thought of doing so came shortly after I had boarded a fully crowded train and found there was a comfort in being underground; in my strange logic at the time I thought of the world above as exposed and therefore vulnerable in ways that the rest of us down below weren't. The idea of branching out to the rest of the city took root from there, and even though I had, after more than ten years, seen what I had always presumed to be a large share of New York, I had never traveled into a foreign neighborhood with the explicit purpose of wanting to be as far removed from my daily life as possible. Finding that remove was even now, with all the riches the city had amassed over the past few years, far easier than I had thought possible. Millionaires were reportedly common in the outer boroughs, and you were rarely far from an expensive, well-lit café, but

when you came down to it, this was still an immigrants' land and
had continued to be regardless of how much they were pushed to
the margins. I sought out hard-to-reach neighborhoods that could
be found only on the minor train lines that seemed to be in a per-
petual state of disrepair, and often, after less than an hour's journey, I found myself walking down wide, open-bungalowed streets
where few people my generation and older spoke English without
an accent. First in Brooklyn, and then later when that had started
to feel exhausted, I roamed sections of Queens. As I did so, I often
wondered what I would say to my students and Angela when I saw
them next. I picked up oily, cheap pieces of fatty lamb and beef to
eat, and after walking for two, sometimes three hours, returned
home to find my wife on the couch waiting for me.

I developed on those walks a habit of continuing the stories I
had told in my class, although now the narrative was expanded to
include anyone who came into my line of sight. I thought if I could
imagine where all of the people I passed had come from and how
they had gotten here, then I could add their stories to my own
basket of origins. To the Pakistani man who sold me my first plate
of overripe lamb curry I gave a slightly distinguished military career thwarted by nepotism, rumors of homosexuality, and a change
in the presidential guard. To the Haitians on the other side of
Prospect Park I threw in a mix of political persecution at the hands
of one of the Docs and several large-scale natural disasters, a mix
of hurricanes and mudslides, to balance the picture out. There
were Orthodox Jews deep in Brooklyn who were descendants of
pogrom survivors who had made their way here immediately after
the end of the Cold War and never once looked back. And of
course there were plenty of Africans scattered throughout the city,
many of whom I knew, despite the reports of torture and impris-
onment on their asylum application forms, were here just because

they wanted to have an easier time getting on with their business plans and dreams, and who could blame them? If my fictional narratives lacked any veracity, it didn't really matter. Whatever real histories any of the people I encountered had were forfeited and had been long before I came along, subsumed under a vastly grander narrative that had them grateful just to be here; it was only a matter of whether they knew that or not.

By the time I returned home Angela had finished eating dinner. Initially I explained my late evenings to her as being the inevitable consequence of new responsibilities, scheduled to begin next semester.

"I'm going to be staying late at the academy to plan the classes I want to teach," I told her. "I want to do something on modern American poetry: William Carlos Williams and a few others, but it's been so long since I last studied them that I have to get my grounding back first."

I couldn't stop there, however. It wasn't enough just to say that I wanted to plan a perfect course for my students, or that I wanted to make the best impression possible on the other teachers when my syllabus was put up for review. These were only minor gains in a game in which, if I wasn't exactly losing, I could hardly claim to have been ahead. There had to be a bigger ambition and a better ending than the one I had come up with so far, and gradually I supplied it.

"There's more to it than just my classes," I told Angela a few nights later as we were getting dressed for bed. "I'm thinking now that these classes could be part of a bigger research project I undertake someday. I mean of course it wouldn't be exactly this, but it would be related. Modern American poetry, or maybe American poetry between 1930 and 1950, when it was great and inventive. Even if you forget guys like Pound and Eliot, it's still amazing. I was thinking that with all the work I put into my classes now, I can use it later for a dissertation. And honestly, even more than that, I forgot how much I enjoyed this type of research. I think it's time I started really considering what it's going to take to go back to school, even if it's only at night."

When I finished, she kissed me once on the lips while holding both my cheeks together, a sign of tenderness that had been common in the early days of our relationship. For the working-class immigrant child and only daughter of a mother who even in the best of times was often missing, great forward strides were being made. More letters of significance were to be added to our portfolio, and when it was over, you'd have a doctor and a lawyer who together no bill or credit-rating agency could touch.

I backed up my story by bringing home books from the library that I pretended to stay up even later reading, as if the five to six hours I had supposedly spent after my class was over weren't enough. The sight of me surrounded by a wall of four-inch-thick volumes of critical studies and anthologies set off a maternal instinct in Angela, prompting her to say one night, as I sat at the dining room table that doubled as a desk, that she was confident someday soon I would make a wonderful father.

"I can see it," she said. "It's so clear. You'll be great."

I tried to make up for my prolonged absences from home with small thoughtful gifts, the kind I had once freely offered to Angela in the early months of our relationship. I picked up strange, obscure books for her on my evening walks—a beginner's guide to Sanskrit, a Jewish holiday cookbook—along with homemade hair pomades from the Caribbean quarters of Brooklyn, all of which she genuinely loved. There were pieces of hand-strung jewelry sold outside a subway station, and a few overly sweet desserts that she claimed reminded her of home. What hurt was seeing just how far these little acts went in restoring her confidence not only in our relationship but in herself as well. The two had been deteriorating along the same path and in equal proportion; it wasn't until she nearly wept at the sight of one of the small gifts I had brought her that I understood that. In our rush to presumably better ourselves we had both missed what had otherwise always been obvious— that it often didn't take much more than careful consideration of each other's needs to secure a degree of happiness.

In normal times it was Angela who stayed up late reading through papers, and now it was my turn to do the same. After she turned off her light, I'd continue to sit well past midnight, occasionally reading from the large texts I'd placed in front of me. I came across a William Carlos Williams poem that I later tried to commit to memory but always forgot after the first three lines:

> *When I was younger*
> *It was plain to me*
> *I must make something of myself.*

I read those words perhaps a dozen times, and after each time I thought that was exactly what I was doing, whether anyone could see it or not: I was making something of myself while I was still young, and even if that something was little more than an ever-growing lie, it was still something to which I could claim sole credit and responsibility. I was, however wrong it may have been, making a go of things.

. . .

As my narrative spilled into a third and then fourth day, my students began to ask questions, shy, almost discreet in nature at the beginning, bolder, and more impossible to answer by the end.

I was asked to fill in narrative gaps that I had deliberately overlooked. Why had my father left? And how had he gotten here? And what were the causes of all these wars that I had hinted at?

I tried to tell my students that these were entirely different stories on their own, worthy of their own proper telling, but the short-changed response didn't hold. They looked at me as if I had cheated them out of something they felt entitled to, and I suppose that was indeed the case. I did the best I could and I trekked backward into a part of the story that until then I knew nothing about.

"Before my father came to Sudan," I told them, "he was in a prison just outside the Ethiopian capital for one hundred and thirty-three days. That may not seem like a lot to you, but you have to understand just how long one hundred and thirty-three days is in a place like that. There are no showers or toilets, just hundreds of large concrete blocks behind a barbed-wire fence where people are crammed together so close that the only way to lie down is on top of someone else. Food, when and if it came, was scarce—mere scraps given to them by the guards. With so many people diseases were rampant, especially cholera and typhoid.

"At that time the government was busy arresting anyone who they thought might be a threat against them, and what's funny of course is that the same thing is still true today. The prison in fact is still there, and the only reason why my father was able to get out of it was because an old high school friend of his had recently been appointed the minister of justice. He saw my father's name on a long list of people who should potentially be executed, and while he couldn't let him out of prison directly, he did get my father a temporary release while his case was reviewed. My father knew that as soon as he was out he would have to leave the country immediately, without telling anyone where he had gone."

And while this part of the story wasn't true to anything I or anyone I knew had ever experienced, it had an air of serendipitous salvation that struck me as being so unlikely that one had to believe it had occurred that way.

As soon as I resolved my students' questions about what had happened to my father before he reached Sudan, I returned to the story of his still-burgeoning friendship with Abrahim. I told them more about how my father spent his afternoons with him learning to fit in at the dusty port town in which he had found himself, and how Abrahim taught him a few words of Arabic and how to make a proper greeting and departure when it came to strangers. While much of what I had said until then was a mix of fact and fiction, Abrahim had a real history I could draw from. Abrahim had played an active role in my father's memory, and by extension mine as well. My father had mentioned him regularly, not as a part of normal conversation but as a casual aside that could come up at any time without warning. Unbidden, my father had often said that Abrahim was the only real friend he had ever had, and on several occasions he had credited him with saving his life. At other times my father had claimed that the world was full of crooks, and that after his experiences with a man named Abrahim in Sudan, he would never trust a Sudanese, Muslim, or African again.

I could never have asked him what exactly Abrahim had done for him, or what their relationship had been like, but I had never asked him anything to begin with, not about his past, his current intentions, or his plans for the future. By the time I was old enough to be genuinely curious about what type of man my father had been before I knew him, I had made up my mind already. He had been a bastard from birth and would remain one until he died. Anything beyond that was irrelevant. Often, however, I did think that it would have been better if Abrahim had let him die, or I remember wishing that at the very least Abrahim had managed to inflict some righteous form of punishment, one strong enough to be felt for decades, right up to and including the moment that had my father standing over me with his fist raised. Some children need heroes to right the imbalances in their world and to settle the scores that they can't; I would have taken a greater villain any day of the week.

The Abrahim who came to life in my classroom was a far nobler man than the one I had previously imagined, and was more likely than not a more decent man than the one who had actually existed, and maybe even still did exist in the port town where my father had found him. This Abrahim had a flair for blunt yet nonetheless poetic statements, like the time he told my father that even the sand in the port town was of a quality inferior to the kind he had known in his home village, hundreds of kilometers west of here. "Everything here is shit," he said. "Even the sand." He had a soft, gentle voice that barely rose above a whisper, and unlike most of the other men in the town, was immaculate in his dress and perfect in his manners.

I relayed all this to my students in a slightly dispassionate voice only marginally different from the one I used to teach my standard English lessons. I wanted to give them the impression that this was a true history being told. And even though it was unnecessary, I began to support my story with dates and figures. "It was late June now and the rains were about to start. Ten to fifteen boats were pulling into the harbor every day, and soon, once the rains had passed, there would be three to four times more.

"My father went to great lengths to disguise his origins; he bought himself two white djellabas and grew a small beard. When asked where he was from, he said that he was a Muslim from As-mara, where barely even the imams spoke Arabic. Did you know what was happening right now in Asmara? he would then add. It was terrible. The communist Ethiopians were killing Muslims by the thousands, bombing their villages into ashes because this was what Moscow and most likely America wanted. That's why he was here. He had barely escaped with his own life, he would add, thanks only to the mercy and grace of God.

"Abrahim got him a better-paying job as a porter on the docks. He told him on their third full day together, 'You're going to be my best investment yet. Everything I give to you I will get back tenfold.' His words were cryptic and yet were said in a tone that made it impossible to be afraid. Abrahim came by almost every day to share a cup of tea shortly after evening prayers, when hun-dreds of individual trails of smoke from the campfires would be winding their way up into the sky along with the prayers that only minutes ago had preceded them. Abrahim would pinch and pull at my father's waist as if he were a goat or a sheep and then say, 'What do you expect, I have to check on the health of my invest-ment.' Afterward, as he was leaving, he would always offer him the same simple piece of advice:

"'Stretch, Yosef,' he would yell out. 'Stretch all the time until your body becomes as loose as a monkey's.'

"At the docks he carried boxes from dawn until midday, when it became too hot to work. Before his shift at the teahouse, he'd take a nap under a tree and look at the sea and think about the water in front of him. Like most of the men he was thirsty all the time, and he was convinced that there was something irreparably cruel about a place that put water that could not be drunk in front of you. He imagined building a boat of his own, something simple but sturdy that could at the very least make its way across the Gulf into Saudi Arabia. And if that was to fail, then he'd stuff himself into a box, hurl himself into the water and drift until he reached a foreign shore or died trying. Even that, he thought, would be better than a lifetime of this."

When I was afraid the story was moving too slowly, I moved the narrative back into the heart of the port town. I filled its streets and harbor as best I could with a sense of mystery and danger not unlike the type that could be found in old black-and-white movies with raincoat-clad men in foreign settings, or even in more contemporary accounts of Africa that never shied away from reveling in the continent's darkness, both literal and imagined. The story needed intrigue and conspiracy and until then was wholly lacking in villains of any sort, and while I initially saw these sidelines as being at best only marginally related to the story I had begun, I quickly found that they had a purpose as well. Somewhere on the blank canvas on which parts of my father's life was starting to take form, there had surely been moments in which he had been forced to take stock of the greater machinations occurring around him, and as I sat in my classroom early each morning, completely alone with the exception of the school's janitor, I tried to imagine, without bias, what some of those moments might have been. He had throughout his life been an ardently politically minded man of the conspiratorial sort and was fond of accusing any government or head of state in the news as being full of lies. American politicians were all liars; the former Soviet Union was full of fucking liars, and all of Western Europe was bullshit. Ronald Reagan had been a hero almost everywhere in Illinois but in our house, except for those moments when the president was threatening war; the same was true of every president who followed, Republican and Democrat alike. The only heroes for him were those who had died, the Lincolns, Kings, and Kennedys, and even then I suspect it was only because in dying they proved what he had known all along about corruption, power, and the hidden forces who really governed things. He was fond of saying that he was certain to see some sort of coup take place in America within his lifetime. "People don't think these things can happen," he would say, not to me or to my mother, but to the television, whose early-evening news often sparked these proclamations. "Because they are stupid and don't know better. But I know how governments really work." And while I had always dismissed such statements as those of a paranoid man who had come to consider his experiences as vastly more important than they really were, I realized now that they must have had their origin somewhere, and here at last with my students I was starting to discover them.

"At least once or twice a week, Abrahim would pick my father up from his room in the evening and walk him down to the docks in order to explain to him how the port town really worked. The two would walk slowly, careful not to disturb anyone or draw attention to themselves, partly out of fear of being robbed. The port was an entirely different town come dark. The only lights came from the scattered corner fires around which groups of men were huddled. Despite the darkness, people moved around freely and in even greater numbers than during the day. It was as if a second city were buried underneath the first and were excavated each night. Women without veils could be spotted along some of the narrow back streets, and my father could smell roasting meat and strong liquor.

"It was down at the harbor, in the shadows cast by the bright lights that illuminated the piers, that Abrahim taught my father how to interpret the ships and cargo that were being quietly unloaded under military guard.

"'The ships that you see at the far end of the port are all government controlled,' he told him. 'They carry one of two things: food or weapons. We don't make either of them in Sudan. You may have noticed this. That doesn't mean we don't love them equally. Maybe the weapons more. Have you ever seen a hungry man with a gun? Of course not. Such things don't exist. It's like saying, have you ever seen a hungry lion? Of course not, because as soon as you did he wouldn't be hungry anymore. The men here with guns are the same. Always stay away from that part of the dock. It's run by a couple of generals and a colonel who report straight to the president. They can shoot, arrest, kill anyone they want. They've done it many times before. They are like gods in this little town, but with better cars. If a soldier sees you there's nothing I can do to help. Not even God will save a fool.'

"'The food is supposed to go to the south. It comes from America and Europe and from all over the world in great big sacks that say USA. Instead it goes straight to Khartoum with the weapons. And do you know why? Because it's easier and cheaper to starve people to death than to shoot them. Bullets cost money. Soldiers cost money. Bombs cost a lot of money. Keeping all the food in a warehouse costs nothing. Even better you can sell it to buy more bullets and soldiers just in case what you have isn't enough already. Everything destroying this country is happening right there.'

"In the course of several evenings Abrahim worked his way steadily down the line of boats docked in the harbor. His favorite ones, he said, were those near the end.

" 'You see the ships at the very end of the harbor? They are full of oil. Barrels and barrels of it. All of it comes from the Middle East, but we have plenty of it right here in Sudan. Enough to make us all rich, but the government doesn't want us to know that. It's true. If you don't believe me, ask anyone. Who knows, though, maybe in ten or fifteen years things will change. Maybe then we will all be like the Saudis and those other Arabs, living in big houses with Mercedeses, rather than living here like rats. If that happens, believe me, you will wish you never left here.'

"On other late-night journeys to the port Abrahim described to my father how he planned to get him out. He showed him a group of newly arrived ships and told him that as far as my father was concerned, those were the most important boats in the world.

" 'And those ships over there, the ones all the way at the other end. Those are the ones you need to think about. Those are the ones that go to Europe. You know how you can tell? Look at the flags. You see that one there—with the black and gold? It goes all the way to Italy or Spain. Maybe even France. Some of the men who work on it are friends of mine. Business associates. You can trust them. They're not like the rest of the people here who will disappear with your money.'

"After several visits to the pier at night, my father began to take seriously Abrahim's advice about stretching. He worked his body into various controlled positions that he would hold for ten, fifteen, and eventually thirty minutes and then for as long as an hour. At night before he went to bed he practiced sitting with his legs crossed and then he stretched his back by curling himself into a ball. After four months he could hold that position for hours, which was precisely what Abrahim had told him he would need to do.

"'The first few hours will be the hardest,' he said. 'You'll have to be on the ship before it's fully loaded and then you will have to stay completely hidden. Only once it's far out to the sea will you be able to move.'

"My father thought about writing letters back to his family, but he didn't know what to say. No one, not even his wife, knew for certain if he was alive, and until he was confident that he would remain so, he preferred to keep it that way. It was better than writing home and saying, 'Hello. I miss you. I'm alive and well,' when only the first half of that statement was certain to still be true by the time the letter arrived."

XIX

For the next twenty-five miles, my father drove in what he believed to be the direction of the Illinois-Tennessee border, full of grand and heady thoughts. If asked what exactly he was thinking of, he would have said that he was remembering the names of every border he had crossed throughout his life, and that there was a time when he imagined that was precisely what he was going to do for the rest of his days, cross and recross different lines on a map until he had touched and memorized them all. The first time he had crossed a border had seemed like something of a miracle to him. The pickup truck he and a dozen other people had been hiding in had pulled over abruptly, and the driver, a tall, lanky man from one of the border tribes who was Ethiopian some days, Sudanese on others, walked over to the rear of the truck and threw the blue tarp off their backs. With the sun suddenly glaring down on them, he had declared, rather proudly in English: Welcome to Sudan. Those who hadn't paid the full fare into town were pushed out of the truck, and for the first time in two days there were only two other people. My father suddenly had enough room to stretch his legs and stare freely out at a blinding midday sun that would soon scorch his lips and leave him faint and nearly dying for water.

The people who got out of the truck gathered their belongings, if they had any, and headed off in separate directions. No one stopped to look back at what had been the border—a thin frayed line of rope stretched between two trees and guarded by two soldiers who were just as gaunt as the half-dead trees they were resting under for shade. Those departing simply walked off, a few alone, most in groups, in the direction of what appeared to be, and most likely was, little more than sand, dirt, and wild thorn brush, with a hamlet of straw-and-mud houses identical to the ones they had left behind in Ethiopia. My father felt like he couldn't have been the only one who wanted to say it, but in the end no one did, perhaps because it was so obvious a thought, or perhaps because there was no simple way to express an idea with so many contradictions inherent in it—so much for so little, and yet still we're left with nothing at all.

Every time he crossed a border since then he remembered that first one. Other crossings were grander in scale and offered more dramatic backdrops—Africa into Europe, Europe into America, and even Europe into Europe, but none bore the weight and meaning of the first. For all the expressed differences between the various nations of the world, none compared to the one made between living and dying. There were still countless ways for him to have been killed in Sudan, and he had already considered nearly all of them, from being thrown from the truck, to disease, to being on the wrong side of a bored government soldier, but the odds were in his favor and had been from the moment he crossed onto the other side of the rope. The rest since then—the languages, currencies, the darker and paler skins, the curlier versus straighter hair, and the lighter shades of eyes, along with the topography of certain cities and the customs people took for granted, from the times they ate their meals to the way they looked at you when you entered their stores clearly poorly dressed for the cold and more likely than not hungry—was just window dressing to him. People imagined their differences as they needed to, so let them if that was what was called for. He would have never said if you've seen one border you've seen them all. He respected and noted their differences. He had his favorites among them—the crossing from France into Italy along the Mediterranean coastline being the best of them all. You crossed only really one, maybe two, such borders in your life where the differences were infinitely greater than those between nations, and none at all if you were fortunate. It was these that you had to really note because nothing would ever compare to them again.

Tennessee he thought could be something similar—not so much a difference between living and dying but between ways of living that were becoming just as vital to him now that the first had been guaranteed. In Tennessee he would see the missteps and errors in judgment that he knew he must have made in his life, and he could begin to make the adjustments necessary to correct them. He would trim his mustache in Tennessee. He would become one of those clean-shaven men in the catalogues his wife spent hours flipping through each evening. There were certain things he would try for the first time, like scented aftershave and saying hello to strangers he passed on the street with a warm and inviting smile that assured them he too was one of the good citizens of the same free world. He would wear white cotton socks and walk with his shirt untucked. They only had two nights in Tennessee, but he had made provisions to stay longer if need be, stuffing his wallet with a couple hundred extra dollars he had kept hidden from his wife in a drawer, money that he had always thought of as being saved

in case of extreme emergency, which perhaps was exactly what
this was.

My mother, for her part, was convinced they were going in
the wrong direction. She had studied the map closely before they had left and seen the highlighted path her husband had
traced days earlier that had them going slightly out of the way
before turning sharply south and then east in the direction of
Nashville. They were supposed to have been on that part of the
route by now, the sun clearly behind them instead of glaring at
them through the windshield with a broad, flat, and seemingly
malicious grin that stretched across the horizon in the shape of
one long, thin stream of pink clouds. When she thought about
telling him, she remembered the numbers. She had done them in
her head earlier, a rough estimate given the number of miles she
had been able to calculate off the map with a pen and ruler, and
knowing her husband's penchant for driving at almost exactly the
speed limit. According to the numbers and the clock on the dashboard, they should be arriving in Nashville in a little more than
an hour, perhaps two at most if traffic was unexpectedly bad or
if a construction detour was forced upon them. And when that
hour or two at most was up, then what? The two of them together
on the streets of a city neither of them had been to and knew
nothing about—two lost immigrant tourists searching for a place
to listen to country music and maybe have dinner so long as the
prices were affordable and no one working there gave her one of
those looks that was intended to remind her that despite what she
may have thought of herself, the rest of the world knew better. No
one needed to tell my mother what absurd and tragic figures they
would have made on the streets of Nashville, she with her half-

swollen face and he with that all-too-eager-to-please look that to her seemed to be the epitome of third-world desperation and poverty—the exact face that Americans expected to see when they asked her how it felt to be in the US of A.

No, there was no reason to rush into any of that. When and if that time came it could do so on its own and didn't need her to assist its arrival. She would never have expected it, but she was surprisingly content just being here in this car with her husband obliviously driving away. That the direction they were heading in was the opposite of what was intended only made it better. It was like being thrown to the wind, flung aimless into the sky with only a breeze to steer you in whatever direction it chose, like the children's song she had heard sung out in the street just below her living room window—*round and round it goes, where it lands nobody knows*. She was sure that not even birds felt as free as she did then, with her forehead pressed against the window and her eyes intently locked on the passing scenery: farm, farm, billboard, billboard, tree, exit, overpass. Again and again, as if there was an almost rhythmic logic behind the landscape, a symphony of normalcy and tedium that she had stumbled onto and was listening to intently. This was how America sounded: flat and almost elegiac— the restrained mournful ballad of a nation that seemed never to be at odds with itself. Given a wish at that moment, she would have asked for hours and hours more just like this—the smooth lullaby that came with drifting aimlessly in a landscape that seemed to have no end. When I finally came to see her after years apart, she would try to describe that feeling to me while we sat sipping tea.

"It was really quite lovely," she said, "lovely" being one of those words that my mother was instinctively fond of and took to, with its slight touch of foreign sophistication and culture—two things that she always aspired to, especially in middle age as her health declined and there was little to do other than recall the sights and sounds of what had been a not-so-glorious life after all.

"Your father drove, and I just sat there staring out the window," she said to me, and while she didn't know it at the time, those were the last moments of quiet that either of them would have on this trip, and so inevitably I'm tempted to stretch them out longer and say although terrible things were soon to happen, for the next thirty minutes or so they both felt comfortable enough to enjoy the view of still-green trees at the end of summer, the last clouds of the day, and the slow onset of night. Right now, as I've imagined it, even the handful of other cars on the road have pulled over, or better yet, they've completely disappeared for them, and while I know it's not geologically possible in this part of the Midwest, I'd like to grant them an elevated plateau from which they could round a bend and look down onto a rolling-green valley dotted with a few homes preparing for dinner.

"It is lovely, isn't it," I'd like to tell them from that vantage point, "even if you never had a chance to really see it this way."

Let them hold that thought for thirty seconds longer, and when those seconds are over, let all the things that are to go wrong take shape, beginning with my father, who despite his best efforts has finally begun to acknowledge what a part of him has known for quite some time—that he's been driving in the wrong direction and that he is, despite what he may have wanted to believe, completely lost and has been for a while. Rather than drawing closer to Nashville as he had hoped, he is farther away from it and all that it promised than he was when he began this trip. He takes careful note of all the road signs around him and looks far ahead for the ones approaching, and not just the brown and white signs that mark potential historical places worth someday visiting, but the large green ones hanging over the road announcing the names of towns he's never heard of. Where are Macon and Fayetteville and Canton, names familiar to him from the map on which he had marked his route? None were coming and none, so far as he knew, had passed. At least a half-dozen small towns go by like this before eventually the sign he's been waiting for shows up on the side of the road, several feet taller and wider than any other sign he has passed, and unlike the others is white and decorated with flowers and large looping cursive letters that can be read even from a considerable distance: "Welcome to Missouri," it says.

He turns over and looks at my mother. Their eyes meet, and even though they say nothing, he is certain that she has known all along that this would happen. There is something approaching rage and fury swelling up in him. He wants to hit, lash out, kick, although he is uncertain about whom or what he wants to injure. His body seems to demand something from him nonetheless. A physical force like this is hard and increasingly impossible to control, even while driving; he gives in and lets his right arm do the rest.

For a few seconds his arm does nothing. It lies harmless against his right leg before finally curling into a fist. It pounds once on the dashboard and then, without warning, takes a strong premeditated jab toward the passenger-side window but finds nothing but air. It retreats and then unfurls. It reaches from behind and makes firm contact with the back of my mother's head, but not as it had hoped for. The contact is only fleeting and falls short of the full grab and hold it had been seeking. It flies straight backward now and finds a nose; it knows to do this again quickly while the odds are still good, and sure enough, it comes up a winner one more time. And while my father's arm swings wildly about, my mother's hands are busy as well and have been so from the moment she first caught

him looking at her. The "Welcome to Missouri" sign had told her
that this could happen, and the look from him had confirmed it.
Everything else fell quickly into place from there, as if she had
planned this all out. She would later insist that she hadn't.

"It was more like instinct," she said. "I had never had to think
about what I was going to do."

First there was her seat belt. As soon as she saw my father's
hand begin to curl, she reached over and tugged at it to make sure
that it was secure. Despite the extra slack, she felt confident that
it was, but for good measure she pulled the remaining part around
the back of her seat so that she felt nearly pinned by it. She felt
somehow safer even though sacrifices in mobility were being
made. It would be difficult to dodge or duck, and even harder still
to throw a hand up in defense, but in this case it would hardly
matter. She could take a few blows, even direct ones at that. In
fact, if asked, she would have said they were necessary to what she
was doing, because just as my father's arm was busy half blindly
searching the car for parts of her head to grab and hold on to, my
mother's arm was also busy quietly reaching over to his side in
search of the metal clasp that held his seat belt in place. He was
overly fond of such devices—seat belts and smoke alarms and even
guardrails. He insisted on their use and after all these years in
America still marveled at their constant, indefatigable presence.
"Everywhere you go," he had told her once, "there is something
there for your safety."

When she found the belt, before pressing down on the clasp
that released it, she let out a loud, piercing scream, one that at
times I imagine I can hear more than three decades later. It was
strong enough to disturb my father's sense of touch and danger so
that he didn't know until it was too late that one of the safety
devices in which he had placed so much of his trust no longer

protected him. The belt retreated not all the way but just far enough to leave his body free, and even though my mother knew that all the way would have been better and more true to what she had imagined—him sailing clear head first through the window like a rocket with both hands at his side for hundreds of feet if not miles—she also knew she had to settle for what she was given, and that even half was better than nothing at all.

Call what she did next self-defense, revenge, or an act of sheer deliberate fury; I'm not sure it really matters. Either way it was never the accident that she and then later my father reported it to be. Anyone witnessing the scene would have agreed. No accident in the world could look like that. The car suddenly swerved hard and fast to the right as if someone had grabbed hold of the steering wheel and thrown it violently in that direction and was determined, despite the consequences, to hold it there, because no one driving a car with their seat belt unfastened would accelerate and swerve straight off the road into a clearly marked irrigation ditch unless they had gone suddenly mad or had been forced to do so.

XX

Two weeks after I had begun telling my students the history of my father's life in Sudan, Angela asked me to meet her at her office after work to celebrate the progress that she thought we were making.

"I want us to have a nice dinner out," she said. "At a proper restaurant. I think we deserve that."

I had only been to Angela's office a handful of times. On numerous occasions I had waited for her downstairs in the lobby or at a nearby bar in order to avoid the awkwardness of standing in an elevator or even in an office where everyone seemed certain of their status as young career-minded professionals. I had always suspected as well that there was something slightly embarrassing for Angela in having a husband whose pay was calculated by the hour, and whose job had been a gift from one of the firm's senior partners. I was resolved, however, to show no signs of my former self, so when Angela asked me to meet her at her office I didn't say that I would meet her in the lobby, or at the corner of Thirty-first and Fifth, or Thirty-second and Sixth. I simply said that I would be there shortly after six.

It was at the reception desk where I met Andrew, the senior

partner who had found me the job at the academy and who over-saw many of Angela's cases. He walked in a few seconds behind me—a slim, towering figure in gray whose hair resembled the color of his suit, down to the thin white pinstripes that were barely visible against the background. He acted immediately as if he knew me, a privilege that affluent white men always seemed to grant themselves when it came to me. He smiled and stared me directly in the eyes without blinking. He placed his hand on my shoulder before introducing himself.

"Jonas," he said. "It's good to finally meet you."

I knew who he was as soon as he said my name, and would recall only later that he never actually said his and that both of us understood that he didn't need to.

I don't know whether Angela heard us from her office or if the receptionist at the front desk had quickly called her to tell her I was there. Regardless, before I had a chance to respond she was standing next to me. She rubbed her hand across my back and kissed me on the cheek, which bought me the necessary time to find the strength to tell Andrew that it was a pleasure meeting him as well.

"Good," Angela said. "You've both met. Now I don't have to do an introduction."

Before we left the lobby, Andrew asked Angela if she had read the message he had just sent. She told him that she had, and that she would get on it right away. He asked next if we had special plans for that evening. Yes, she said. We're having dinner at a new restaurant in Chelsea called Le Coeur. Andrew had heard of it as well. The food there was supposed to be excellent and worth the price. He was happy to see her making time for herself. He di-rected his attention back to me. He told me that there was a period there when he was worried that she was never going to leave the office. She worked so hard, he said, that he was eventually going to force her to take a vacation. And how was I doing, he wanted to know. Was the academy still treating me well? He was on the school's board now. His youngest son would be attending next year. The school had a special place in his heart. What exactly did I teach again?

"Freshman English," I said.

"Still the same class?"

"Yes. Just the same class for now. That's going to change, though, next semester," I told him. "I'm being promoted. I'm going to be teaching some of the more senior-level English classes, hopefully a course on literary modernism in American poetry."

"I didn't know there were changes in the faculty for next semester," he said.

"There are," I told him. "I wanted to teach the class last year, but I was preparing to apply to graduate school so I thought it was better to keep my time for studying, but that's finished now so I'm doing it this year."

"And where are you applying?"

"Columbia, and maybe Yale—it's still close enough to New York to commute from sometimes."

"Best of luck with that," he said. "I'll have to tell my son to look out for you. Too bad you won't have him in your class."

"Yes," I said. "It's a shame."

I would ask myself several months later if I didn't know exactly what I was doing when I said all of that to Andrew, and whether or not his last words were a parting shot or were spoken sincerely. The best answer that I've been able to come up with for the former is that it doesn't really matter whether or not I had examined the consequences beforehand—I said what I did out of necessity. I had met my challenge head-on.

Angela waited until we were on the street to ask me what had just happened. "Why did you say that?" she said.

"Say what?"

"Everything—about your job, graduate school. You never told me any of that."

And now it was my chance to dare her to tell me I was lying. We stopped walking near the intersection of Thirty-first and Sixth Avenue, which at that hour was crowded with people rushing to get to the subway; we instantly became barriers to what had been a rapid flow of human traffic up and down the sidewalk. Several people bumped directly into us. One man told me to fucking move as he passed by, but I didn't. I stood there and stared at Angela and waited to see if she had the courage to say that I had lied, or at the very least stretched the truth as she knew it, while we were upstairs talking to Andrew. Only after I was confident that she wouldn't, and that we were both culpable, did I take her hand and begin walking toward the restaurant as if nothing had just happened. I was more convinced than ever that we were going to be okay.

When I returned to the academy the next day, I realized that my father's story had already gone on longer than I had intended, and that soon it was going to have to come to an end. There was a feeling among my students that we were all engaged in a quiet and perhaps even subversive act of deception as we passed our days ignoring the school's requirements for all first-year students. I noticed them lingering together in the hallway after class, convinced that they were privy to a private history that only they could understand. Even though large parts of what they had been told were fabricated, I took pride in feeling I had brought them together. While the rest of the teachers were fulfilling their mandate to prepare the students for what most assumed would be a bright, affluent future, my students indulged me by letting me pass off this story as being somehow relevant to their own lives. I told myself that it was for their sake that the story of my father's life and near death in Sudan had to have a fittingly moving dénouement.

Four months and three weeks after my father arrived in the port town in Sudan, war broke out in the east. A garrison of soldiers stationed in a village five hundred miles away revolted, and with the help of the villagers began to take over vast swaths of territory in the name of forming an independent state for all the black tribes of the country. There were rumors of massacres on both sides. Who was responsible for the killing always depended on who was doing the talking. It was said that in one village all the young boys had been forced to dig graves for their parents and siblings before watching their executions. Afterward they were forced to join the army rebellion that still didn't have a name.

Factions began to erupt all over the town. Older men who remembered the last war tended to favor the government since they had once been soldiers as well. Anyone who was born in the south of the country was ardently in favor of the rebels, and many vowed to join them if they ever came close.

Neighbors began to shutter themselves off from one another. Children were pulled from schools. The streets became increasingly deserted at night. Abrahim and my father stopped going to the port. "If fighting breaks out here," Abrahim told him, "they'll attack the port first. They'll burn the local ships and try to take control of the government ones."

Every day more soldiers arrived. There had always been soldiers in the town, but these new ones were different. They came from opposite corners of the country and spoke none of the local languages; what Arabic they spoke was difficult to understand. The senior commanders, who rode standing up in their jeeps, all wore bright gold sunglasses that covered half their face and made it difficult to see their eyes, but it was clear regardless that they were foreigners and had been brought here because they had no attachments to the town or its people.

Abrahim guided my father around the newly set up garrisons for his safety. He gave him a list of streets and neighborhoods to avoid. "Stay away from the post office," he said. "Never go to the bank. The cafés that have a view of the port are no good as well."

At night my father often heard sporadic gunfire mixed in with the sound of dogs howling. If the war came closer, soon there would be only minor differences between shooting a dog and shooting a man. He was determined not to be there for that. Every day he pleaded with Abrahim to help him find a way out.

"I have plenty of money saved," he said, even though it was a lie. If there was an honest exit, he would find a way to pay for it. Abrahim's response was always the same. "A man who has no patience here is better off in Hell."

Two weeks after the first stories of the rebellion appeared, there was talk in the market of a mile-long convoy of jeeps heading toward the town. The rebels were advancing and would be there by the end of the afternoon. They would spare no one. They would attack only the soldiers. They would be greeted as liberators. They were like animals and should be treated as such. Within hours the rumors had swirled the town into a frenzy. Soldiers were on the move in every street, but it was hard to tell if they were running or taking up defensive positions. The convoy was now two miles long and there were possible tanks in the background. A general from the army had defected to the rebels and had moved his troops with him. Even the capital, Khartoum, was no longer safe and possibly even under attack at that moment.

My father watched as the women who lived in all the nearby houses folded their belongings into bags and suitcases and made for the road with their children at their side or strapped to their backs. Where are they going? he wondered. They have the sea on one side and a desert on the other.

Abrahim found him during lunch resting under his usual tree. They walked back to the café where my father had once worked. There was no one to serve them tea.

"It's very busy," Abrahim said. "Maybe we should come back when it's less crowded?"

"Give me a few minutes," my father said. "I know the owner. Let me try to find us a table."

It was the first joke he had made in months, and as if to acknowledge that, neither one said anything for a few seconds, long enough for my father to wonder if he shouldn't try to offer Abrahim tea after all.

"Are you leaving?" my father finally asked him.

"I already have," Abrahim said. "A long time ago. My entire family is in Khartoum. I'm just waiting for my body to join them."

Abrahim didn't ask my father if he was planning on leaving. He knew my father had nowhere to go—no relations in neighboring villages he could turn to. To be a refugee once was hard enough—you abandon home and family in order to start all over again in a foreign country with nothing. To be one again, before you had even settled, was pointless. After that, one had to accept that you could never run far enough; God or the devil would always find you.

Abrahim suggested they watch whatever was going to happen from the roof of the boardinghouse.

"At least that way," he said, "we have a good seat."

By late in the afternoon they could hear mortar shells slamming into the desert.

"They're like children with toys," Abrahim said, pointing west, toward where the rebels were supposed to be advancing from. "They don't even know yet how far they can shoot with their big guns. There's nothing out there—or maybe they'll get lucky and kill a camel. They'll keep doing that until eventually they run out of shells, or camels. It's just a question of which one is going to happen first."

They were the only two men standing on the roof, but across the town they could see other men in similar positions, with their hands raised to their brows as they stared west. Every now and then there was another shallow explosion, and a burst of sand could be seen flying into the air.

"It's going to be terrible what happens to them," Abrahim said. "They think they can scare away the soldiers because they have a couple of big guns. They think it's 1898 and the Battle of Omdurman again, except now they're the British."

My father never thought that war could look so pathetic, but from that rooftop it did. The rebels were loudly announcing their approach, and, from what my father could see, the soldiers in the town had disappeared. He began to think that Abrahim was wrong, and that the rebels, despite their foolishness, would sweep into town with barely a struggle. He was debating whether to say this to Abrahim when he heard the first distant rumbling over his

head. Abrahim and my father looked out toward the sea, where a
plane was approaching, flying far too low. Within less than a minute it was over them.

"This will be over soon," Abrahim said. They both waited to
hear the sound of a bomb dropping, but nothing happened. The
plane had pulled up at the last minute. Shots were harmlessly fired
in its direction and the convoy kept approaching—a long, jagged
line of old jeeps trying to escape the horizon.

Neither one of them spoke after that. Nothing had happened
yet, but soon something terrible would take place and it would be
over so quickly that there would hardly be time to acknowledge
it. They were trying hard to do so before the moment passed.

When the same plane returned twenty minutes later, three slim-
mer and clearly foreign-made jets were flying close to it.

"The first was just a warning," Abrahim said. "To give them
a chance to at least try to run away. They were too stupid to understand that. They thought they had won."

The planes passed. My father and Abrahim counted the seconds. Forty-three for my father, twenty-one for Abrahim, before
the first shots were fired. Even from a distance they made a spectacular roar—at least seven bombs were dropped directly onto
rebels, whose convoy disappeared into a cloud of smoke and sand.
From some of the other neighboring rooftops there were shouts
of joy. Soldiers were soon spilling out into the street singing of
their victory.

"They should never have tried to take the port," Abrahim said.
"They could have spent years fighting in the desert for their little
villages and no one would have really bothered them. But do you
think any of those big countries was going to risk losing this beautiful port? By the end of tonight all the foreign ships will come

back. Their governments will tell them that it's safe. They've taken care of the problem, and soon, maybe in a day or two, you'll be able to leave."

A week later, during his midafternoon break on September 4, 1975, Abrahim found my father resting under his normal spot in the shade, staring out at the water. He kicked him once in the ribs, like a dog.

"Look at you, resting here like a typical Sudanese. Maybe you belong here after all."

The two of them walked to a nearby café, and for the first time since my father came to Sudan someone brought him a cup of tea and lunch.

"This is your going-away meal. Enjoy it," Abrahim said. "You're leaving tonight."

Abrahim ordered for the both of them: a large plate of grilled meats—sheep intestines and what looked to be the neck of a goat—cooked in a brown stew, a feast unlike anything my father had eaten in four months. When the food came he almost wanted to cry and was briefly afraid to eat it. Abrahim had always told him never to trust anyone, and of course my father had extended that advice to Abrahim himself. Good men were hard to find anywhere, and here there seemed to be none at all. Perhaps this was Abrahim's final trick on him. Perhaps the food would disappear just as he leaned over to touch it, or perhaps it was poisoned with something that would send him off into a deep sleep from which he would awake in shackles. My father reached into his pants and untied the pouch in which he carried all his money. He placed it on the table.

"That's everything I have," he said. "I don't know if it's enough."

Abrahim ignored the money and dipped into the food with a piece of bread.

"After where your hand has just been, I suggest you wash it before eating. Take your purse with you."

When my father came back, all the food except for a small portion had been pushed to his side of the plate.

"Eat," Abrahim said. "You're going to need all of it."

When they were finished, Abrahim walked my father to a part of town he had never seen before—a wide, dusty street that gradually grew increasingly narrow until the tin-roofed shacks that lined it were almost touching. The few men they passed along the way walked quickly, with their heads turned, as if they were being issued from a factory with explicit directions to walk and move in unison. They stopped in front of one of the houses and Abrahim pulled back the curtain that served as the door. Inside, a heavyset older woman with her head partly veiled sat behind a wooden counter on top of which rested a row of variously sized glass bottles. Abrahim grabbed one and told my father to take a seat in the corner of the room where a group of pillows had been laid. He negotiated with the woman for several minutes until, finally, he pulled a large bundle of Sudanese notes from his breast pocket. He counted off three and handed them to the woman before choosing a bottle from the counter. He sat next to my father and handed it to him.

"A drink for the road," he said. "Take it slow."

If Abrahim's intention was to harm my father, then so be it, he thought. A decent meal and a drink afterward were not the worst way to go. If such things had been offered to every dying

man in this town, my father imagined, then the line of men waiting to die would have stretched for miles.

"Give me your little purse now," Abrahim said. He handed
him the pouch and Abrahim flipped through the bills quickly. He
then took a few notes from his own pile of money and added it to
the collection.

"This will buy you water, maybe a little food, and the silence
of a few people on board. Don't expect anything else from them.
Don't ask for food or for anything that they don't give you. Don't
look at them in the eyes and don't try to talk to them. They will
act as if you don't exist, which is the best thing. If you do exist,
then they will throw you overboard at night. It's happened many
times before. Men get on board and they begin to complain. They
say their backs hurt or their legs hurt. They say they're thirsty or
hungry. When that happens they're gagged and thrown into the
sea where they can have all the space and water they want."

My father took a sip of the spirits, whose harsh, acrid smell
had filled the air from the moment Abrahim popped the lid.

"When you get to Europe, this is what you are going to do. You
are going to be arrested. You will tell them that you want political
asylum, and they will take you to a jail that looks like Heaven.
They will give you food and clothes and even a bed to sleep in. You
may never want to leave—that's how good it will feel. Tell them
you were fighting against the Communists and they will love you.
They will give you your pick of countries and you will tell them
that you want to go to England. You will tell them that you have
left behind your wife in Sudan, and that her life is now in danger and you want her to come as well. You will show them this
picture."

And here Abrahim pulled from his wallet a photograph of a
girl, no older than fifteen or sixteen, dressed in a bizarre array of

Western clothes—a pleated black-and-white polka-dot dress that was several sizes too large, along with a pair of black heels, and makeup that had been painted on to make her look older.

"This is my daughter. She lives in Khartoum with her mother and aunts. She's very bright. The best student in her class. A town like this is no place for a girl, so I sent her there some months back. When you get to England you're going to say she's your wife. This is how you're going to repay me. Do you understand?"

And although my father didn't understand, he knew it was better to wait silently until an explanation was given.

"This is proof of your marriage," Abrahim said. "I had to spend a lot of money to get that made."

Abrahim handed him a slip of paper that had been carefully folded and unfolded perhaps only twice in its lifetime, since such paper didn't last long in environments like this. Everything on it had been neatly typed out, once in Arabic at the top and then again in English, with an official-looking stamp at the very bottom of the page. The words spelled it out clearly. My father had been married for almost two years to someone he had never met.

"You will give this to someone at the British embassy," Abrahim said, laying his hands on top of my father's, as if the two were entering into a pact simply by touching the same piece of paper. "God willing, maybe you will even give it to the ambassador. You should try to give it only to him. It will be better that way. It may take some weeks but eventually they will give her the visa. You will call me then from London, and I will take care of the rest. We have the money for the ticket and some more for the both of you when she arrives. Maybe after one or two years her mother and I will join you in London. We will buy a home. Start a business together. My daughter will continue her studies."

Even for a skeptical man like my father, who had little to no faith in governments, the story was seductive: a tale that began with heavenly prisons and ended with a premade family living in a home in London. He didn't want to see how much Abrahim believed in it himself and so he kept his head turned in the direction of the large woman behind the counter, who seemed to be listening in with approval, as if she had been thinking of the same thing. It was obvious to my father from the moment Abrahim began speaking that he was completely convinced that everything he said was not only possible but seemingly inevitable, in part because this plan had already been in place for years—

"I've thought about this for a long time. Ever since my daughter was born. There is no certainty in a place like this. You've seen that. I've been expecting something terrible to happen for quite some time. It didn't happen the other day, but eventually it will, and how can a man live like that. Always in fear."

—and in part because what else was there to believe in. When it came to Europe or America, men supposedly hardened by time and experience like Abrahim were susceptible to almost childish fantasies. They assigned to these faraway lands all the ideals of benevolence and good governance lacking in their own, because who among us doesn't want to believe that such places exist.

My father took the photograph from Abrahim and placed it in his pocket. He didn't say, "Of course I will do this," or even a simple "Yes," because such confirmation would have meant that there was an option to refuse, and no such thing existed between them. He expected Abrahim to place a hand on his shoulder, a type of gentle almost fatherly embrace, but there was nothing of the sort. Instead he motioned for him to finish his drink. "Your ship is waiting," he said.

XXI

The last thing my father claimed he remembered seeing were the golden tips of a thousand heads of corn rushing toward him as the car descended into the ditch. After that he went completely blank, his head battered by the dashboard and his neck severely strained but not quite broken. There were deep cuts under his eyes and thumb-sized gashes above his eyebrows. Only the strange incline on which they had landed had kept him from flying through the windshield, out into the same rows of corn he had just gazed upon. The steep angle of the descent had folded him almost cleanly in half over the steering wheel, breaking his bottom two ribs, while leaving my mother only dazed from the knock her head had taken against the sun visor. Her belt, which she tugged at from the ceiling as soon as she knew how to, had protected her after all, and even though she had no right to think so, she felt certain that her child was safe as well.

When she opened her eyes she would have seen roughly the exact same scene that I'm staring out at now—a vast and seemingly unrestrained portrait of wealth in the heart of America. It's long been a dream of mine to pull my car off the side of the road and enter into one of these great fields, ever since I was a child and my mother and I would make our aborted getaway attempts. Why, I used to wonder, worry about making it to St. Louis or Chicago as she had so often planned when right here before us there were thousands of acres of crops in which we could just as easily get lost. If it was in the afternoon and if the sun was out, then I even imagined the warmth that must have radiated outward from the center of such fields, one that could sustain life throughout even the coldest of winters and that would provide us with enough comfort to live on for years. And while my car is not in a ditch as theirs was, it is sitting half balanced on the side of the road, somewhat precariously positioned, as if a slight push could send it tumbling down. If asked by anyone what I'm doing here, I'll say I'm looking for something I lost, something important that I accidentally let fly out the window somewhere right around here more than thirty years ago, and now I've finally come back to retrieve it.

After taking account of the dashboard and windshield, my mother would have seen that field at eye level, from a perspective that suggested she could glide through the windshield and straight into the rows of corn, hovering just slightly above them so that their tips tickled her stomach as she flew over. Only after that would she have remembered my father sitting next to her, unconscious, and for all she knew barely breathing, and everything that she had done to bring him here, from unclasping his belt to waiting for his hand to take hold of her head before leaning over and, for a few seconds, seizing full control over the steering wheel. She hadn't expected it but a great violent storm of regret was preparing to swell up in her as she considered his possible death. What neither of them had ever said to each other, she said to him now: I'm sorry; or maybe it was, Forgive me. With this part I've always had a hard time deciding whether if she said either or nothing at all matters.

. . .

There were a number of competing desires and options for her to consider. There was a desire to comfort and stay close, to pull a tissue from her purse and wipe away the blood from my father's head, and maybe even cradle it in her lap as she would a child. Only once, shortly after they were married in Ethiopia, had she been able to do that, and that was on the evening before he left. He had placed his head there out of his own free will and let himself be comforted. He was supposed to leave the next day with two friends for safer borders but had been picked up and arrested before he was even out of the city, an act that had hardly surprised him. That was the last memory she had of him before he disappeared and resurfaced years later in America, and for much of that time it had spurred her on to keep him close even after others had assured her that he was dead.

Poor man, she thought. Without even knowing it he had become something else. If he died now it wouldn't be a stretch to think that it was for the second time. She considered what would happen if she ran away in search of help. By all measures this was the right thing to do, and she knew that if she succeeded she could be branded a hero for helping to save her husband's life. He could say nothing to her then, and if asked to explain what had happened she could say it was an accident, or that she had acted quickly in fear of her own life. There would be no one to blame, and all, at least in her mind, would be equal.

There was also a suitcase with enough clothes to last a few weeks, or to comfortably make it through the night sitting quietly right here with her husband until he completed his last breath.

Before opening the passenger-side door, she told herself two things: I'm going to go search for help, and I should be prepared in case I never find it. She reached behind her and grabbed the smallest of the two valises, the one that would be necessary to get through the night somewhere else, and then from her husband's side pocket his wallet, which was easily accessible because for the first time in its short life it was bulging with money. She didn't know yet how these things worked in this country. If you could walk into a hospital and say, "Here is my husband. Do something to save him." Or if first you have to be cautious and make some sort of down payment to prove that you are serious and do indeed want this man to live. If she found someone on the road, she could say, "Here, take this money and get us some help," and more likely than not the person would, because that is what money does. It commands and dictates in a way no earnest words can. And if there was none of that, if there was only her walking at night by herself for hours along the side of the road, then she could do so until she came to a small-town motel, or maybe even a boarding-house, and with the money in her pocket she could say, "Please, I'd like to have a room for the night. My husband has just died." And because of her money and her loss, she would be granted a room for as long as she liked.

She tried not to think of all the options at once but there they were. She opened the door and got out slowly, one careful foot at a time since she was standing at an angle and her balance was uneven, and there was the risk that the weight of her suitcase would tip her too far to one side and send her tumbling back down into the ditch. She was surprised to find how cold it had gotten, as if all the warmth accumulated over the course of the day had been casually abandoned, let loose with no regard for the people who lived here, and instead been replaced with a wide half-moon that seemed impossibly large rising directly in front of her. As a final consolation before closing the door, she whispered into the car, suddenly convinced that her husband could hear her, "Don't worry, I'll be right back," in English, which was the language she preferred to use when she was uncertain if what she was saying was true.

XXII

As soon as my father's ship was ready to set sail, stories about him began circulating freely around the academy. I had snippets of my own narrative played back to me in a slightly distorted form—in these versions the story took place in the Congo amid famine. By Thursday it was said that my father had been in multiple wars across Africa. Another claimed that he had lived through a forgotten genocide, one in which tens of thousands were killed in a single day. Some wondered whether he had also been in Rwanda, or in Darfur, where such things were commonly known to occur.

Across the academy, huge tides of sympathy were mounting for my dead father and me. Students I had never spoken to, even when they were in my class, now said hello to me when they saw me in the hallway. Standing outside my classroom, before or after the bell had rung, I was a figure to consider, and at least for a few days no one passed me without a flicker of recognition. There were smiles for me everywhere I went, all because I had brought directly to their door a tragedy that finally outstripped anything my students could have personally hoped to experience.

Once the story had reached that size, I knew it was only a mat-

ter of time before I was called in to account for what I had been
teaching my students. I expected some form of mildly stern lecture
from the dean reminding me of the school's principles and obligations not only to the students, but also to the parents who were
spending a substantial amount of money to send their children
here. My job was to teach freshman English, not African history.
Once that was addressed, I expected as well that he would want
to know how much of what I had told them was true, given the
gross exaggerations that he must have heard, and what I was going
to do to set the record straight, for my students' benefit as much
as my own.

On Friday the dean caught me in the hallway just as I was
preparing to enter my classroom. There was nothing threatening
or angry in his voice. He simply said, "Come and see me in my
office when your class is over."

That day I decided to skip the story and return to my usual
syllabus. I said to my students, "We have some work to catch up
on today. Here are the assignments from last week. I want you to
work on them quietly." If they groaned or mumbled something, I
didn't hear it, and could have hardly cared. When class was over,
I walked slowly up the three flights of stairs that led to the dean's
office. He was waiting for me with the door open. He motioned
with his hand for me to take the one seat opposite him. The other
chairs in the room had been deliberately pushed to the side to
make for a more direct conversation. His wide and slightly awkward body was pitched over the large wooden desk far enough so
that it might have made it difficult for him to breathe. As soon as
I sat down, he leaned back and exhaled.

"How was class today?" he asked me.

"Fine," I told him. "Nothing exceptional."

"I've heard some of the stories about your father that you've been telling your students," he said, and at that point I expected his tone to reveal at least a hint of anger at what I had done, but there wasn't even a dramatic folding of the arms.

"It's very interesting," he said. "What I've heard, at least. Awful, of course, as well. No one should have to live through anything even remotely like that, which leads me to ask: How much of what they're saying is true?"

"Almost none of it," I told him. I was ready to admit that my students weren't the only ones who had exaggerated the truth. I had made up most of what I had told them—the late nights at the port, and the story of an invading rebel army storming across the desert. More likely than not, nothing he had heard in the hall-ways was true. Had he called me a liar directly I would have been braced for that, but before I could say anything further he gave me a sly, almost sarcastic smile. The facts in this case didn't concern him at all.

"Well, regardless of that," he said, "it's good to hear them talking about important things. So much of what I hear from them are shallow, silly rumors. Who said what to whom. That sort of thing. They can sort out what's true for themselves later."

And that was all it came down to: I had given my students something to think about it, and whether what they heard from me had any relationship to reality hardly mattered; real or not, it was all imaginary for them. That death was involved only made the story more compelling. Had I taken that away I could have easily imagined a certain level of outrage at my distortion of his-tory and geography, but there was just enough suffering to claim that neither really mattered.

I suddenly felt disappointed that I hadn't taken my story further. I could have given my students a full-on massacre in which hundreds of thousands of imaginary Africans were killed, and for that I would have been commended.

I was almost standing when the dean asked me to sit back down.

"We're not finished," he said. It was only then that I heard hints of the anger I had been expecting earlier.

I returned to my seat; he leaned back and exhaled again. I wondered if he did that only for effect.

"I had a phone call yesterday from the school's president," he told me.

He paused before continuing so I would have time to understand the direction this conversation was going. It was a cheap interrogation tactic meant to inspire an immediate rush of guilt. I doubt it worked even with the students who were called into his office daily to account for their infractions.

"He wanted to know why I hadn't informed him of the changes to the teaching staff. He assumed someone was leaving or retiring in the English department and that you were being promoted to take their place. I told him that no such thing was happening. All of our teachers are staying. Imagine how confused we both were when we hung up the phone."

When I didn't say anything he continued.

"Apparently you spoke to someone on the school's board and told them you were going to be teaching some new classes next year. You know that's not true. We've never talked about that before."

"I know that," I told him.

"Then why did you say it?"

I never thought of trying to apologize, much less back out of

what I had said. As the dean sat there waiting for my defense, I
thought, if this is the only truth they were concerned about, then
fine, they could have it, but they would never get it from me.

"I didn't say that," I told him. "I never spoke to anyone about
teaching here."

"Mr. Harris says you did. He said that you told him that you
had intended to teach here full-time since last year but couldn't
because you were too busy. He said you were planning on leaving
soon as well."

"He must have been confused," I said.

"Then what did you tell him?"

"Nothing. We only spoke once for three or four minutes in my
wife's office last week, but that was it. He seemed distracted at the
time. He asked me what I was doing there even though we were
clearly on our way to dinner."

"So he invented this himself?"

"You'd have to ask him. He's a busy man; I imagine he makes
mistakes sometimes."

"It was on his recommendation that we hired you."

"Yes. I know. I even thanked him for that when I saw him. I
told him how much I enjoyed teaching here."

"And that was it?"

"Yes, that was it. I didn't say anything else about the school.
You can ask my wife. She was there as well. Although I'd rather
not involve her since she works at the same firm."

The dean gave himself a moment to consider what I had said.
Hundreds of students had sat here before me and denied their
culpability, and undoubtedly he considered himself an expert
when it came to detecting a lie. He had nothing on me, though;
the only thing he could have registered was my complete indifference to what he said.

"We'll pick this up on Monday," he said. "I'd like to schedule a meeting so we can clear this up quickly."

I returned straight home after that, an act made easier by the fact that I hardly carried anything with me to the academy. The black leather bag Angela had given me contained only a few minor artifacts from my time as a teacher—a large spiral notebook, a collection of pens, and an in-class assignment that I had never handed out. As soon as I left the academy I felt that it was necessary for Angela and me to leave town immediately, even if it was only for the weekend. That feeling was confirmed once I stepped out of the subway and stood face-to-face with our apartment. I looked down at the steps leading to our home, and the thought occurred to me that as long as we were living there we were never going to make it; we would never have enough space to get through. Time was running out. The solid, yet thin walls around us were on the verge of caving in.

When Angela came home from work, I had two bags of heavy winter clothes packed for us. There was a motel at the far end of Long Island with a view of the Atlantic Ocean and a windswept, sandy beach. It was empty this time of year and now had a reservation in our name for what I said would be at the very least two nights. I had packed for six, and if I could have done so without alarming Angela, I would have packed for much longer.

"I have a surprise for you," I told her as soon as she came in. Over the past couple of weeks she had steadily grown used to the idea that I was still capable of surprising her, and she greeted the news with a broad, enthusiastic grin.

"We're leaving tomorrow for Long Island," I said. "It'll be the first vacation that we've taken together in years."

As a general rule Angela did not operate well when it came to whims. She tried to take this one, however, as further proof of the progress we were making as a couple.

"The ocean in winter," she said, betraying at least a hint of her usual skepticism. "Okay. With you? Why not?"

The train ride out of New York together was one of the best leaving experiences that either of us had ever had, and if I could do that part all over again, I would. We were never afforded a final sweeping vista of the city before the low-level homes of the suburbs began, but I think we could both feel ourselves slowly shedding some of its pressures and burdens until suddenly it was evident to both of us that we were miles away from home now and had never felt better about it.

"What do you think about living in the country?" I asked her.

She was still feeling excessively charitable toward me. She pushed herself over to my half of the seat and said, "If we were together I would."

"Really?"

"No," she said laughing. "Not really. What the hell would we do?"

I wanted to offer her a pitch, much like the one she had offered me years ago about the job at the academy. In this one, however, I would be the one selling. What we needed to do, I wanted to tell her, was start from scratch. We had been stuck on the wrong narrative, one that left us cold and bitter at each other; the only way to get off was to leave and begin again. We could have space out in the country, I wanted to tell her. Miles and miles of it, and there would be no one who could find us.

For the next hour and a half we both stared intently out the

windows. There was something about being in motion together
that set us off into our own private reflections. Angela, I assumed,
was taking close notice of the suburbs we were passing through
and imagining what it would have been like to grow up in one of
these nice, semi-gated communities. She romanticized precisely
what she claimed to hate the most—isolated and homogeneous
privilege, which she had never had but was now in almost daily
contact with. I was concerned only with the landscape, with the
broad, flat stretches of the horizon that sometimes came into view.
I pictured myself kicking a soccer ball across an empty stretch of
grass or running with my arms slightly outstretched like a child
pretending to be a bird.

W hen the train finally pulled into our station, we were the
last ones in our car still left on board. A storm high over
the Atlantic had caused it to snow thick, white flakes that appeared to be meticulously cut out of paper, and it was still doing
so as we pulled our luggage off the train. The ground was too
warm for any of the snow to accumulate, but we were draped in
it by the time we arrived at the motel. It was just as I had hoped
for; we were the only two people there and the wall of gray clouds
blended straight into the ocean with the white sand dunes on the
beach clearly standing out.

Once we had settled into our room and begun to unpack I
noticed Angela staring at me puzzled from behind the doors of
the armoire where she was busy hanging our clothes.

"Is something wrong?" I asked her.

"Why are we here, Jonas?"

"For a vacation," I told her. "I thought you wanted that."

It was the first notable sign I'd had that Angela wasn't completely convinced by my performance, but looking back, I can see that there were others. She had been staying up later and later at night, and for several days prior to then, had watched me as I pretended to work at our kitchen table. She had unexpectedly called from her office late in the afternoon on four separate occasions simply, she said, to say hello.

We had a small dinner delivered to our room. We pulled the bed up against the window so that we had a view of the snow drifting out over the ocean and onto the beach. I knew we had at least one night together where we could happily coast along, and I thought this was going to be it. We fell asleep in each other's arms. In the morning Angela and I opened our eyes to a bright, cold sun blazing in through the windows, a sight unlike any we had seen in recent memory, our normal mornings being ones of muted shades and car horns blaring. For the first time in months we made love after waking up, and were content to later bask in the glare of the frigid sun, which offered no warmth but was lovely to look at.

Later that afternoon we took a taxi to the center of the village and walked slowly up the main street, staring idly through the windows of the handful of stores open on a winter Sunday morning. The town felt as if it had been abruptly abandoned in preparation for a natural disaster, which only the most committed were determined to see through. We had expected a street full of picturesque Christmas decorations and large cardboard turkeys taped to the windows. Instead we were at any given moment two of maybe four people walking down the road.

"It's kind of depressing, isn't it," Angela noted. "I thought white people loved the cold. I thought I would see them walking around in flip-flops and shorts, but it's just us. We're probably the only two black people to ever come here in winter."

"Maybe that's why everyone left."

"You think they heard we were coming?"

"Word travels fast in small towns."

A few minutes later, while we were browsing through an antique store whose oldest items dated back to the late 1970s, Angela told me that I was a terrible liar. She said it jokingly but there was no humor in her voice, only a forced and slightly pained smile that did a poor job of masking her intentions.

"You think you can lie," she said. "But really you can't. You're terrible at it."

"That's not true."

"When was the last time you lied to me?"

"I can't remember."

"You're lying to me now."

"No, I'm not."

"You lied to me yesterday when you said this was a vacation."

"How was that a lie? Look at us. That's what this is."

Angela picked up a music box with the figure of a ballerina doing a pirouette on top.

"What do you think of this?" she asked me. She held the box close to my face so I could make out its poorly carved details and the flecks of paint missing from the nose.

"I think we should pay for it with your Discover card. Or it deserves to be right here in this shop where no one will ever see it."

"I don't believe you when you say that."

"So you think I like it?"

"No. I think you know I don't like it, and before you can even decide, you say you hate it because that's what I would say. You do that because you want to make me happy. I know that's true sometimes. But you also do it because you don't want me, or I think anyone, to ever be angry at you, or to say something that will make you upset."

"You've been angry at me for years."

"That's probably true. But I can say the same about you as well, Jonas."

"I've managed to live with that."

"No. You haven't. You haven't lived with me in a long time. You've slept in the same bed as me, you've had dinner with me, gone to the grocery store with me, but you haven't really lived with me again until just a few weeks ago."

"That's not true."

"Yes, it is, and you know that as well. You don't want to say that though because you think it will hurt me, or you or the both of us. Do you remember when our fights started to get really bad?"

"Of course."

"I was miserable."

"I know. You hardly tried to hide it."

"But do you know why?"

"It was a lot of things. We were under a lot of stress. We were short on money, my father died. You were working long hours."

"That had very little to do with it, Jonas."

"That had everything to do with it."

"I was convinced that I could no longer love you, or us. I'm not really sure which. Every time I thought about us I had this picture of two damaged little kids trying to heal each other's wounds and failing miserably at it. I began sleeping with someone else; I think you know who already, someone I hardly even cared about, just because I thought it might make me feel better. Less alone. Less frightened and nervous. You knew that even then, didn't you, and yet you didn't want to admit it. Even now you don't want to admit it. We could fight about anything else so long as it was stupid and trivial but not that."

"I never knew that," I said, but neither of us was convinced I meant it.

"You're lying again. I came home late from work. I left condoms in my purse for you to find. I deliberately showered before going to bed. I couldn't have been more obvious unless I waited for you to come home before fucking someone else. What I want to know is why you didn't say anything. I stayed away from you night after night to see if you would say something. When you didn't I just assumed it was because you didn't care and so I thought fine, fuck it. Let me sleep with Andrew. Let me rub his face in it. It killed me that you never even asked me why I was doing that."

"How could I? After you left for the summer, that would have been impossible."

"I was gone long before then, and so were you. Every time we had a fight or argument you disappeared."

"I never left. I never even threatened to leave, even when you asked me to."

"You didn't have to. But I think it would have almost been better if you had. You'd shut down so completely that it was worse than if you weren't even there. I felt like I was talking to myself; I've done enough of that in my life, Jonas. It's the one thing I know I can't do anymore. I can't be ignored, especially not by someone who's supposed to love me. That was why I was so happy when I found you. But then you would shut down like that on me and it was a thousand times worse than being completely alone. You could be so distant and polite that I was nearly convinced that you had never cared about me until the day you almost hit me. Do you remember that?"

"It was an accident."

"It wasn't an accident. You squeezed my wrist so tight that you left a bruise around it. You had your fist curled. It was only at the very last second that you released it. I could tell you wanted to hit me hard, and not on the hand."

"That's not true."

"It is true. And do you remember why? I said I was going to be coming home from work very late."

"You were always coming home from work late."

"You knew what I meant. And honestly, Jonas. If you hadn't done anything, I wouldn't have stayed much longer. I would have never let you grab me like that again, but I also wouldn't have been able to stand your indifference anymore."

"I was never indifferent. That was just how you chose to see it."

"I know, although it's a bit too late for that now, isn't it? I only understood this part about you later. You run and hide when anything dangerous comes too close. You seek comfort wherever and however you can, regardless of the consequences. I didn't even mind that much that we fought after you grabbed me. At least now every once in a while I could tell what you were really feeling. I think maybe it was because you knew I never slept with Andrew or anyone else again. We were unhappy, but at least we weren't strangers, and of course, I still loved you and was convinced that we could make this relationship work."

Angela put the music box down and took me by the hand and led me outside. I didn't have to tell her that I was having trouble breathing. Once we were on the street, she kept close hold of me. For the next fifteen or twenty minutes neither of us said anything, except once, when someone pulled their car over and asked us if we knew where the nearest beach was. We both laughed as we told them no. We had almost reached the motel when Angela picked up the conversation from where we had left off.

"I feel like we've come really far in these past couple of weeks. I've been happier with us than I have been in a long time, but it's not real, is it?"

"I don't know," I told her, and at that moment, I thought that was the best I could come up with.

"You don't have to worry. It's fine, Jonas. Tell me. This isn't going to last like this, is it?"

"No," I told her. "It's not."

"Okay, then. That's all I needed to know."

That night we went to bed early. We were going to take a five a.m. train back to the city so both of us could make it to work on time. The Angela and Jonas we had both grown used to would have gone to sleep quietly after reading side by side, first one light and then the second clicking off ten to fifteen minutes later. Those two would have maybe exchanged a quick kiss in the dark and a wish for a good night's sleep, and then backs would have been turned and neither one would have felt comfortable closing their eyes first. An hour or more would have passed in the dark like that until eventually one of them fell asleep, and the other resented them for it. The couple who went to bed this night, however, had nothing to read. They lay next to each other and talked at length about purely trivial matters, from the paintings hanging on the wall to the exceptional water pressure in the shower. They kissed affectionately on the lips and even risked a slightly awkward but not perfunctory "I love you." They left one light on until the woman fell asleep with her head on her husband's chest, a position she held until early the next morning, even though in her normal life she was a restless sleeper, prone to getting up in the middle of the night and turning constantly throughout.

XXIII

What happens next between my mother and father is best told in her words. It was the last conversation that we had in the state-subsidized housing complex where she was living, two hours outside of Boston. It was also lacking a decent view, but she claimed that was fine because no one there bothered her. After I finally left Angela, that was where I eventually landed, although at the time I wasn't exactly sure where I was heading. It had taken us five months to completely pull apart. Much of that time had been spent sleeping on the spare couches of mutual friends, including Bill and Nasreen, who had let me stay with them for six weeks and had treated me almost like a son.

"This is what happens when you don't have children," Bill had joked. "You end up taking in any old stray."

Rather than immediately settle into a new apartment that would have once again involved the long-term company of strangers, I packed one suitcase worth of clothes and rented a car from an airport in New Jersey. At the time I had thought only of driving along the coastline. It seemed important that I see the ocean, and as much of it as possible. It wasn't until I was an hour or so away from the apartment where I thought my mother was still living that I realized I had been headed there all along and would finally have to accept that. It had been more than three years since I last saw her and so it took the better part of a slightly overcast spring afternoon before I found the building. When I rang what had once been her apartment's buzzer, a heavily accented voice completely different from my mother's asked me what I wanted. I told the voice I was looking for Mariam Woldemariam, who I knew of course must no longer live there; my mother was never one for strangers.

"She's moved," the voice said, and that was all I would ever get out of it. I spent the next several hours waiting outside the building for a familiar or at least friendly face, one that might have known my mother when she lived there. Eventually a middle-aged black man who had occupied the same floor as her pulled up. As he made his way to the entrance, I approached him slowly from the side so he could clearly see me coming and know that, unless I was armed, I posed no threat to a man his size.

"Excuse me, sir," I said. "I wanted to know if you knew where Mariam Woldemariam lives now. I'm her son. I visited her several years back and remember that you lived on the same floor."

It took him a moment to respond, and I'm sure in that time he must have wondered what kind of son I was to have had to ask a stranger where my mother lived.

"She don't live here," he told me.

"I know that."

"Why don't you call her?"

"The last phone number I had was for the apartment here."

"Try her cell phone."

"I don't think she has one, or if she does, then I don't know the number."

"Maybe, then, she doesn't want to see you."

"That was never it," I said.

He reached into his memory and found a conversation he had once had with my mother about me.

"She didn't show me a picture," he said, "but I remember she said she had one son. What did you say your name was?"

"Jonas."

"That's right. I remember that. Jonah and the whale."

"Yes," I said. "Almost exactly like that."

The man asked me to wait downstairs while he checked to see if he had an address in his apartment. I wanted to be nostalgic for a time when someone like him, skeptical but generally good-natured, would have invited me to his apartment and offered me a drink while I waited, but I had no such memories like that of my own and had a hard time believing that anyone did. Ten minutes later, from an open second-story window, the man shouted down an address to me.

"It'll take you at least an hour to get there," he said. "There's construction all along the way." He disappeared into his window frame; I doubt he heard me say I appreciated his help.

Sometimes the world blesses you with small gifts such as traffic precisely when you need it most. I had less than forty miles to travel, but the roads were worse than what the man had said. Four lanes reduced to two going in opposite directions meant that everyone moved at an inelegant but synchronized crawl. I enjoyed it immensely and never once thought about what I wanted to say to my mother when I finally saw her.

When I arrived at her apartment almost two hours later, she seemed hardly surprised to hear my voice on the other end of the intercom. All she said was, "It's the third floor. Take the stairs because the elevator doesn't work." In form and content the building was almost exactly the same as the last—squat, built out of ugly dark-colored bricks, with tiled hallways and bright fluorescent lights that were likely put in place to keep the cockroaches out of sight. I wondered if my mother hadn't moved here simply just to move because it was in her blood, but now she no longer had the energy to cross even a county line. I never did know all the places she lived in after she left my father. For years we had only stayed in touch through sporadic phone calls and occasional e-mails.

I'm in Rhode Island.

I'm back in Virginia.

I'm heading off to Maryland soon.

There were more than a dozen other places, although I was only able to remember the exact locations of four others: two of them not too far away from the last apartment complex, with the others split between Vermont and Virginia. And perhaps while more of an effort could have been made on my part to track her locations, I always understood she would have never wanted that. If I had come too close, settled in a town nearby, or even made frequent visits to see her, then the relentless forward progress she had strived for would have come to an end. There wasn't a trace of her to be found anywhere in my life—not a coffee shop, restaurant, or bar that I could have associated with her, which was precisely how she wanted it. Had it been any different it would have been impossible to have claimed that she had gotten away from anything or anyone.

She left the door open for me. She had situated herself awkwardly in the center of a cream-colored couch that looked to have cost more than she could have afforded. Whatever indulgences she had developed to brighten her days manifested themselves in furniture.

She remained seated while I bent down to kiss her three times—formal, ritualized gestures delivered by a culture that I had never really believed in. She told me tea was brewing in the kitchen before she asked me how I was doing, how my wife was doing, while pointing to a chair opposite her for me to sit in. The last time I had visited her I had told her briefly about my job at the immigration center and Angela, whose apartment I had just moved into.

"What's she like?" she had asked.

"She's wonderful," I said. "I'm sure you would like her. She's smart, tough, and never lets anyone take advantage of her." I pulled from my wallet a picture of us on the corner of Broadway and Canal, Angela's lips pressed against my cheek as I held the camera high in the air with one hand to capture the traffic behind us. My mother held the picture in her hands briefly, staring at it with no more or less of a passion than with which she watched her sitcoms at night.

Her response after she returned it to me had been her usual one, "That's lovely, Jonas. Are you happy?" She claimed at the time that she herself was perfectly content where she was, and had been so for quite some time, even with all the wandering that she did. Since leaving my father, she had supported herself well enough with odd jobs—mainly working in people's homes or on occasion as a sales clerk in a grocery store or restaurant. She had a little in savings, not much but enough to live on after she retired.

We talked about a number of things during that last afternoon visit, much more so than in previous ones. I understood from the gauntness of her frame that she was, or had been recently, sick. When I asked after her health, she smiled and said, "It's getting better," which was one of the tricks that we once had for communicating. We both always understood what couldn't be stated directly. My mother would have never told me, especially at that point, about the extent of her illness, even if it was grave, nor would I have asked her directly, but then again, neither of us needed to say anything for me to understand that something was wrong.

It was near the end of my visit that she began to talk about what happened between her and my father the evening he reportedly drove the car off the side of the road. The events of which weren't a myth in our family so much as a shadow marriage behind which the true forces that governed their relationship played out. One of the more common accusations my father made against my mother was that she still wished him dead. Not that she wished him dead at any particular moment, but that she had once done so in the past and had never stopped since.

"I know what you want," he would shout. "You want me to go back and have me dead." In the way he phrased it, death always sounded less like a condition and more like an item from a grocery list. You want me to go back and get the fish. Or, You want me to go back and get more bread. Over the years I had time to come up with dozens of variations on what it meant to go back and be dead, a sentence that my father always followed with a quick, backward thrust of his hand against whatever part of my mother's body happened to be near. This would generally go on for several minutes.

Later, when he was finished and his arm was tired or his hand was sore and he needed to justify what he had just done, he would grumble, from whatever corner of the house he had retreated to, that he could not be easily fooled. How else would he have survived this long? How else would he have made it to America and gotten a job and a car if he didn't know how to protect himself?

"I'm not stupid," he would add. "I know what's going to happen," which was mostly how he saw the world—as a series of traps against which he must remain vigilant, because the threat, as he believed it, could come from anywhere.

With time he began to consider everything my mother said as being a conspiracy against him. If she asked him, "Why not move to somewhere else?" his response would be slow and measured as he considered all the calculated risks the question posed.

"Why not move to somewhere else, huh? This is what you want to know. Why not move to somewhere else? What do you mean by that?"

During which an immovable fury would begin to swell, a force that as a child I often pictured as taking the shape of a comically large wave in the midst of a vast blue ocean slowly growing larger as it headed toward the shore. Sometimes I would plug my ears closed with my fingers so I could better imagine the crash when it finally came.

"That would make you happy, wouldn't it? To see us with no home, so I could go begging like a dog for a new place to live."

All angry men are depressingly the same, and my father was no different. Once he reached the apogee of his fury he had to let loose; this was when things would begin to fly. My father was a spectacular thrower, with a world-class arm that in another version of his life could have landed him in the minors. He threw whatever was near, mainly within reason. On several occasions I watched his better judgment take hold of him as he picked up an object that was far too heavy (there was nothing too precious to throw in our house) or dangerous—a category that included a range of objects from chairs to glasses and cutlery, a copper vase, and every lamp we owned. A brief list of things that were eventually airborne: books, spoons, plastic cases full of pens, my school notebooks, markers, crayons, a pack of cigarettes that he found in my bedroom, bottles of liquid soap, multiple types of fruits—bananas, oranges, apples— and one flashlight. All flew, as did a couple of pillows, which my mother easily caught, causing both of us to spontaneously burst into laughter.

The worst of these fights often left my mother plotting our escape the next day. Over the course of my childhood I must have missed out on at least three months' worth of school because of these attempts at leaving. After my father left for work, my mother would wake me up by telling me to hurry and get dressed because we were going on a trip. I don't remember the first time she tried this. I imagine she must have begun shortly after I was old enough to walk. I know that on later occasions I was excited at the prospect of going somewhere just with her, and at that age any distance greater than a few miles seemed epic in scale. We would walk half a mile together to the nearest bus stop, with me holding her left hand while she carried a suitcase in the other. By the time we arrived I was always exhausted and ready to go back home. We tried this several times a year, and for a long time afterward I considered my mother foolish for doing so. How could she see these attempts as anything more than desperate measures? I didn't understand yet that these were all just trial runs. She was gauging my strength and courage and testing the waters to see how we would fare on a long journey from home together. By the time I was ten we were taking bus trips out of the city. Two years later we even spent several nights away from home, once in a motel just outside of Chicago, on another occasion in Springfield supposedly on our way to St. Louis. My mother spent most of that time asking me if I wasn't afraid being so far away from home by myself.

"Are you scared, Jonas?" she had asked me at least once each morning and again several times at night.

I had wanted to tell her at the time that I wasn't scared or alone. I had her with me, but I suspected even then that might not have been completely true. Only a part of her was actually in the motel room with us—the other part was imagining how far she could get if she was by herself. She was afraid that once she abandoned her husband, leaving her son was no longer such a stretch of the imagination; the longer she stayed away, the farther she traveled, the easier it became for her to picture herself leaving me in the care of strangers.

A few years later and I was almost old enough to travel without her, but by then she had calculated that it was already too late. I was starting high school. She wouldn't be able to pull me away whenever she wanted. I'd resist, even if I never could have lived with my father without her, and so it wasn't fair, was it? All that time spent waiting for me to grow up, and now that I had, she felt more stuck than ever.

The night of the accident my mother had only the slightest sense of what awaited her. They still had their moments back then. My father could surprise her with an offhand joke, and even though he was far more somber and withdrawn than she remembered, it wasn't hard to find traces of the man she had met through a friend of her father's at a café in Addis.

"Yosef, come here. I want to introduce you to my dear friend's daughter. A very bright girl. She was at the top of her class at St. Mary's Academy," was how Dr. Alemiyahu had brought them together.

When he came over she could see that he styled himself after some brazen image of a modern American gigolo, with the wide butterfly-collared shirt that was in fashion with all the affluent boys or those who dreamed of someday being rich. She could still hear his country accent when he spoke.

"It's an extraordinary pleasure to meet you," was how he introduced himself, using a florid language that would have been better suited to a woman three times her age and of a much greater stature. He pulled up a chair next to them and for the next hour spoke of nothing but politics.

"We will finish this tired old government," he said. "Crooks, liars, thieves. They take and take from the poor, and look at what's happening. People are starving, and they are growing fat."

She knew the same speech could be heard in all the cafés and bars, not only in Addis but throughout Africa, where the dream of revolution was endemic and seemed to almost be a birthright for this generation of men. It was charming to hear him talk in such grand terms, even if he lacked the convictions that she had heard in others. If no revolution came, then he would find another way to make his money and he would be just as happy. Of course it would be easier if it did come, regardless of the sacrifices that would have to be made, since those on the front lines would be the first to benefit. For all his talk she was convinced that he was a safe bet, a man who caught hold of the changing winds and bent with them before he could be blown away.

. . .

When they finally met again in America they did not talk about "old times." They made no mention of their previous lives together in Addis—the two-day-long wedding or the home they rented after they were married; friends, cousins, landmarks were all equally forgotten, as were the details of what had happened to him after he left.

"I went to Sudan," was all he said when she asked him where he had disappeared to. "Then I took a boat to Europe."

"He never wanted to say more than that," she said. "I asked him several times to tell me, but he refused. After a short time of knowing him, I didn't care."

The present was insistent enough to demand their full attention, and yet there was the possibility that some of who they had been would find a way to reassert itself here in America, if not now, then perhaps soon, in another few months, six at the most, Mariam hoped.

When my mother left the car with him inside it, she was weighing several options at once. If he died while she was gone, then she would be free to do as she pleased. She could find a job as a nurse, or even if need be as a maid until her son or daughter was born. There was the chance that her husband would survive as well and that she would be the one to rescue him. If she found a house or a passing car and got him "immediate medical attention," as all the poison labels on the cleaning supplies in the house said to do, then for all the remaining days of his life he would stand in her debt. A man who owed a woman his life would have to treat her like a queen. He would have to be if not kind and gentle, then at the very least guarded and in full control of his emotions when it came to her—a sort of stoic knight whom you never really knew but who was pleasant to be with and in whose presence you always felt safe.

She tucked her suitcase under her arm and prepared herself for the long lonely walk in front of her, confident that regardless of what happened or whom she found, she was certain to come out of this ahead.

XXIV

Angela and I parted at the train station in New York. She agreed to take the suitcase home while I headed north to the academy.

"You don't have to go home before going to class?" she asked me.

I shook my head no.

"I have everything I need in here," I said, pointing to the satchel she had given me. There was enough evidence of neglect in that gesture to confirm all the doubts that Angela already had about my supposed future at the academy. We kissed twice on the same cheek, and held each other briefly afterward. Neither of us was comfortable making a scene in Penn Station, but every moment after we separated was going to divide us further, an understanding that we shared and which could have been expressed by saying we might not feel this close to each other ever again. I resisted the urge to apologize, and I think Angela did so as well. There would be time for that soon enough.

I was the only teacher at the academy when I arrived. The school was closing early on Wednesday for Thanksgiving, but by tomorrow many of our students would have already left for extended weekend vacations to country homes up north. This was supposed to be the last day of the week for serious learning, but it was always tinged with too much holiday nostalgia and restlessness for the upcoming break to get much of anything done. While all the teachers pretended to treat it as a normal day, most had partly checked out and were worrying about their own upcoming holiday fates. In years past it had always been one of the days of the school year that I hated the most, with the distractions to my class almost too numerous to mention. This time, however, I wanted to take the day in, and before entering the academy, I spent a good fifteen minutes slowly walking in circles around it. There was the faint light of an early fall morning, but even more critical to the particular mood I was searching for was the slightly frigid breeze blowing in from across the Hudson River that felt as if it had been put in place that morning strictly to remind me of the value and vigor behind life. The wind came in steady bursts, shuffling thoroughly the dimly colored leaves that instead of turning colors would simply wither and fall to the ground. I didn't want to think about the conversation that Angela and I had yesterday, much less worry about more abstract thoughts like whether we were going to survive it, or what we could do next to make things right between us. Nor did I want to think about what the dean had recently said to me, or what I had said to my students over the past two weeks. There were vast swaths of my life that I knew if I looked at closely I would come to regret, and I was certain that soon enough I was going to find the time to do that. I'd regret and wonder, and then do so again until all known ground was covered. This was certainly part of the cost that had to be paid. Before that was forfeited, however, I had this repose, and it was important to take it. I didn't know when or if I would see the academy again, and I wanted to admire it briefly in its own right. An awkward

blend of neo-Gothic and late Renaissance styles, it had undoubtedly come out looking all wrong, but time had healed those errors,
so now one was struck by details such as the elaborate molding
over the cornices that on any other building would have seemed
like too much but on the academy appeared to be natural expressions of the school's ethos. Time had also done justice to the
stones. They seemed to have aged more rapidly on the small hill
on which the school was built. They were a darker and more mot-
tled shade of brown near the top, full of texture and slight grada-
tions in color that made them perfect to stare at that morning.

Half an hour after the Angelus rang I went inside. I had almost
an hour until my class began—time that I would have previously
happily spent in my classroom. Even though I had been at the
academy for three years, I still didn't know its hallways intimately.
I rarely walked down corridors where I didn't belong. As a result,
there were entire floors of the school that I had barely seen and
had taken almost no notice of. I wasn't interested in attaching
myself to them now, but I did want at the very least to be able to
say that I had really seen all of the academy and not just the selected portions of it that I felt comfortable in, that because I was
there it had made a full, proper impression on me. I had already
spent enough years without noticing anything; I had walked for a
long time with my eyes half closed. I wasn't suddenly passionate
about the hallways of the academy that morning, and made no
effort to search for any distinguishing detail other than noting, as
I had always done, that the walls were painted a terrible shade of
yellow. Such efforts weren't really necessary and couldn't be sus-
tained, regardless; if one was really looking, which was what I felt
I was finally doing—looking, with neither judgment nor fear at
what was around me—then that was enough to say you had truly
been there.

Thirty more minutes passed like that—time enough to cover the missing three floors. Once I was finished, groups of students started entering the building in steady droves. The hallways were soon flooded with their bodies; without knowing it, they took up more space than rightfully belonged to them. They constantly reached out to touch one another, affectionately or violently or both at the same time. Their limbs and voices were everywhere.

It was with the full appreciation of this spectacle that I finally entered my classroom, a few minutes before the first bell was to ring. I was still waiting for it when the dean's secretary came and knocked at the door. Most messages that came from the fourth floor were passed down through students and other teachers. It was rare to see Mrs. Adams anywhere other than in her office. My students knew as well as I did that something important was happening, even if they didn't know what it was yet. To save me the embarrassment of being publicly summoned, Mrs. Adams was careful to whisper into my ear that the dean and the school's president would be waiting for me upstairs once my class was finished. I thanked her in the kindest voice I could for the message. "Tell them I'll be there," I said, but a part of me doubted already if that was true. The whole exchange lasted only a matter of seconds—thirty to forty at most, and yet undoubtedly it changed the mood, enough so that when I turned and faced my students, it felt as if they had been replaced by a whole new class, one slightly more nervous and on edge than the previous.

XXV

Just what my mother hoped to find after she left the car was never clear. She claimed to have seen lights in the distance as soon as she stepped out, but it was never certain that she expected to reach them, much less find anyone there.

"They weren't very bright," she said when I asked her to describe them, "but there was nothing else out there, so they were easy to see."

She spoke with a rehearsed conviction, her hands nearly but not quite gently folded on her lap, as if she was attempting to model to her long-lost son a form of good behavior and proper decorum that she had never quite practiced but was willing to pretend to do now. Her voice was perceptibly sterner and less nostalgic than it had otherwise been until then, and yet, despite her best efforts, I had a hard time believing her, both then and even more so now. Having walked along the side of the road for over an hour, I have seen lights only from the few passing cars that have gone by, helmed by overly cautious drivers who have turned their headlights on early even though dusk is still at least an hour away, because it's true, you never know what you might find along these quieter back roads. There are no nearby towns, and all the houses are set far back from the road and are blocked by trees or bends that keep them hidden. It's possible that thirty years ago there was more here. Plenty of homes since then I'm sure have been destroyed— sold off to make more room for farming or just simply abandoned as corn prices fell and small fortunes were lost, and so perhaps this is what my mother saw—a few twinkling porch lights on the horizon that may very well have been there, even if it was only because she wanted them to be.

According to her, after she left the car she walked in the general direction of the scattered lights for close to an hour in search of help.

"I didn't know what else to do," she told me, and at least in this regard, I was fully convinced. She would have never claimed to be at a loss for anything unless she really was. It wasn't in her nature to do so.

"I was afraid of sitting in the car by myself, and I saw the lights. I didn't know how far away they were. I thought I would reach them after just a few minutes, but it didn't turn out that way."

To hear her tell it necessitated a belief that she began her search with the best of intentions, and that it was only because of an error in perception that things had gone wrong. The lights were too far. Distances were deceptive, especially in the dark, and given how empty this road generally is, particularly after dark, what else was she to do.

She stopped at least once to put on a sweater.

"It was much colder than I thought," she said. "I was freezing once I left the car."

And again later to briefly catch her breath.

"I didn't have much energy, you know. I was pregnant with you and always tired."

She thought several times about turning around, or simply stopping where she was and giving up.

"I almost went back," she said. "I kept looking behind me expecting to see your father waving at me. He could do something like that. He used to do that all the time. He'd leave and then come right back a few minutes later or he'd get up in the middle of the night, but I'd always find him next to me in the morning. I thought if I walked a little bit farther he'd find a way to get the car back on the road and would come and find me. When I couldn't see the car anymore, I wanted to stop and give up, but then I remembered that I had you to think about as well."

The first half hour was the hardest.

"It was so dark out there you wouldn't believe it. I kept thinking there was something hiding in the fields. I didn't know about these things back then. No one had ever told me what happened in those places. The only thing we had ever really learned in school about America was that it was very rich and they treated the black people terribly. Maybe it sounds stupid to you, but my father had told me to be careful of strangers in America. He said they would kill you if they saw you. He knew about these things and I believed him."

Finally she saw a car approaching, perhaps a mile or so away. Its headlights were far brighter than those of the houses that she claimed to have seen. While for most the sight of an approaching car would be more than welcome, my mother, after a fleeting burst of relief, was confronted by a host of doubts and worries.

"I know I should have been relieved," she said. "But I wasn't.

I think maybe for a few seconds there I was. That didn't last long, though."

When the car was less than a half-mile away, she was certain that she had to get out of its line of sight.

"There was a tree not too far away on the other side of the road. I remember that. I thought of hiding there. But then I was afraid they would see me running across the street."

And so she made a quick, impetuous decision to duck back into the ditch that ran along the side of the road. She scurried all the way to the bottom for safety, lying flat against the embankment to make sure no one could see her.

"It doesn't make sense to you now why I would do that. I know that. It was different at the time, though. I didn't know who was in that car. I kept thinking that maybe they were going to try to hit me with it. How did I know that they wouldn't? What if I had stood in the road and they crashed right into me. We would both be dead then. There were so many things I didn't know back then. I was only twenty-eight. I never used to be afraid of anything, but it was completely different once we came here. I was always afraid. I used to hate to leave the house by myself. What if someone yelled at me or hit me? I never knew what was going to happen. A little boy with red hair once swore at me. I think he called me dirty. Or something like that. I didn't understand it at the time, but I was very afraid of him, even though he was just a boy. What could he have done to me? I don't know. You don't know what that feels like. To be afraid of everything, even children. My English wasn't very good then. Most people were very nice and they would say, 'Oh, where are you from?' but not everyone was like that. Some people would get very angry, and it wasn't just at me. It was at your father as well. The people in that car could have done anything they wanted to me and no one would have known. I was afraid of getting lost and disappearing all the time."

She hid in the ditch by the side of the road until the headlights came and then passed. For good measure, she waited at least five more minutes to make sure they were completely out of sight before she even attempted to stand up again. Once she did she found that she was tired and nauseous and more comfortable lying on the ground.

She staked out a space next to a newly erected wooden fence, on the other side of which were hundreds of acres of more farmland. Today, this is all part of the same estate, everything that stretches from where my mother sat down to rest to the place where the accident occurred belonging to one company known for its cereal. The estate continues on for another two miles before breaking open to allow for a now half-dead small town.

The barbed wire along the fence is surely new. My mother made no mention of it and would have been less likely to stay had it been here then. She always thought Americans were too territorial. "All those fences and flags," she had once said, seeing very little difference between the two. Take the barbed wire away and it's easy to see the appeal in resting here. The road remains relatively untrafficked even today and were it not for the private property markers along the border I'd be inclined to do the same as her. She, for her part, did the best she could to make herself comfortable, pulling out another sweater from her valise to use as a blanket around her shoulders and a second to rest her head against. She leaned back against the fence and drew her knees into her chest for warmth. She said she had never felt so tired.

"It was like I had walked a hundred miles," she said. "I was so exhausted. Every part of me was tired."

She drifted off to sleep. For the first time she had a dream of a house that resembled the one she had grown up in, except larger and in this version dressed in the same type of furniture she had picked out for herself from the catalogues—all of it sleek and dark with smooth, clean lines that nearly hugged the floor. When she woke up a few minutes later, she was convinced that her husband had finally gone ahead and died without her.

"I was sure of it," she said. "I don't remember why anymore. Maybe it was because of the dream. He wasn't in it. Maybe there was no reason. Maybe it was just because I thought it would be better for the both of us if he had."

I was struck by that sudden hint of concern for my father. Never once before had she made any mention of how he suffered or how deeply miserable they were when together.

"Was he that unhappy?" I asked her.

She looked at me briefly stunned, as if I had spoken to her in a language similar to the ones she knew in form and tone and yet still completely incomprehensible.

"I don't mean him," she said. "I mean you and me. Better for us."

She leaned in at that moment and almost touched her hands to mine, but pulled back before she could complete the gesture; she didn't know if I was fully on her side, and was afraid of finding out that I wasn't.

It was with that thought of her husband already dead that she picked herself up and continued her walk along the road, this time no longer worried about who she would or would not find to rescue her. Suddenly it seemed to her as if there was nothing out there that she had to fear, neither cars nor man, and that if called upon to do so, she could walks for miles, straight through the night and into the morning.

"A great weight," she said, "had been lifted off my shoulders."

Night in the rural Midwest, miles away from any large towns, can be a remarkable thing precisely because there is often so little to behold. There are plenty of stars, but a greater number could always be found in other remote corners of the country. I've seen more of them for example on a single clear night outside of Boston than I've ever seen here, and I've stared up in obligatory wonder. Still, that doesn't mean that I loved this place any less. The insects, whether they're cicadas or crickets, are going at it right now, and their pulsing, whirring hum more than makes up for what the sky may lack. They haven't quite yet reached their full force, and won't until hours after the sun has completely set, their sound more of a persistent hum than the full-fledged chorus that it will soon be. My mother was kept in their company for the last thirty minutes of her walk, and I'd like to think that she also reveled in their sound, even if she made no direct mention of them. There isn't much time left for her to enjoy these things. When the next set of lights finally approached, they obviously came with her and my father in mind. Someone, most likely the car that had passed, had spotted the tail end of the red Monte Carlo sticking out of the ditch and had done the right thing and called for help, and now help was finally coming, bringing with it a cavalcade of lights and sirens. Very soon they are going to be the only things that she can hear. The rest will fade into the background, and for the next eighteen-odd years she'll spend much of her solitary time remembering how it felt to have briefly wandered even one small piece of earth with absolutely nothing and no one at all to fear.

"It was lovely," she said when I asked her what those last minutes before she was picked up by a policeman and returned to the scene of the accident had been like. "Really, absolutely lovely. I can say that, can't I?"

"Of course," I told her. "You can say whatever you like."

XXVI

I began my final lesson from where I had left off, with my father and Abrahim walking to the pier on their last morning together. They didn't say much along the way, but every now and then a few words slipped out. Abrahim had important ideas that he wanted to express, but he had never known the exact words for them in any language. If he could have, he would have grabbed my father firmly by the wrist and held him there until he was certain that he understood just how much he depended on him and how much he had begun to hate him for that. To pin so much hope to a man seemed cruel and stupid in equal parts. My father meanwhile was desperate to get away. He was terrified of boarding the ship, but he was more frightened of Abrahim's desire. A man could easily be crushed under an obligation like that, and he felt himself already being weighed down, as if his shoulders were slowly being loaded with stones as he waded into water.

When they reached the pier Abrahim pointed to the last of three boats docked in the harbor.

"It's that one," he said. "The one with the blue hull."

My father stared at the boat for a long time and tried to imagine what it would be like to be buried inside it, first for an hour and then for a day. He didn't have the courage to imagine anything longer. The boat was old, but almost everything in the town was old. The cars, the tin roofs on most of the homes, the fabric that the men, women, and children wrapped themselves in, and then the very same men, women, and children themselves—all were engaged in a long-running state of gradual decay, one that may very well have been sustainable for as long as or perhaps even longer than a normal lifetime, as if the key to survival wasn't living well but dying slowly, in such gradual increments that actual death would bypass you all together.

There was a tall, light-skinned man at the end of the docks. He was from one of the Arab tribes in the north. Such men were common in town. They controlled most of its business and politics and had done so for centuries. They were traders, merchants, and sold anything or anyone. The effect was noticeable. They held themselves at a slight remove from other men, spotless white or, on occasion, pastel-colored robes that proved immune to the dust that covered every inch of the town.

"He's arranged everything," Abrahim said. "That man over there."

My father tried to make out his face from where they were standing, but the man seemed to understand that they were talking about him and kept his head turned slightly away. The only feature that my father could make out was that of a rather abnormally long and narrow nose, a feature that seemed almost predatory in nature.

Abrahim handed my father a slip of yellow legal paper on which he had written something in Arabic. He handed him another piece of paper with an address and phone number in Khartoum, the capital. He understood that the first was for the man standing near the pier and the latter for him, but he wasn't sure as to what to do with either. Did he fold them into his pockets or did he clench them tightly in his hands? He would have liked for Abrahim to say something kind and reassuring to him. He wanted him to say, "Have a safe journey," or "Don't worry. You're going to be fine," but he knew that he could have stood there for years and no such false reassurances would have ever come.

"Don't keep him waiting," Abrahim said. "Give him the note and the rest of your money. And do whatever he tells you."

My father walked away from Abrahim wishing that he had never come here. He looked around him and saw the same scene that he had seen every day—a long, poorly organized parade of men, mostly black with a few occasional shades of light brown, stripped down to their barest piece of clothing and almost always loaded with something on their backs. There were herds of donkeys who fared only a little worse than those crowding the one unpaved road that ran adjacent to the harbor, with a sun that shone down harshly on all of them. He tried to get a read on the man's face as he approached him, to see if there were any signs of hidden malice that could be detected in his eyes or smile, but the man kept his head turned away from him so that the only thing my father could see were the folds in the blue head scarf the man was wearing as they trembled in the breeze.

When he was halfway to the ship, Abrahim called out to him: "I'll be waiting to hear from you soon," and my father knew that was the last time he would ever hear his voice.

My father handed over the slip of paper Abrahim had given him. He couldn't read what was written on it and was worried that it might say any one of a dozen different things, from "treat this man well" to "take his money and do whatever you want with him."

He told himself that he was a fool for being so trusting and that there was nothing else he could do but be a fool; it was too late already, events had been set in motion and the only thing was to silently follow the man up the gangplank and into the boat, where they entered unmolested, as if the crew had either failed to notice them or had been expecting them the whole time.

The man pointed to a group of small storage slots near the stern of the boat that were used for holding the more delicate cargo. These crates were usually unloaded last and he had often seen people waiting at the docks for hours to receive them. They always bore the stamp of a Western country and carried their instructions in a foreign language—*Cuidado; Fragile*. He had unloaded several such crates himself recently, and while he had never known their actual contents, he had tried to guess what was inside: cartons of powdered milk, a television or stereo, vodka, scotch, Ethiopian coffee, soft blankets, clean water, hundreds of new shoes and shirts and underwear, anything that he was missing or knew he would never have he imagined arriving in those boxes.

There was a square hole just large enough for my father to fit into if he pulled his knees up to his chest. He understood this was where he was supposed to go and yet he naturally hesitated, sizing up the dimensions just as he had once sized up the crates he had helped unload. He considered its angles and its depth and then imagined all the ways in which he could and could not move inside it. He could lean his body slightly to the side and rest his head against the wall when he needed to sleep. He could cross his legs. He could not raise his elbows above his head.

My father felt the man's hand around his neck pushing him toward the crate. His father had often done the same thing to him as a child, and also to a goat or a sheep when it was being led into the compound to be slaughtered. He wanted to tell the man that he was prepared to enter on his own and in fact had been preparing to do so for months now, but he wouldn't have been understood, so my father let himself be led. He crawled in on his knees, which was not how he would have liked to enter. Headfirst was the way to go, but it was too late now. In a final humiliating gesture, the man shoved him with his foot, stuffing him inside so quickly that his legs and arms collapsed around him. He had just enough time to arrange himself before the man sealed the entrance shut with a wooden door that was resting nearby.

Before getting on the boat, my father had made a list of things to think about in order to get through the journey. In the preceding weeks he had come up with several items he recorded in his head by repeating them over and over until he fell asleep. They were filed away under topic headings such as: The Place Where I Was Born, Plans for the Future, and Important Words in English. He wasn't sure if he should turn to them now or wait until the boat was out of the harbor. The darkness inside the box was startling, but it wasn't yet complete. Light still filtered in through the entrance and continued to do so until the hold was closed and the boat began to pull away from the shore. He remembered that as a child he had often been afraid of the dark, a foolish, almost impossible thing for a country boy, but there it was. Of the vast extended family that lived around him, his mother was the only one who never mocked him for this, and even though he would have liked to have saved her image for later in the journey, at a point when he was far off at sea, he let himself think about her now. He saw her as she looked shortly before she died. She had been a large woman, but at that point there wasn't much left of her. Her hair hadn't gone gray yet, but it had been cut short on the advice of a cousin who had dreamed that the illness attacking her body was buried somewhere in her head and needed a way out. Desperate, she had it cut completely off, which had made her look even younger than her thirty-odd years. This was the image he had of his mother in an almost doll-like state just two months before she died, and while he would have liked to have a better memory of her, he settled for the one he'd been given and closed his eyes to concentrate on it. It would be some minutes before he noticed the engine churning as the ship pulled up its anchors and slowly headed out to sea.

When I reached this point, I knew it was the last thing I was going to say to my class. The bell rang, and as when I had first begun this story, there were a good ten to fifteen seconds when no one in the classroom moved. My students, for all their considerable wealth and privilege, were still at that age where they believed that the world was a fascinating, remarkable place, worthy of curious inquiry and close scrutiny, and I'd like to think that I had reminded them of that. Soon enough they will grow out of that and concern themselves with the things that were the most immediately relevant to their own lives. They will opt for the domestic and local news any day of the week; they will form rigid political alliances and dogmatic convictions that place them in good standing with one group or another, but at that time these things had yet to pass.

Eventually one bag was picked up off the floor, then twenty-eight others joined in. Most of my students waved or nodded their heads as they left the room, and there was a part of me that wanted to call them back to their seats and tell them that the story wasn't quite finished yet. Getting out of Sudan was only the beginning;

there was still much more ahead. Sometimes in my imagination, that is exactly what I tell them. I pick up where I left off, and go on to describe how, despite all appearances, my father did not actually make it off that boat alive. He arrived in Europe just as Abrahim had promised he would, but an important part of him had died during the journey, somewhere in the final three days when he was reduced to drinking his urine for water and could no longer feel his hands or feet and was certain that if death came to him he would welcome it without the slightest hesitation. He spent six months afterward in a detention camp on an island off the coast of Italy. He was surprised to find that there were plenty of other men like him there, from every possible corner of Africa, and that many had fared worse than him. He heard stories of men who had died trying to make a similar voyage: who had suffocated or been thrown overboard alive. My father couldn't bring himself to pity them. Contrary to what Abrahim had told him, there was nothing remotely heavenly about where he was held: one large whitewashed room with cots every ten inches and bars over the windows. He had a hard time understanding most of what the guards said. They often yelled at him and the other prisoners. The guards spat at their feet and made vague, animal sounds when they looked at them confused. He quickly learned a few words in Italian and was mocked viciously the first time he used them. He was once forced to repeat a single phrase over and over to each new guard who arrived. When he tried to refuse, his first meal of the day, a plate of cold dried meat and stale bread, was taken away from him. "Speak," the guards commanded, and he did so dozens of times in the course of several days even though there was no humor left in it for anyone.

"You speak Italian?" the guards asked.

"No."

After which the subject of the sentence was always dropped and the question transformed into an order.

Speak. Talk. Or more rarely, Say something.

In Italy he was given asylum and set free. From there he worked his way north and west across Europe. He met dozens of other Abrahims along the way, men who promised him that when they made it to London, the rest of their lives would finally resolve into the picture they had imagined. "It's different there," they always said. They placed their faith in difference, which is to say they placed their faith in the idea that there had to be at least one place in this world where life could be lived in accordance with the plans and dreams they had concocted for themselves. For most that was London; for a few it was Paris; and for a smaller but bolder few, America. That faith had carried them this far, and even though it was weakening, and needed constant readjustment ("Rome is not what I thought it would be. France will surely be better"), it persisted out of sheer necessity. By the time my father finally made it to London eighteen months later, he had begun to think of all the men he met as being variations of Abrahim, all of them crippled and deformed by their dreams.

Abrahim had followed him all the way to London to test him, and my father was determined to settle that debt. On his first day in the city he found a quiet corner in Hampstead Heath. A guidebook for Americans that he had picked up in France had said that he would be afforded a wide, sweeping view of the city from there. At the edge of the park, with London at his feet, he set fire to all the documents that he had brought with him from Sudan. The fake marriage license turned to ashes in seconds. The picture of Abrahim's daughter melted away near a large green hedge with ripe, inedible red berries hanging from it. For many nights afterward he refused to think about her or her father. There were no rewards in life for such stupidity, and he promised himself to never fall victim to that kind of blind, wishful thinking. Anyone who did deserved whatever suffering he was bound to meet.

Let me be honest and admit that many more days if not weeks would have been needed to have told this properly, and that most of my students would have lost interest by then. My story would have slipped into the curious but rather boring file into which these things were logged, and long before the end they would have gone back to staring at me blankly.

When the last of my students had left, I finally took my seat behind my desk, even though I knew the dean and the school's president were upstairs waiting for me to join them. I pictured them sitting around the coffee table near the front entrance to the office casting stray glances at their watches. Scones were neatly arranged on a plate; coffee had recently been made. They would go to such lengths to make me comfortable. When I arrived they would want to hear for a second time everything that I had said earlier to the dean when it was just the two of us in his office. They would ask me to repeat exactly what I had said, and one or both of them would record it. They would counter my response with Andrew's version, and then demand to know if I was telling the truth, and if not, then why hadn't I been honest with them from the beginning. Before I stood up and left my classroom I knew I couldn't go through that. To have sat there and lied once was enough, and what I wanted was to come clean. My stories, all of

them, were over, and the first person I wanted to tell that to was
Angela. Rather than go upstairs, I left the building through a
rarely used side door that opened up immediately onto the avenue.
I walked two blocks south, to a quieter side street, and called
Angela from the steps of a brownstone whose façade was being
repaired.

Angela processed bad news better while she was at work. In
her office, surrounded by colleagues, she kept her profes-
sional demeanor intact and was never anything else but a lawyer. When her mother passed away, the call had come into her
office and she had accepted it as she accepted all of her clients'
calls, and while I wasn't there with her I did see the notes that she
recorded from the conversation, written as if they were to be billed
at a later point to an imaginary agency charged for tallying up the
costs of our deaths. In her neat, formal penmanship, under that
day's date, she had quickly scrawled a series of questions on a
yellow legal pad:

> What time/Time of death?
> Cause of death suspected?
> Proof of cause?
> Autopsy to be expected?
> Name of doctor on staff?
> Name of hospital administrator?
> Name of hospital counsel?

She recorded the answers for the first three questions next to
each one:

11:34 a.m.

Coronary heart failure aka heart attack

Speak to coroner, "I'm just the hospital family counselor"

After that she gave up on answering the rest of the questions. My guess is that she had gone through and asked them, just as she would have liked to have done under the most ideal circumstances, but that in the end she hadn't found the energy necessary to care what the response was. She could only be a lawyer for so long, and on that day she had held out for a good ten minutes before giving in.

She took her lunch in her office. She passed on to one of her colleagues two memos due the following day. In an e-mail she wrote that she wasn't feeling particularly well and needed to go home. When I came back from the academy late that afternoon, I found her tightly coiled on the bed with one tissue still waiting to be used in her hand. Her mother's death had left her nothing to speculate over.

"I'm not surprised," she said. "I knew this was coming. Even when I was a kid I always thought she was going to die. It used to terrify me, and then after a while it didn't anymore. I've hardly even thought of it these past few years, and now that she's dead I'm not even the least bit surprised. It's like someone had called me a long time ago and told me to wait for exactly that phone call. But they didn't call just once. It was like they called every few months to check in and make sure I remembered to keep waiting.

"You know, I almost didn't come home from work. I hung up the phone and I felt sad, but I said to myself, 'You knew this was going to happen. You can't even pretend to be surprised, so why make a big fuss about it. You have a ton of work to do.' I finally decided to come home because I was afraid she would be mad if she found out that I didn't. She'd say, 'I raised you better than that. How dare you not mourn your mother,' and I'd want to say back to her, 'No, you didn't,' but of course I could never say that to her. So maybe she did raise me better than that."

She sent an e-mail to her supervising partner and took one more day off from work. She stayed in bed and waited for her grief to find her.

When I called I wanted to be greeted by the same Angela who took notes on her mother's death, even if that Angela was no more real than the fictional portrait I had recently made of myself. What I got instead was my wife, tender and soft-spoken.

"Jonas?"

It was unlike her to answer her phone like that, but I had never called her at that hour. I tried my best to be direct, although the first thing I said to her was that I hoped I hadn't disturbed her.

"No," she said. "You haven't disturbed me at all. I was just sitting here staring into space."

That was what Angela claimed she did all day at work. "They only think I'm being busy," she said. "When in fact, as soon as I close my door, the first thing I do is find a corner of the wall to stare at. I do it for hours."

"Do you remember what I told you last week?" I said. I waited a moment for her to tell me that she did, or at the very least, for her to ask me to be more specific. Instead she countered with her own question.

"None of it was true, was it?"

I tried and wanted to say no, but the only thing that came out was a silly gasp of air that had been lodged in the back of my throat from the moment I called.

"I knew that already," she said. "I had a meeting with Andrew on Friday, just before I left work. He said he spoke to someone at the school to congratulate them for promoting you. I don't really believe that was why he called, but I couldn't argue with him. Whoever he spoke to told him they knew nothing about that. He called me into his office and asked me if it was true what you had told him, and I said of course it was. He hasn't said anything about it since."

"Why didn't you say something to me?"

"Because when I came home on Friday and saw you sitting there with our bags packed, ready to take this imaginary vacation, I wanted to have that with you. We were suddenly happy. I probably would have done almost anything to have kept that going for as long as possible. I even began to fantasize on the train that maybe you really would find something great, at the school or someplace else, and that everything we talked about would still be possible."

We slipped into a pained, awkward silence.

"This wasn't to get back at me, was it?" she asked.

"No," I said. "It was never that."

"If I told you I wasn't going to come home tonight, you would know that I wasn't saying that to hurt you, and that I wouldn't go see someone else?"

"Yes. I would know that."

"Okay. Then maybe I'll see you tomorrow."

She hung up before I had time to question her. Even though I knew it was unlikely, I waited that night for several hours for her to come home. I perched myself on the edge of the bed and re-garded the clock from time to time. At a few minutes before ten p.m. I gave in and called her on her cell phone. The phone was off and went straight to her voice mail:

"This is Angela Woldemariam . . ."

She came back home early the next morning, still dressed in the dark gray flannel suit she was wearing when I last saw her. I had fallen asleep fully dressed and there seemed to be something in that, as if somehow we had successfully deceived time and gone back to the previous day when we had both woken up together and parted in the train station. It was that morning all over again, except now we knew how the day was going to end and could act accordingly.

Angela placed her palm against my cheek once I sat up to greet her.

"I don't want us to fight over this," she said. "There's no point in doing that anymore. I think if we're careful we can do this properly. We don't have to yell. We don't have to be angry."

Her words were undoubtedly rehearsed but never once as she spoke did they feel like that. She was careful to never say I'm leaving you, or this marriage is over, much less something as harsh as I want a divorce. No one was leaving and nothing was over and neither of us wanted what we were about to have.

"Where did you go last night?" I asked her.

"To a motel. I thought I was going to stay someplace lavish where I could take a bath and look out the windows onto the city, but in the end I went to an overpriced motel six blocks away from here. I didn't want to see you, but I didn't want to be far away from you either. I thought, What if I get up in the middle of the night and change my mind. I want to be able to run straight home."

"Did that ever happen?"

"No. It didn't. I wanted it to, but it didn't. I spent the night thinking, though, that actually, if you looked at us from a distance, we haven't done that bad by each other."

"Are those the standards now?"

"I don't know. But maybe they should be."

"And if they are?"

"Then I think we both can come out ahead. Or that at least it's still not too late for us to do so."

Those were the final words we spoke directly on that topic. We weren't leaving or quitting each other so much as we were strategically retreating while taking account of our mutual gains and losses before one or both of us was resolutely defeated. The next day while Angela was at work I packed a small suitcase and went to a friend's apartment deep in Brooklyn. I called Angela during lunch and told her that I was going to be staying with friends for a while. Up to the very end that was how we conducted our separation. We neither denied its permanence nor tried to enforce it. For several weeks we spoke almost daily about small things that I had forgotten to pick up until eventually there was nothing left; the only reasons we would have had for calling after that would have been to say I'm sorry, or I miss you, both of which we knew already.

XXVII

Before I left my mother's apartment, she asked me why I had finally come to see her after all these years.

"Why now?" she wanted to know.

I had been expecting that question since I arrived, although I expected it in a blunter form, something along the lines of "You should have told me you were coming," or worse, "Why didn't you leave me alone?" I had anticipated that, and yet still didn't have an appropriate answer.

"It must have been difficult to find me," she said, as if my efforts, which she hoped were extensive, provided some consolation for the intrusion placed on her.

"No," I told her, "it wasn't difficult at all."

"Oh," she said, "that's good to know."

The disappointment in her voice was barely disguised when she spoke. I'm certain it was intended for me to hear. I waited for it to pass before I offered her something more.

"I came to see how you were doing."

I should have known in advance, however, that that could have never been an appropriate answer. She sighed when I said it; small lies had always bored her. She herself had been exceptionally gifted in the stories she told. As a child I had heard her tell hundreds. One evening she told the social worker who had been recently assigned to visit us every two weeks following a neighbor's call to the police, that before she came to America, she had been like royalty in Ethiopia. The woman was wearing a dark gray suit and every few minutes looked down at me over her glasses as if to tell me not to listen. She had what I thought of at the time as fairy-tale skin— white with touches of red from the cold on her cheeks.

"Our family," my mother told her, as the three of us stood awkwardly in the kitchen, "was very close to the emperor."

I was old enough to worry that she was going to continue talking like that, but fortunately she was always sensitive to other people's reactions and knew that it was better if she didn't continue.

On other occasions she escorted me to school in order to explain to teachers and principals that my recent absences were the result of family losses back in Ethiopia. "His grandfather," she said, "passed away," or "A sister of his father died on Saturday."

When these became too numerous, mysterious childhood ailments that had left me almost too weak to walk until just the other day were invented.

"The doctors," she said once, "think it might be serious."

Had I said I was coming to say good-bye before being shipped off to war in Afghanistan, she would have at the very least appreciated the effort. To say I missed her meant nothing.

"Well, then," she said. "I'm glad you came."

She wanted more. This conversation had exhausted her. These were events she hadn't thought of in years, and most likely she would try as hard as she could never to do so again. Bringing those memories back meant that she would have to sit with them for a while—they would remain in the room long after I had left, and for days she would be haunted. Turning on a light switch, or a slight, subtle shift in the temperature at night, and there she'd be standing on the side of the road with my father all over again, or locked in her bedroom early on a Sunday morning, refusing, unless God came down himself, to leave. Because of that I told her what I knew most likely was the real reason I had come to see her. It had nothing to do with honesty or compassion or even a concern for her well-being.

"I wanted to know what my life might look like in ten years," I said.

It wasn't meant to be a hard comment, but I knew she took it as such. She held the door open for me and kissed me only once on the cheek as I left.

"Take care," she said. "Call next time before you come."

As soon as I was in my car I drove to the nearest gas station and bought maps for Illinois, Tennessee, and just in case, Missouri. I took my time driving back here. I avoided most of the highways and tried as much as possible to stay on quiet semi-obscure back roads. I spent many minutes waiting for freight trains to go by in the small towns I was passing through. I often stopped for coffee and oddly timed meals at diners and cafés that reminded me of the ones I once knew. When there were finally no more hills or rolling valleys, when all of the land was as flat as I remembered it from my own childhood, I began to search for glimpses of my parents as they must have looked when they first came here, when they were far better people than I ever knew them to be. It was only once I began to do so that I understood just how tightly I had been holding on to them all these years.

.   .   .

It seems to have taken hours for evening to finally settle in; the sunsets in the Midwest tend to linger, drawing the last moments of the day out much longer than one would expect. For the past twenty minutes I've stood on the side of the road watching the standard colors that come with it, until now, finally, there are none left. In the meantime I've caught a number of strange glances from passing cars surprised to see a man standing on the road's narrow shoulder with his hands in his pockets as he takes turns staring out in all four directions. I can see them wondering as they drive by a few miles an hour slower than usual if I'm lost or perhaps even injured, or in a worst-case scenario completely mad. I don't doubt that I give off that impression, especially since I seem to have appeared from nowhere. I'm miles away from my car, so it's difficult to tell, and yet because we're at a point in our history where almost anyone driving along this road would be hesitant to stop and ask, the mystery behind my presence here seems inevitably more unsettling. No one, for the past two hours, has bothered to try to find out what I'm doing here, and nor would I have expected them to.

I suppose I could say my parents were unfortunate in that regard. Theirs was not a gentler age, only a less nervous one, everyone not quite yet on the lookout, perhaps simply because no one had told them to be. Hitchhikers were common back then, and even as a child I remember often seeing one or two on roads exactly like this, although I don't ever remember stopping to pick any up even though my father always insisted that it was safe and proper to do so.

The state police who stopped my mother near here were inclined to see things in the simplest possible light. They came in

with their sirens blaring, but once they saw her, a small, even fragile figure standing on the side of the road, they cut the horns and
gently eased their car onto the shoulder a few feet ahead of her so
as not to alarm her. I doubt they approached her cautiously or
even skeptically, and more likely than not, they exited their cars
completely unguarded with their hands safely at their sides or
pulling at the rims of their wide state-trooper hats. They waved
her toward them and she complied. When she was close enough,
they saw the swelling on her forehead and took it as proof of
trauma induced by an accident and the suitcase by her side as part
of the confusion that came with it.

Armed with their good intentions, they loaded her and her
belongings into their car and drove her back to the site of the accident. They might have noticed that she seemed nervous about
returning, and that when one of them asked her if that was her
husband who was driving the car, she seemed to hesitate, as if she
wasn't exactly sure as to what the right answer was, even though
there were only two possible choices, but again, this could be assigned to the general fear and confusion that anyone would face
after an accident. The troopers had undoubtedly seen far worse,
with plenty of death included, and so by their esteem all of this
was far from extraordinary.

In a few minutes they arrived where the red Monte Carlo had
spilled off the side of the road. That surprised my mother. She
would have thought that it would have taken at least three or four
times longer at the very least, but in fact, the distance that she
assumed she had traveled had been nothing, just barely more than
a mile, while in her head it had felt as if a whole vast terrain had
been conquered. She wanted to ask the troopers if they would go
back to where they found her so they could do the journey all over
again, this time slower, at a pace that matched the distance she felt

she had traveled in her heart. How fast that would have been would have been incalculable. They would have had to travel at a fraction of a mile an hour, so that hours, if not a day, would have had to pass in order to get it right.

Under the glaring headlights of two squad cars, a tow truck, and a pair of ambulances, the entire scene seemed more deliberate and plotted than it had before. She spent several minutes reassuring herself that she wasn't responsible for what had happened. "I am good," she told herself. Good, good, good, until she finally half believed it. She had been staring out the window when it happened, and only God knew how long it had been since either of them had spoken to the other. She had done nothing wrong, she told herself, and she was prepared to say the same to anyone who asked.

They had arrived just in time to see two paramedics pulling my father out of the car and loading him onto a stretcher. He was half conscious and had been so more or less since my mother left him.

Before they drove away, a second pair of paramedics examined my mother. They flashed a light into her eyes and felt the swelling on her forehead. At least one of them might have noticed that there were signs of earlier bruises, one at least a few days old, under her right eye, and that there were other, even older bruises along her arm, including one on each wrist. One of the paramedics asked her, repeatedly, if she was feeling okay. If she had any medical conditions that he should be aware of? If she was pregnant, or thought she might be pregnant, and if she didn't, perhaps, want to talk to someone else? And how did she respond? Appropriately, of course; her sense of decorum never failing her, least of all when other people were involved. Say everything is fine and people will believe you, and so it's my turn to say it for her.

"Thank you. I'm fine," she responded.

And when asked again if she was certain.

"Yes. Everything is okay."

The car was towed out of its ditch. Both headlights were missing and the windshield was badly cracked. The hood of the car had recently popped open; my mother thought there was something almost embarrassing about seeing its engine exposed and briefly turned her head in the other direction. When it was finally hooked on to the tow truck, one of the officers who had found her on the side of the road leaned over and told her, "You're incredibly lucky to have walked out of this alive." It took her several seconds before she was certain that she understood what he meant by that.

He led her gently by the elbow back to his car. He promised her they would follow the ambulance all the way to the hospital, and in fact, he said, he'd try to catch up to it so she could see its lights. "You'll feel better once you can see them," he told her. "And that way you'll know exactly where your husband is."

Once they reached the hospital she knew that if she wanted to she could eventually get up and leave on her own. After an hour or two, no one, not even the policemen driving her, would be there to stop her. She could leave her husband's wallet at the reception desk, just as she had found it, along with a note addressed to him that said "Take care," or "I'm sorry for what happened," or better yet "Please leave me alone." She pictured herself walking out afterward through a pair of double glass doors with a small bandage affixed to her head and a prescription for painkillers in her pocket. From there she saw herself shuffling across the street in her own blue hospital slippers carrying nothing, not even a purse under her

arm, toward a large field of wheat that seemed to have been erected
solely to receive her. The sun would be rising but still below the
horizon; large flocks of black-winged birds would be flying over-
head, and everywhere there would be the sound of cicadas. She
would slowly part the field with her hands as she entered; the
stalks would quickly bend and then fold around her so that within
seconds it would look to anyone watching as if she had never been
there at all. Eventually, she was certain, if she walked in that field
far and long enough, for years, perhaps even decades, there wouldn't
be a trace of her, not even a footprint that could be found.

One of the last things Angela told me once we had agreed to
a divorce was that she was afraid of disappearing.

"If we're not together," she said, "then I wonder what's left.
I'm afraid to find someday that there's no one who knows me
anymore. I could disappear and who would care."

Once I would have had a hard time finding fault in that. I
would have thought that there was little else that one could look
forward to in life other than being set free from others' demands
and the obligations they placed on both your time and heart. The
invisibility that came with that freedom was a small price to pay
for all the damage and pain that could be avoided as a result. By
the time I had packed my bags and was preparing to leave Angela,
I was grateful I no longer believed that. I hope that when I settle
into someplace for the evening that I will have the courage to call
her and tell her that while the legal terms of our marriage may end
soon enough, we are still not finished, and won't be I hope for
many years yet to come. Our marriage, for all its shortcomings
and failures, has taught me as much. I tried to explain this to

Angela while we sat one last time on our bench, worrying about our fates once we were separated.

"You will never disappear," I said. "Even if it may feel like you have at some point. We're going to remain a part of each other's lives for much longer than we think. There's nothing we can say or do to change that."

And while at the time a part of me may have questioned the veracity of that statement, I no longer do. We do persist, whether we care to or not, with all our flaws and glory. If Angela, my mother, or even my father were here I would gather them close to me so I could tell them that despite what we've gone through, and despite our best attempts to escape one another, I'm certain beyond the slightest doubt that if there is one thing that has to be true, it's this.

ACKNOWLEDGMENTS

To my parents, Hirut and Tesfaye Mengestu; my sister, Bezawit; my family in D.C. and in Ethiopia, thank you, as always, for your love and support. To Jonathan Ringen, Mark Binelli, Jonathan Hickman, and Aamer Madhani for always being there, regardless of distance. To Rattawut Lapcharoensap, Kalpana Narayanan, Shawn McGibboney, Pervaiz Shallwani, Pru Rowlandson, Julia Holmes, Jessica Lamb-Shapiro, Marcela Valdez, Steve Toltz, and Julian Chatelin for your steady, unwavering friendship. To Gerard and Nicole Robicquet for everything you've done for us. To my agent, PJ Mark, for your guidance, advice, and friendship. To my editor, Megan Lynch, for once again helping to make this a better book, and to Sarah Bowlin, Mih-Ho Cha, and the staff at Riverhead for all of your efforts. To the Lannan Foundation, whose generous support helped make this book possible. For Gabriel.